THE JEWELS OF HALSTEAD MANOR

The
JEWELS
of
HALSTEAD
MANOR

LADIES *of* DEVON 1

KASEY STOCKTON

AUTHOR'S NOTE

Giulia Pepper is a young woman of British and Italian heritage. Her parents chose to name her Julia, but with the Italian spelling. While this is explained throughout the course of the book, I (as a fellow reader) understand the frustration of not knowing how to pronounce the main character's given name in the beginning of a book. For that reason, I want you to be able to start off with confidence that Giulia, the feisty, strong heroine in this story, is called Julia, but given the Italian spelling.

Happy reading,

Kasey

CHAPTER 1

*G*iulia stood in the center of the lane and watched the carriage bound away down the pocked road, jarring the passengers seated on top of the swaying conveyance. She had only just been among those who couldn't afford passage inside the stagecoach, and cringed watching Mr. Bradley, the older gentleman she'd sat beside earlier, clutching his seat to remain upright on the careening vehicle.

Cold autumn air rushed into her lungs as Mr. Bradley nearly toppled off the roof. She squeezed her hands together as if maintaining a rigid posture would keep the elderly gentleman atop the carriage and waited for what felt like ages. Mr. Bradley righted himself, lifting one hand in a tentative wave and she eagerly responded, trying —and failing—to ignore the pity she could detect in his kind, old eyes.

The conveyance turned out of view and Giulia spun in a full circle slowly taking in the vast expanse of empty land that seemed to continue in every direction without end. The sun brushed the edge of the sky, already dipping behind the horizon. Looming darkness nipped at her heels and she picked up the rope Ames had tied to her trunk. Gripping her valise over her shoulder, she pivoted away from the declining sun and walked in the opposite direction.

According to the stage driver, this road would end at Halstead Manor. The long, empty lane looked daunting, and Giulia's stomach complained as she began her trek. Or, rather, continued the rather long and tedious journey that had begun eight months prior when her father took his final breath on Africa's soil. Or any soil, for that matter. It was not entirely possible to take a breath anywhere when one was dead.

Giulia moved as briskly as her trunk would allow and tried not to watch the distance for buildings, gates, or obvious signs that she was nearing her uncle's home. That would only make the walk longer.

Uncle Robert. The *elusive* Uncle Robert. How had she come to be in a position where the only person she could turn to was the man who was single-handedly responsible for keeping her own father from his childhood home? She swallowed the apprehension that bubbled up into her throat and shook her head.

Uncle Robert had written to her. She had proof. He had invited her to come. She dropped the rope tethered to her trunk and opened her valise, feeling the folded missive tucked into the pocket and absorbing the calming balm of hope. She would not be turned away, she reminded herself. She was invited.

The sun continued its descent and Giulia felt the lack of warmth on her back as it fell behind her. She trudged down the lane, pulling her trunk and readjusting the valise on her shoulder. The luggage was heavy and beginning to slow her down. She was tempted to hide it away on the side of the road, but there was no bush or ditch sufficient to lend coverage. Sighing, she pulled harder. What else could she do? In it was every earthly possession she owned.

Ames had seen to that.

A smile tugged at her lips at the memory. His dark hair falling over his brow and the half-smile that tilted his mouth up. The footman-turned-valet-turned-man-of-all-work had been in Giulia's life since before she could remember. As her lifestyle had altered, his job had altered with it. He was eight years her senior, but that had never stopped her from fantasizing over a future shared with the man. She hardly cared if marriage to Ames would lower her alleged station in life, for she had lived like a servant for half of it anyway. At least, she had done so after her mother left.

Giulia pushed thoughts of Ames from her mind. Dwelling on the man would do her no good, at present. He was in London starting his business, and she would make do with clandestine letters until they could be reunited again.

She had devised a plan. Ames would address his letters to her father, which would naturally be passed on to her. It was foolproof. No one need know she was corresponding with a man whom she was not yet engaged to and Ames's notes would fall in with the rest of them easily enough. Letters addressed to her father were bound to pour into Halstead Manor since she had given her new direction to her father's publisher. Adventurers of the world seemed unlikely to give up on Patrick Pepper and his assistant, Jules, anytime soon.

Giulia's foot collided with an object and she pitched forward, sprawling on the rough dirt road. Pushing up onto her knees, she looked behind her to find a heap lying prostrate in the lane. Shadows fell behind the dark figure, blending it into the road.

The heap shifted slightly, and a low groan emanated from one end —the end which had snagged her foot. It was a person.

No, it was a *man*.

Giulia quietly got to her feet and rounded the edge of the crumpled form toward her discarded luggage. He groaned once more, causing her to jump. Shaking herself, Giulia focused. Father had taught her to be cautious, but he had also taught her to be kind. And this man was clearly hurt. Squaring her shoulders, Giulia straightened her spine and looked in unabashed courage toward the fallen man.

"Sir?"

Nothing.

She stepped closer and bent slightly, hoping to ascertain the man's status from his clothing. The near darkness made that an impossible feat. But what sort of man would find himself in this position? Could he be a ruffian? Or perhaps a drunken workman fallen on his way home from the pub? Giulia glanced around her again. Unlikely. There was no building in sight, let alone a pub. And according to the stage driver, this lane led to one place, and one place only. Halstead Manor.

Giulia bent lower and raised her voice slightly. "Sir? Are you alert?"

A mumble came from the man. It was as easy to discern as his clothing in the fading light. So, not at all.

She stood, hesitating. It was growing far too dark to see what she was dealing with.

A hand shot out and grabbed her ankle before she could move away. A heart wrenching cry escaped the man and his grip immediately slackened.

Worry moved into Giulia's gut and churned. The sudden and inappropriate feeling of the man's hand on her ankle was instantly overshadowed by the pain in his voice. This was no drunken farmer; he was hurt.

Giulia dropped to her knees and did not hesitate as her nursing instincts kicked in. She felt up and down each arm before moving to his neck. He lay face down, his head bent away from her. Her eyes were adjusted to the dim lighting and she took notice of his clothing. Even if the dark made it utterly impossible to see, she would have known who he was by the feel of the fine wool that made his coat. The high-quality neckcloth circling his throat. The polished shine of his hessians caught out of the corner of her eye.

This man was a gentleman.

His neck and head fully examined, Giulia moved lower, feeling along his broad shoulders. Part of her hoped not to find injury, but she knew it was a fruitless wish and waited in anticipation for the recoil that would show her exactly where he hurt. Hopefully before she had to move much lower.

Her fingers kneaded the muscle of his far shoulder and worked their way inward. She reached the shoulder blade closest to herself and he cried out again, a split second before her fingertips landed in something wet.

Wet, warm, and gooey.

Blood.

Oh, heavens. It was a blessed thing she wasn't the fainting type.

After feeling a little further, she dug her hand under the man's body and felt the underside of the wound. Well, that was a relief. It had to be a bullet and it must have gone clean through.

Shifting to access the bottom of her petticoats, Giulia ripped off a length of fabric and turned back to the patient. How was she to wrap him if she could not get him into a sitting position?

"Sir, are you alert? What is your name?"

He mumbled, but the sound was incoherent.

Giulia did her best to focus her gaze. "I need to wrap your shoulder and it would ease my job immensely if I could get you to sit up. Or lean, perhaps. Do you think, sir, that you might be able to lean?"

A muffled groan sounded in the darkness. Giulia tried to take a calming breath and crawled to the opposite side of her patient before leaning down to get close to his face. Groaning was a good sign usually; it showed a level of consciousness. Now she only needed to determine just how conscious he was.

She placed a finger beneath his nose and felt his breath. It was coming in short, rapid spurts, but she already knew that by the quick rise and fall of his back. She could see enough of his face to determine that it was pinched, and sent a prayer up asking for guidance. How was she going to help a nearly incoherent stranger when she was stuck in the middle of nowhere, no buildings for miles?

She brought her face nearly level with the patient's, her body contorted so that she could look him in the eyes without actually lying down in the dirt.

"Please open your eyes," she murmured calmly. "I need to be sure you are awake so I may talk you through my treatment plan." What she truly needed was to assure herself that the man would remain alive long enough for her to fetch help, but she would keep that to herself.

His eyelids fluttered slightly before peeking open.

Success!

Then they closed. She frowned.

"I would like to turn you over and lay you against my valise. We need to elevate your torso to slow the bleeding. And it will make my job of wrapping you a tad easier." She waited a moment and watched his lashes flutter. He grimaced deeper, if that was possible, and opened his eyes again with what appeared to be determination.

Giulia grinned. That was a welcome trait for a man in his position. She retrieved her bag in haste, returning to his side. "Do not strain, sir. I do not wish to cause further stress to your injury."

She positioned her valise near the man's good shoulder.

Giulia took a breath. "When I count to three I am going to roll you onto the bag. Ready?"

She slid her hands under the man's chest and wished, not for the first time, that Ames was with her. His strength would have made this an easy task. Harnessing power from the inner confidence that this was a necessary action to save the man's life, and the simple truth that she had no other option than to attempt it alone, Giulia took a sustaining breath.

"One. Two. *Three!*" She grunted on the last count and heaved with every bit of strength her body possessed. To her astonishment, he rolled easily. Whether by sheer will or the unlikely possibility that he may have helped, the injured man was turned over and propped up on her valise, making his shoulder accessible and elevated.

Perfect.

"Splendid," Giulia said cheerfully as she clapped her hands together and sat back on her heels. "Now, don't you go anywhere. I am going to fetch my sewing shears and then we will have this coat off of you in a jiffy."

He grunted, seemingly in response, and she moved to her trunk to retrieve her scissors. Father often said her excessive talking was a virtue and not a failing, but she sometimes wondered if it would be better for her mouth to remain closed. This man seemed somewhat lucid; just *how* lucid, she could not determine. If she could do anything to distract him from her poking and prodding, it was worth trying.

"I suppose I ought to introduce myself, given this extraordinary circumstance. I am Giulia." She sighed. "I wish I knew your name. That would make our situation less awkward, do you not agree?

Perhaps I should give you one." She slid the scissors between the man's neck and her valise, using her fingers to guide them, and began carefully snipping the coat away. She was used to assisting the doctor in the dim light of a ship's cabin as it rolled upon the waves, but even then she'd had at least one candle to light the room.

"Just a nickname, of course," she continued, then wrinkled her brow. "Though I cannot see your face clearly, so that adds a level of difficulty to the act of naming you. I must come up with something, however." She hummed for a moment while she thought and continued to snip away the fine coat. "This is certainly a shame, is it not? What a fine coat to utterly ruin in such a barbaric manner. Though, to be fair, the large hole in the shoulder rendered it ruined long before I came at you with my sewing shears."

Giulia clucked her tongue. The wound was substantial, from what she could tell. She only hoped she was successfully distracting him. "I've got it! I will call you Trouble! That is what we are in, don't you agree?"

He groaned and she ceased cutting. "You do not like Trouble? No, you are right. It does not roll off the tongue so easily, does it?" Giulia looked up as clouds began to move away from the moon on the horizon, lighting the scene around her and giving her a better view of her patient. "Glorious. We must thank the moon. How kind of her to come out right when I could use her light. Now, where were we?" She resumed cutting and noticed the grimace back on the man's face. It was easier to decipher now, though not by much. The blood that dripped from his wound gleamed in the moonlight and hastened her work.

"Right, we were naming you. Hmmm, I think...yes! I've got it! *Danger.* I shall call you Danger. It is fitting, don't you agree? You clearly are in some yourself, though how that came to be is not hardly fathomable to me, given our location. And has your horse run off, Danger, or were you walking along this lane alone?" She unbuttoned the front of the coat and pulled off the portion she had cut off, talking while gently removing the clothing. Then she moved on to the waist-coat, working as quickly as her chilled fingers allowed her to. The man's injury was alarming enough, but in the back of her mind, Giulia couldn't stop thinking about *who* caused the injury in the first place; she had no guarantee the aggressor wasn't still a threat. She would not be comfortable until they were removed indoors somewhere, safe.

Nerves loosened her tongue further. "I suppose I cannot say it is totally unreasonable to go without a horse, since I was walking along the lane alone myself. But I cannot say it is *normal* behavior, for it certainly is not normal for me."

Giulia made quick work of the waistcoat, removing it from the injured shoulder while leaving what she could on the rest of the man to warm him. His loss of blood was evident in the pallor of his skin and she did her best to distract him with her chatter while no doubt adding to his pain. Once she got to his shirt, she removed his cravat and set it aside while cutting a hole in the shirt for access. Whoever this gentleman was, he clearly maintained activity that built his physique, for Giulia had done her fair share of nurse work on other men, and few had come near this man's breadth or firm display of muscle. Had he not worn the clothing of a gentleman, she would have assumed him to be a laborer.

She threw the inappropriate thoughts from her mind. How could she examine a man's physique so thoroughly? What would Ames think if he knew how she was admiring this complete and total stranger? Her vicinity to the man and the intimacy involved in her care of his wound was questionable enough. Now that she was back in England, she would have to take care, to act the part of a lady—as Father had asked of her.

She mentally shook herself and returned her attention to Danger with a smile on her face. Not that it mattered, for his eyes were screwed shut. But she liked to think the smile could be heard through her voice.

"I do wish I had some laudanum to give you. It would put you to sleep though, and then I would be forced to talk to myself. That is not quite an attractive idea, I feel." She wadded up his cravat and pressed it against the wound on the front of the shoulder where the majority of the blood was pooling before picking up the strips of ripped petticoat and using them to wrap underneath his arm and around his neck to firmly hold the cravat in place.

"Danger, you must not think me selfish." Giulia tied off the bandage and then dropped a hand to his and squeezed his fingers in a show of support. He did not squeeze back, his cold, calloused hand still beneath her touch. She swallowed. "I do promise that if I had laudanum at my disposal, I would not hesitate to administer it to you. It would be much more pleasant to talk to myself than to sit here and know that I am causing you pain. Please keep in mind though, that what I am doing will undoubtedly help you feel better eventually, for I have staunched the bleeding. You must feel more secure with this wrap in place, yes? Now, for the chill."

She released his hand and moved to her trunk before pulling out her winter pelisse, a nice, fur-lined garment of blue wool. "This should do the trick," Giulia murmured as she laid the pelisse over the large man, covering his torso and legs down to his knees. She stared below his knees for a moment, her brow furrowing.

"I am afraid I have nothing to cover your legs. Nor any food to give you for sustenance." Her stomach growled on cue. "I promise that was not to prove my innocence," she said with a smile and tucked the pelisse around Danger's shoulders and waist. "Now, I am trying to determine if it would be foolish to continue on this road, or if I should go back the way I came and attempt to flag down any passing carriages. I do think that given the late hour, I may have more luck if I continue onward. My father always said I was a quick runner, though that is entirely unladylike so you must promise never to reveal that tidbit of information. I have only shared it with you now, Danger, so that you will not be alarmed at my choice to leave you. I cannot possibly sit around here and wait on this deserted road for help. And that is no exaggeration; it truly does seem quite deserted."

She wondered briefly if it would be safe to leave him alone. He'd found some reason to get himself shot in the first place. Could Danger's foe return to finish the job? Unlikely. Given the blood loss and incoherence of her patient, it had been some time since the wound had been inflicted. The assailant was surely long gone. She *hoped.* No, if there was any danger in leaving Danger, it was only the possibility of a carriage coming this way and not seeing him.

Giulia chewed on her lip and looked at the strained expression on the stranger's face. He did not have much time. He needed a doctor right away.

She shot to her feet. "I will be quick, Danger. I am leaving all of my possessions with you, so you must guard them. I am trusting you with everything I own."

Danger's lip twitched and Giulia stifled a gasp. It could have been a trick of the moonlight, but it looked as if he was fighting a smile. That was a very good sign and her heart soared. She took off in the direction of Halstead Manor and ran with all of her might.

CHAPTER 2

G iulia sprinted faster than she ever had before, and she'd had plenty of reasons to flee with haste in her short twenty years. She ran without slowing, watching the ground for holes that would lead to twisted ankles, and glancing up periodically to watch for the manor. As she neared her breaking point, she had to talk herself out of slowing to a walk more than once.

The lane trailed around a copse of trees and dipped slightly. As Giulia rounded the trees, a large castle bounded into view, halting her in her tracks. Chest heaving as she gulped for air, she trailed her gaze up the tall towers framing the castle, faintly glowing in the moonlight. The bulk of the building leered in the dark, its vast size and dark windows ominously taunting Giulia. She swallowed the fear that made its way into her throat.

Her father had spoken countless times about the castle he'd been raised in, but given the name Halstead *Manor*, Giulia had naturally assumed him to be exaggerating the claim. Father had made his living creating outlandish stories stemmed from fact. But it appeared this was not one of those times.

Evidently the perfect rendition of this very castle she had seen in her father's journal was not, as she had assumed, a product of his imagination.

Giulia shook off her surprise and ran over a vast drawbridge, lowered over the remnants of what once must have been a deep moat but was now utterly dry, with pale grass, just visible in the moonlight, growing down the sloping sides of the ditch. Whether this was her uncle's residence or not—though how could it not be—she needed to find help. And there was bound to be someone willing to help inside.

Reaching the vast wooden door, Giulia lifted the heavy, iron knocker and banged it against the metal plate, the vibration reverberating through her arm. It had been loud enough to wake the dead, a stark contrast to the silence now consuming the air.

She counted to ten to stem her impatience, all the while envisioning Danger lying on the road and a carriage unknowingly coming upon him. The vision stirred her anxiety. She hadn't much time to lose. Giulia stepped forward and banged the knocker again with fury until her arm grew sore.

A muffled sound reached her ears as the door whipped open, yanking the knocker from her hand and pulling her arm forward with a snap. She clutched her shoulder, gazing up at an older gentleman in a dressing gown and cap, his mouth screwed up in a scowl and his bushy white eyebrows drawn together. A candle in his hand lit the doorway and cast shadows on his face, deepening the effect of his frown.

"Please, sir, you must help! There is a man down the lane that suffered a—"

"Do you know what hour it is?" he fumed.

Giulia bristled. It couldn't be too terribly late, for the sun had only set an hour or so before. "No, nor do I care."

This seemed to shock the man. She took advantage of his stunned silence. "As I said, there is an injured man on your lane. He suffered a gunshot wound, and I fear if he does not see a doctor soon, his life will be in danger." She tried to sound calm and collected but had yet to restore her breathing to normal. She attempted to relax her irritation and offered the man a gentle smile.

"Who is he?" he asked.

She spoke with patience. "I do not know the man. I came upon him and did what I could to stop the bleeding, but he will need antiseptic and possibly surgery. He needs a doctor. *Now.*"

The man's mouth formed a frown. "How do I know he is not some ruffian deserving of his gunshot wound?"

"I cannot answer for how the wound came about, but I know he is dressed like a gentleman. And it is my belief that one must do all one can for one's fellow men, despite whether or not one deems them *deserving*."

The man stared at her for a moment, moving his gaze from her rumpled, blood stained dress to her frizzy black hair which was undoubtedly in shambles. She clasped her hands together, willing them to stay down and not feel along the coronet braid that rounded her head just to see how unkempt she looked. The movement sent a sharp pain down her arm, but she ignored it.

"Now, will you help me, sir? Or shall I continue to another residence?"

This seemed to pull the man from his trance. "I will order the carriage right away and send my man to assist you."

My man? So this was not the butler. Could it be…

Clearing her throat, Giulia said, "Thank you, sir, I am most obliged. I am sure the injured man will be as well when he regains full consciousness."

He was distracted, his eyes settling on anything but her. "A gentleman, you said? On my road?"

"Yes, sir. Very fine clothes. I was unable to get a proper look at his face, but I can attest to his attire."

He muttered a mild expletive and glanced at Giulia quickly. "Sorry," he muttered.

She ignored it. A lady would never admit to hearing such language. At least that is what her father had told her time and again. She'd always believed it was his own strange way of saying what he wanted and reminding Giulia to not be phased by it.

"Do you know him?" she asked.

"I may." The man turned and shouted, causing Giulia to jump. "Wells! Wells! Come, man!"

A moment later a tall, gangly man strode into the room. "Yes, m' lord?"

My lord? There was no denying it, now. The older man had to be her uncle. She took an involuntary step back. The implication was clear, but she was not ready to give credence to that line of thinking yet.

"Have Baker hitch up the traveling carriage. And prepare an additional horse. I may need him to ride for Mason."

"Yes, m' lord."

"With haste!" the lord yelled after his servant. He turned back to Giulia. "I will meet you out here."

"Sir?"

He spun back around, irritation written on his face.

"We may need blankets too. To protect your seats."

The man stared at Giulia and she smiled, trying to ease his irritation. He only grunted and moved back into the house. But not before slamming the door in her face.

———

Burning. All Nick could feel was the tight, hot sensation of burning in his left shoulder. Pain clouded his vision and made it difficult to count. And he needed to count. He needed to do something, *anything* to pass the time, for waiting was going to kill him. Possibly literally.

He would even welcome back that chatty little thing that had helped him if it meant the waiting was over. He nearly yearned for the girl's unceasing monologue. What an odd creature she was. Though, if he had to be honest, he'd hardly had time to consider his pain when she'd been about; he was too busy listening to her rambling and questioning whether she was meant for Bedlam or was just this side of eccentric. Regardless, her distraction—for surely that's what all the chatter was—had worked. Whoever she was, she definitely knew what she was about. He'd give her that.

Now, for the waiting.

Nick struggled to open his eyes. The pain clouding his judgment caused dark splotches to close in whenever he opened them. He had done it for her, longer than he probably should have, because she'd needed to know he wasn't a hopeless cause. But that had taken all of his strength. Or so he had thought.

Who knew waiting could be so much work? The struggle to remain awake was sapping every ounce of energy he had managed to retain. Slowly, the life was draining out of him. The sensation was palpable and certain.

What was taking her so long? Halstead could not be more than two miles down the road. She had mentioned she was a fast runner, had she not?

A soft rumble shook the ground, steadily growing until he could hear the pebbles beside his head jumping to and fro. A carriage was coming.

Oh please, please *let it be Little Miss Chatty and not an unknown vehicle.*

He braced himself for the possibility that the oncoming team of horses did not know he was there. Moments later, and vastly to his relief, the pounding slowed. There were a few voices, all decidedly male, and then a moment later a lone horse thudded past his head and down the lane at great speed.

He had to assume they were sending for a doctor.

Footsteps crashed toward him and the pounding in his head increased tenfold. He had the woman to thank for that nice kick in the head. But given her role in saving his life, or so he hoped, she could be forgiven.

"Nicholas? Is that you?" a deep voice questioned, panicked. Robert. It must be Robert. Nick grimaced and tried to nod but couldn't move his head. He opened his mouth to answer but no words would form. He was losing control of his faculties.

Robert was satisfied, apparently. Most likely due to the moon that the woman wanted to thank. Thank! She actually wanted to *thank* the moon. He had most definitely leaned toward deeming her loony in that particular moment.

And what reason did she have for thinking the moon a *her*?

"Wells! Come!" Robert snapped. "We must move him to the carriage. Girl! Can you hold the horses?"

Girl? She had returned with Robert then. She'd told Nick her name during her monologue, but he couldn't call it forward now.

She must have answered Robert favorably, for within a moment four hands were under him and he was being lifted and carried. Pain seared his shoulder and sliced down his torso and arm. His head throbbed painfully. He wanted to speak but could not find the energy to open his mouth. Never before had he felt such fatigue, pain, and complete, utter exhaustion.

Before he knew it, he was being laid across a plush seat.

"Wells, let us be off!" Robert barked.

"Sir, my luggage," a feminine voice called. "I must retrieve it from the road."

There was silence and then a grunt. Little Miss Chatty must have retrieved her belongings. A moment later, the carriage rocked with the motion of someone entering. A heavy someone—it must have been Robert. A thud on the boot of the vehicle and a motion behind him. Her trunk being tied on to the back.

"Wells, be quick about it," Robert snarled. If the irascible earl was so bothered, Nick's condition must appear as dreadful as he felt. He swallowed against the dryness of his throat. If only he'd seen the man who had shot at him; if only he could think of a single person who wanted him dead.

Another rock of the carriage and a hesitation. How odd that he could actually feel the woman hesitate.

"He needs to be elevated," she said. "It will slow the blood loss."

Robert grunted.

She huffed, but so very quietly. Her voice came out sickeningly sweet. If she was trying to cover her frustration, she was doing a very poor job of it. "You do not mind sharing a bench with my valise, do you my lord? *I* will do the elevating."

The bag thumped onto the seat and Robert huffed loudly. Then Nick stilled. Two small hands snaked under his head and good shoulder and lifted him gently before laying him back down onto something warm and soft.

Her lap. She had laid his head onto *her lap*.

It was such a kind and inappropriate thing to do that Nick did not know what to think. The carriage rolled forward, and the woman's fingers began weaving through his hair. The soft motion was so soothing he almost forgot about the pain that was searing through his shoulder with every bump and jostle the carriage made. She combed through his hair, comforting him with her quiet murmuring. For a brief moment, he felt so content and, oddly, confident. He knew without a doubt that as long as this strange woman was around, he was going to be taken care of.

With that thought, Nick submitted to the overwhelming exhaustion and darkness that threatened the corners of his mind and slipped quietly into unconsciousness.

CHAPTER 3

"*H*e has lost quite a bit of blood. He may not come to for some time." The doctor wiped his hands on a cloth and then adjusted the spectacles on his freckled nose. He was young, entirely too young to be a doctor, in Giulia's opinion, but the *my lord*—she had yet to confirm his identity—and the man called *Wells* were both listening intently. They must've trusted his opinion.

She hesitated on the edge of the bedchamber, standing beside the fire. The injured man slept soundly, tucked into the bed against the far wall. The room was dim, and the voices hushed, but she could clearly hear the conversation taking place just beside the bed.

The doctor ran a hand through his shock of red hair. "I have cleaned and treated the wound, but you must watch for infection. Contact me if he fevers, otherwise I will check back in tomorrow. There is not much else to be done for him until he wakes."

"Thank you, Mason." Wells shook the doctor's hand and walked him to the door.

"The wrapping was good and tight," Dr. Mason added as he moved toward the exit. "That could very well be what saved his life."

My lord grunted, which seemed to be all he did. Wells nodded and walked the doctor out. Giulia wanted to huff but refrained. She did not *need* credit for her work, but it would have been nice.

The older man scanned the motionless body, his white eyebrows drawing together. Concern pulled at his features and he shook his head slightly before turning from the injured man.

"Sir?"

He glanced back, eyes widened in surprise. Had he already forgotten her? "You are still here?" he asked.

She tried not to be offended. "Yes, I am. I was hoping you could help me."

"Wells can see to that." He turned to leave again.

"My lord!"

He grunted and spun back slowly.

"I am sorry to have put you out so horridly, but this little adventure with your friend has eaten up my daylight hours, and if you cannot return my kindness toward your friend then please at least have the decency to answer my question directly."

He looked at her for a moment, his eyes narrowing. "What is your question?"

She lifted her chin. "Are you my Uncle Robert? The Earl of Hart?"

He stared at her unblinkingly for several moments. Then he began to laugh. His ample belly shook with mirth and he plopped down in a chair near the fire until his humor dissipated. Giulia hesitated to ask what had amused him. Could her uncle be gone? Could she have been wrong about the castle her father drew in his journal?

"Your *Uncle* Robert, you say?" he asked.

"Yes. My uncle."

He laughed again and Giulia could not help the frown that formed on her face.

She was exhausted and put out. She'd dealt with a gunshot victim, ran several miles, and hadn't eaten since breakfast. "Sir," she said, commanding his attention. "I am in a strange area and in a strange house. No, a strange *castle*. I have traveled all the way to Devon to visit a relative I have never met. I have had a trying evening helping a man who has suffered from a *gunshot wound*, and I would like nothing more than to assure myself that I have, in fact, reached Halstead Manor so I may beg some mercy and a pillow and sleep for the next three days. Please discontinue this behavior, I beg of you, and explain yourself."

He sobered and stood. "Very well. Follow me."

Giulia raised her eyes to the ceiling and let out a silent sigh. She followed the man from the room, down the stairs and into the entryway, pausing before the massive oak door.

Taking a step back, she folded her hands in front of her, awaiting his pleasure, for the fact that he was ruminating on something was plain. But why this conversation needed to occur in the foyer went beyond her.

He muttered something incoherent and Giulia said, "Pardon?"

The man held her gaze and Giulia forced herself not to step back further. "I said, indeed. If your uncle is Lord Hart, then I am he."

A measure of relief fell over her shoulders. "I am so pleased to be here, Uncle Robert."

He looked taken aback. "You must not call me that. Lord Hart, the Earl of Hart. Only Robert to my close friends. And why are you here?"

"But you *are* Robert Pepper then?" Giulia asked, her body humming with nerves. He did not seem at all pleased to see her. "Brother to Patrick Pepper?"

"I've not had a brother for many years, no."

Giulia wanted to scoff, but his question rose to the surface of her thoughts. "Why am I here? Because you wrote to me."

"I've done no such thing." He had the gall to look affronted.

"It is not such an offensive accusation." Giulia spoke calmly. "I am your niece, after all. And I did receive a letter signed by Robert Pepper begging a visit."

She fished the missive out of her valise where it had been plopped on the floor just beside the front door and handed it over. Robert took it slowly as if it were a snake ready to strike and unfolded the paper before reading it, his eyes narrowing.

"I do not know who wrote this to you, but it was not me." He thrust the note back to her, unbothered and unrepentant.

They stood in the foyer of the grand castle, staring at one another. Clearly the Pepper stubbornness ran strong in both of them.

He was the first to avert his gaze. "You may sleep here for the night, but I want you gone in the morning. Return to your father and explain that it was a mistake and I will have none of his offspring under my roof." Lord Hart turned and shouted, his booming voice echoing in the cavernous room. "Wells! Wells, come!"

A scurry of footsteps preceded the butler. "Yes, m' lord?"

"Have a room made up for the girl. You are to feed her in the morning and send her away."

And with that, her estranged uncle strode from the foyer. It was not until she was safely deposited in a room of her own and sinking into the plush feather bed that she realized what he had said.

He did not know her father, his *brother*, was dead.

Despite the cold greeting and unfortunate encounter with the earl, Giulia managed a deep and restful sleep. She slept late into the morning and woke on her own with the sun shining through the window and birds fluttering by. Waking in the castle, she would have assumed she was in a fairy tale if it hadn't been for the ever-present knot in her stomach. The earl had kicked her out, and she had nowhere to go.

Sighing, Giulia rose from the bed and splashed water on her face from the washbasin. She dressed herself, as she had for many years, and pulled her thick, frizzy hair into a coronet braid. It was the only way to style her hair that gave her a semblance of order.

Rubbing her shoulder, she winced. Her arm ached from the encounter with the door the previous evening. There was slight bruising, but aside from the soreness she was sure it would heal quickly.

Giulia closed the door to her room and stopped short. She'd been directed in the dark the evening before, and the corridor was foreign in the light of day.

She was located in the west wing, she had been told, a section of the castle that had been uninhabited for years. Finding her way to the breakfast room that Wells had pointed out on his short tour the previous evening was going to prove difficult, but not entirely impossible.

She walked in what she deemed must be the right direction until she came to a dead end. Giulia frowned, then spun and walked back the other way. She made a mental note of when she passed by her door but kept walking until she reached a fork. There was no clear way to tell which direction led to stairs or even the front of the house, so she decided to cross off incorrect lanes by process of elimination.

The entire ordeal took an inordinate amount of time, but Giulia eventually found the split staircase that led to the foyer, broken in the center by a wide landing. The adventure had given her a clear layout of the entire west wing, enticing her to explore further—if she weren't being kicked out within the hour.

It wouldn't do. She had nowhere to go. The only option was to come up with a solution regarding how she might stay on for a while longer; the sprout of an idea took form in her mind. It just might work.

First she would put food into her empty stomach and then she would locate her grouch of an uncle and propose her plan to him.

The scent of bacon, bread and gravy wafted into the foyer, and Giulia followed them to the breakfast room. She took a plate from a footman and moved to the sideboard, filling it with a little bit of everything. She had not eaten since the morning before and the scent of bacon was making her salivate.

"Will the earl be eating as well?" she asked the footman who pulled out her chair and helped her to sit.

"He ate hours ago, miss."

"I see. Where might I find him?"

The footman's gaze shifted nervously before returning to Giulia. "Our instructions are to help you on your way, miss."

"Lovely," she said wryly. She speared a slice of bacon and shoved it into her mouth, closing her eyes as the food filled her stomach. She could not quit her campaign yet. Swallowing another bite, she addressed the footman again. "And your name is?"

"Denny, miss."

"Denny, I would like the opportunity to thank my gracious host before my departure. You would not deny me that, would you?"

Denny looked to the open doorway. Afraid someone might overhear, perhaps?

"If you tell me where I can find the earl, then I will do so on my own. You've no need to introduce me. And no need for anyone to ever find out who my informant was." She looked him squarely in the eye. His Adam's apple bobbed as he swallowed.

He was not quite ready to go against his master, and she did not blame him. It could not be comfortable, working for such an ogre. Giulia dipped her head, affecting a helpless look. "It was a horrible thing, coming upon a body in the road last night. A woman could certainly swoon over less. And now, to be tossed into the cold without delivering a very important message to the earl? I do not know how I will live with myself."

Denny cleared his throat. "If you would like to write a message—"

"Oh no," she said at once, her voice grave. "It is nothing I could put to paper. My father entrusted only me for the job. I cannot let him down."

Denny maintained his post beside the wall, but she could see that his resolve was weakening.

Giulia sighed, drawing out the breath as she pushed pieces of broken bread around her plate.

Despite her overwhelming hunger, she could only eat so much before her stomach threatened to explode. What a disappointment. Her plate had hardly been touched, and she knew she would be hungry again soon. Such was the process of regaining her full appetite, as she had learned numerous times over the years.

Her motivation to convince the earl to let her stay was now multiplied as she stared at the uneaten rolls and bacon smothered with gravy.

"Very well," Denny said at last, and Giulia did her best to look grateful. "As you leave this room, go east. Pass the stairs and turn north down a long corridor. You'll find the earl in his study through the door at the end."

She thanked the man and slipped from the breakfast room before he could think better of having helped her. Winding her way down the dark corridor, she found the door at the end swathed in colorful light. A beautiful stained-glass window was positioned high on the wall beside the door, light streaming down through it. Gathering courage, she tapped at the door and waited.

"What?" the earl barked.

Giulia opened the door and stepped inside. The earl spoke without looking up from his desk. "What is it now?"

"I was hoping for a moment of your time, my lord."

The earl glanced up, eyes widening under bushy, unkempt brows. He quickly shuttered his expression and frowned. "I thought I instructed that you be on your way."

"Yes, I heard as much. Only, I thought that we should clear up a misunderstanding before I do so. And I have a proposition for you."

This seemed to pull his interest. "Be quick about it," he muttered. His shoulder-length, scraggly hair was salt and peppered, and Giulia wondered how she had not caught the Pepper family resemblance right away. Her father had maintained a close shave and trimmed his hair on a regular schedule. Giulia knew because it was her job to do so. In fact, it was something she did with the very sewing shears that she had used the previous evening to cut off the injured man's coat. Whatever had she done with those shears? Had she put them back before running for help?

Obviously now was not the time to ruminate.

"Well?"

"I apologize, my lord. It is just...your eyes. I have not looked into those eyes in nearly a year."

The cool gray eyes pierced her. If she ignored the unkempt, bushy hair, she could very well be looking into her father's face. The revelation moved through her and pricked the back of her eyes. She quickly cleared her throat and snapped out of it. The earl, it seemed, was not the sort of man to be moved by emotion. In fact, it would probably harm her cause.

"You see," she continued with a flat, unaffected voice, "my father is dead. It happened about eight months ago in Africa." She paused to gauge the earl's reaction and was disappointed to see that he showed no sign of emotion. In fact, it looked as if he was holding his breath. She shook off her disappointment. "On the journey back to England I was under the care of a doctor and his wife, the Hendricks. Since I have done my share of nursing over the years, I was taken on as an unofficial nurse and assisted the doctor with his patients during the journey, as his wife was struggling with sickness from the boat."

The earl continued to stare at her. She smiled and made her plea. "I want to offer my assistance. I understand that you did not invite me here, but as it is, I have nowhere else to go. In order to—"

"What of your mother?"

The question caught her off guard. She must have looked it, too, for the earl pinked slightly in his cheeks. "She left when I was four, my lord. She went back to her family in Italy."

He nodded once, slowly, holding her gaze.

She continued, shoving away thoughts of her mother as she had for the last sixteen years. "Since I was falsely led here," she said, then paused. She searched the earl's face for any sign that he *had* written the letter but found nothing. Sighing, she continued, "I plan to look for a position, but in the time it will take me to find employment I could nurse your injured friend. He would not be my first gunshot wound patient, and I do know the signs to watch for to catch infection early on. If it is agreeable to you, my lord, then I will do so in trade for room and board; the moment I find a position elsewhere, I will leave."

He brought a pudgy finger to his lips and tapped. "No."

Giulia deflated. She tried not to show it, but she could not help her disappointment.

She would have to beg. She opened her mouth to speak but the earl stayed her with a hand. "You will remain until he is healed and fully well. If I am going to engage your services, I would like to see the job finished. I cannot abide a half-given effort."

That was better than she could have hoped. The weeks it would take the man's wound to heal would give her sufficient time to obtain a position. She tried not to look as relieved as she felt. "Very well, my lord. These terms are agreeable to me."

He nodded once more before returning his attention to the papers on his desk in dismissal. Giulia bobbed a curtsy and turned to leave.

Relief flooded her as the door clicked shut and she leaned against the opposite wall. She ran her hands over her arms in a comforting self-embrace and closed her eyes. She was going to be fine.

CHAPTER 4

*G*iulia didn't have much time to lose. She needed to begin perusing her uncle's newspapers and search for a position so she might have a place to go once the injured man healed. Perhaps as a governess or companion. Or maybe she could find a position as a schoolteacher's assistant close by.

Nearby would be ideal. She hadn't money for travel anyway, and would like to remain in Devon, if she could manage it. For as many countries as she had visited, this was one area of the world she'd often dreamed of as she traveled from one place to the next. Her father's stories hadn't done the countryside justice; it was a far cry from the busy streets of London that she was used to—for they never left the metropolis during their brief stints in England.

Father would take her to all the ends of the earth, but he had staunchly refused to return to Halstead. To know the land and the people who raised her father was not a chance she would squander. She found herself grasping for any connection to him now.

Perhaps she could visit the shops and learn of a position that way. There had to be a village nearby. In fact, she knew there was. Gordley? Grandon? It started with a G, she remembered that much.

Giulia climbed the grand staircase and halted on the landing, where it split in two. The castle was quiet. She tipped her head back, tracing the gray stone walls that rose on either side of her and met at the top far above. It was a sturdy house, prestigious enough for an earl. And yet, somehow the dignity and grandeur made the castle feel all the more lonely in its silence.

Drawing in a steadying breath, Giulia imagined her father as a boy, running up and down these very stairs. He should have been with her now. *He* should have been the person to show Giulia her ancestor's home. But the earl and his anger had forbidden it while Patrick Pepper was alive, and now it was too late.

Questions filled Giulia's mind. Lord Hart had not sent for her, but someone had.

Someone had sent her a letter inviting her to Halstead Manor. She had wondered for a brief moment if the earl had written the letter but then decided to pretend otherwise, but he proved that theory false with his conversation in the study.

That left very few people that could have deceived her, and none of them made logical sense. Could it have been Wells? The man was an old family retainer. He had been at Halstead when her father was growing up—Giulia remembered his name from her father's stories—only then he'd been a footman. Could Wells have written the letter in an effort to mend broken fences?

If it was Wells, he likely had the best of intentions. He could not have known that Lord Hart would not care one whit for his deceased brother's child.

Shaking her head, Giulia lifted the hem of her plain, gray gown and started toward the next set of stairs.

One direction would lead to the west wing, so she turned the opposite direction. Presumably the east wing.

The room her patient stayed in was easily accessible, near the top of the east staircase—identifiable by a tray sitting on the floor outside the door. She halted beside the tray and knocked softly. Light footsteps approached before the door swung open and a young girl stood on the other side in a maid's uniform.

"I am Giulia Pepper, and I am going to be taking care of the patient."

The maid looked equal parts relieved and wary. Had she also been aware of the earl's plan to remove Giulia from the premises as soon as she'd had her breakfast?

"The earl himself has sent me," Giulia said. "If you will show me in and explain how the patient has been since the doctor's call last evening, I would be much obliged."

The maid nodded and turned back into the room. Large tapestries lined the walls, sandwiching a fireplace so large Giulia could easily step inside it—if a fire were absent. The drapes were mostly drawn, leaving a hand-width's space open to allow the sun to light the room. The four-poster bed in the center was enormous and dwarfed the man lying on it, further proving its grandeur, for he was anything but small.

There was a plain wooden chair pulled near the bedside and a small table beside it that held some mending. The maid's gaze flicked to the pile of fabric and her cheeks grew pink.

"I was watching him, Miss Pepper. I only thought I could get some work done while he slept."

"I see no problem with that." Giulia smiled. "When the doctor asked us to watch him, he did not mean endlessly. Has he awoken at all, miss…?"

"Tilly, miss. Just Tilly. And no, he hasn't. I've been with him since they brought him in last night."

Clasping her hands together, Giulia shot a worried glance toward the man in the bed. Perhaps there was no room for panic yet. Head wound victims sometimes took hours, and other times took days before awakening. She wasn't certain he had a head wound, but if he'd been riding a horse while he was shot, it was entirely possible he hit his head when he fell. And she couldn't disregard her own mistake in kicking him in the head. "Does his wrap need to be changed?"

"No one told me to do it, miss."

"Very well, Tilly. That will be all."

Tilly hesitated.

Giulia tried not to be irritated. "Go on and check with Wells if you doubt me. I have an agreement with the earl, and I am going to be looking after this man for the time being."

Tilly nodded her head slowly, coming around to the idea. Or at least realizing she had the ability to check with the butler. "Nicholas Pepper, miss. The man is Mr. Pepper."

"*Pepper?*" Giulia said, louder than she'd meant to. Her father had been under the impression that Robert Pepper had never married. But had he done so and had a son? She glanced back to the slumbering man but found no immediate resemblance between Mr. Pepper and Lord Hart. "Is this my cousin, then?"

Tilly shook her head, then paused, her nose scrunching in apparent thought. "I suppose he is a cousin of yours, though somewhat distantly. Lord Hart was forced to track down Mr. Pepper when no other heirs were apparent."

Giulia's gaze drew back to Mr. Pepper. He was the next Earl of Hart and he'd been shot. It was no wonder Lord Hart had been so concerned last night.

"Do you know the relation between this man and Lord Hart?" she asked Tilly. "In what way are they cousins?"

Tilly's eyes widened. She shook her head. "I don't know, miss."

Giulia swallowed a sigh.

"Can I get you anything, miss? Tea?" Tilly asked, inching toward the door.

Giulia knew the maid was going to run straight to the butler when she left to verify Giulia's claims, and she didn't fault her for it. Giulia would have done the same thing. "Tea sounds lovely."

Tilly bobbed a curtsy and fled.

Giulia ran her hands down the front of her serviceable gray dress. It was one of three she owned. Or possibly one of *two* now that the one she wore the previous day had an array of bloodstains, dirt stains, and rips from kneeling on the road. It was hard losing a possession when she had so few to call her own; as soon as her mourning period was over and she could acceptably wear colors again, she did not want to look at a gray dress for the rest of her life. Though, it could be worse. At least she was through with black.

She shivered and brushed away the revulsion. Black had been horrid beside her skin tone, making her look pale and sickly. If only she had gotten her mother's beautiful Italian skin, she would be able to wear any color with grace. But no, of all the traits she'd inherited from the Italian blood, her skin color had not been among them. Her ridiculous, unruly hair was. And her boring brown eyes. But every other part of her was English—including her language. Father had made sure of that.

Giulia approached the bed and laid a hand across Nicholas Pepper's forehead. He was warm—too warm. It was hard to know exactly, but she was fairly sure he was beginning a fever. Not *entirely* a surprise. Dr. Hendricks had explained to her how the body would fever to fight potential infection, but she would need to make certain it didn't rise too high.

She got a good look at his face with the light of day peeking behind the drapes, and her breath caught. He had to be one of the handsomest men she had ever encountered. And in her adventurous life, she had encountered her share of the species. Not that she was a proficient, for none of them had ever shown any interest in her. No one except Ames, that is.

A motion under the blankets caught her attention and Giulia's gaze flicked back to Mr. Pepper's face. Lines formed between his brow and outlined his eyes. He was waking.

"Nicholas Pepper," she murmured, lowering herself onto the chair beside his bed. "You are going to be fine." Giulia felt his brow again, assuring herself he was the same temperature. Warm, but not hot.

Nicholas Pepper's pale eyelashes fluttered, and he squeezed his eyes closed. The laudanum must be wearing off.

The door opened and Tilly stepped in carrying a tray.

"Wonderful timing, Tilly. Would you be so kind as to fetch some broth for our patient? I believe he's waking."

"Yes, Miss Pepper. Right away."

Tilly set down the tea tray on a table beside the bed and scurried out. Giulia leaned over the invalid and picked up another pillow. Sliding her hand under his neck she began to lift.

"I am going to lay a cool pillow under your head, and I would like you to try and sip some broth. I know, broth sounds like the last thing you would like to eat. But, you must do what you can to regain your strength. Your body is going to do its part to heal you; the least you can do is nourish it." She placed the fresh pillow under his head and laid him back down.

His face was set in an eternal grimace.

"Do not bother pretending you are still asleep. I can tell you are rising from the fog. You looked much more peaceful a moment ago when you were sleeping." She paused, debating the merits of changing his dressing while he was still somewhat unconscious. No, it would be easier while he was alert. "It cannot be comfortable recovering from a gunshot wound. But the doctor did say you were fortunate in the placement of the bullet and will likely have a full recovery with use of your arm. Is that not wonderful news?"

Tilly entered the room with a bowl of broth, setting it on the tea tray.

"Thank you Tilly, that will be all."

Giulia sat on the chair beside the bed and pulled it as close as she could.

She leaned in and lowered her voice. Mr. Pepper was most likely suffering from a headache due to the medicine, if not from the kick she had given him last night. "Are you ready to eat a few spoonfuls of broth? If you could open your eyes it would make my job easier, but if not, I will tell you when to open your mouth."

She waited patiently while his eyelids fluttered. He hardly peeked at her before closing them again. "Oh, is it too bright? Allow me to darken the room."

She crossed to the window and pulled the drapes shut, closing out the last bit of light. She was able to see from the rays peeking around the curtains, but only just.

Mr. Pepper's eyes were a brilliant green, and still quite hazy. She imagined they were stunning when they were clear. He opened his mouth, but nothing came out. Perhaps he was waiting for the soup, but he looked frustrated.

"Do not push yourself," she said, settling beside him. "The broth will help."

Giulia lifted a spoon to his mouth, and he drank. It was tedious and unpleasant to watch. The poor man was struggling nearly as much to swallow as he was to stay awake. And it was no secret that his injury pained him.

He turned toward her, and she noticed a dark bruise on his temple. Giulia gasped and her hand flew to the bruise, grazing it lightly with the tips of her fingers. "Did I do that? Oh, please forgive me. I feel terrible about tripping over your head."

His startled eyes held hers, and she tore her gaze away, focusing on her task. She managed to help him swallow four more spoonfuls before he went back to sleep.

Giulia set down the broth and sighed, settling in for the long and tedious process of nursing Nicholas Pepper back to health.

***

Tedious was an understatement, but Giulia knew what she had agreed to when she asked for the nursing position.

Furthermore, no one could quite figure out where the gunshot wound had come from. Nick—Giulia had come to know him as such in her own mind for he did not look at all like a Nicholas and calling him *Mr. Pepper* reminded her too painfully of her own father—had left Halstead in the early afternoon of that fated day to attend to business in Town and planned to be away for at least a fortnight. His horse was discovered in Graton by the innkeeper and brought back with Dr. Mason on his subsequent visit. But the injury had occurred on the road from Halstead Manor, which implied that the man responsible likely knew of Nick's plans that day.

Giulia spent her days and the majority of her nights looking after Nick with the help of his valet, Jack. She fed him when he would awaken in spurts of lucidity, which was not as often as she would like, and she checked and rebandaged his dressing each day. Dr. Mason came every day to check Nick's progress and was happy with his improvement.

"Perhaps we should decrease his laudanum?" Giulia suggested as Dr. Mason replaced the bandage and moved away from Nick's bed.

"Yes, he is healing well. He would probably benefit from more time awake. As long as we can keep him in bed."

"That should not be an issue." She smiled at the doctor. "He cannot possibly have regained his strength so quickly, surely?"

"No, but men are stubborn." Dr. Mason leveled his gaze at Giulia, and she blushed. His smile was warmer than the jest warranted, and his gaze settled on her longer than she was comfortable with.

She cleared her throat and circled the large, plush armchair she had dragged near the bed to replace the small wooden one. The comfortable wingback had been a lot easier to sleep in.

"When he awakens, shall I attempt a more substantial meal?" she asked.

"No, broth is good for the time being." Dr. Mason glanced at Nick and then back at Giulia. "Would you like me to send my sister to assist you? You must be exhausted, and she is quite used to nursing my patients."

"You have a sister?" Giulia asked, her voice rising in hope. She had not had anyone to speak to besides Tilly for nearly a week. In fact, she had hardly left the room at all in that time.

The earl had come up a few times to check on Nick, but he usually timed his visits for when Giulia was out. The one time she had come face to face with Lord Hart in the corridor, he had refused to make eye contact with her. She wondered if he was harboring displaced hatred toward her or was just simply uncomfortable. Regardless of his reason, she was happy to stay out of his way. His eyes were haunting.

"I do have a sister, and she would welcome the acquaintance," Dr. Mason said. "She is recently widowed and would love the company."

"I do not need the help, but if she has a free moment, I would love a visitor."

"Lonely here, is it?" Dr. Mason colored immediately, his face growing red and his freckles standing out further. "I only meant—"

"I know what you meant." Giulia smiled encouragingly. "Yes, it is quite lonely. I would welcome a friend."

"I will send her along," Dr. Mason said, his eyes boring into hers. "I do not know how you stand it here." He stepped back as though recalling his situation and delivered a bow before taking his leave.

Giulia sat beside Nick. Leaning forward, she fluffed his pillows and pulled his blanket up over his shoulders, tucking it in around his sides. These actions had become second nature to Giulia given the frequency at which she did them, but the tingle they left in her fingertips from his warmth was unceasing.

She told herself she could not be attracted to a patient—let alone the heir to Halstead—and made herself picture Ames's hair falling over his brow and his handsome half-smile. Just imagining the way Ames looked at her with such care was enough to banish unruly thoughts about Nick.

But the lack of any correspondence from Ames thus far was *not* very comforting.

He was beginning a business in London with the money he had received from her father's death. Her father had always thought of Ames like a son, and he'd left Ames nearly every penny in his will, aside from Giulia's dowry. And when Ames's wood-working shop was running and profitable, he would send for Giulia and they could marry.

That her father did not leave everything to her was not a surprise. He was kind but controlling. This was no doubt his way of making sure Giulia and Ames married so they could both benefit from the inheritance.

She desired answers, naturally, but they would come about in their own time. Though it was in her possession, Giulia struggled to read her father's journal, the writing and stories a painful reminder of his absence. Aside from Ames's constant companionship, Father was the only family Giulia had ever had. She had never met any of her grandparents or aunts and uncles, and if she had cousins then she did not know about them; aside from Lord Hart, they were all in Italy.

Neither did she claim a mother. Any woman who would leave her daughter without a touch of correspondence at the ripe age of four years old did not deserve that title.

Giulia closed her eyes to reset the images which bombarded her when she thought of her parents. She had endured her share of trials in life, but she could not say she was ever bored.

A small smile graced her lips at the memory of a Christmas when she was twelve and Father had taken into his head that India was where they were meant to be. Giulia had been stung by a scorpion and laid up in bed while Father celebrated with a few other families of nobility in the area. Despite his family having cut him off financially, Patrick Pepper was still welcomed in the first circles everywhere he went. And Giulia hadn't minded his absence during the holiday; it had meant she got Ames all to herself.

It was while Ames cared for her during the episode of the scorpion sting that she had first begun to look at him as more than just a friend. Of course, it took years before he returned the sentiment. Long, unrequited, painful years.

The sting had not been fatal, but it had kept Giulia bedridden for nearly a week. When Father returned from the Christmas festivities, he had presented her with a beautiful jeweled pendant—an elephant, featuring nearly every color of the rainbow in its bright, beautiful glory. Father had told her the necklace was meant to be a good luck charm and perhaps he should have given it to her earlier. Of course, she had laughed at the strange local customs and put the necklace on, not thinking much about its proffered luck. But coincidence or not, since that day she had not fallen ill once.

Father had always credited the elephant. Giulia had always let him.

She opened her eyes and found her fingers absentmindedly stroking the elephant around her neck. She dropped it and stilled when she saw that not only were Nick's eyes open, but they were focused right on her. And they were alert.

CHAPTER 5

The woman sat an arm's length away, doe-eyed and frozen. Could she tell that Nick was seeing without the haze for the first time since the attack?

He reached toward her and paused, squeezing his eyes closed and dropping his arm instantly. It may feel significantly better, but his shoulder was far from healed. And somehow, he had forgotten.

"Do not try to move," the angel said. What had he called her before? Ah. Little Miss Chatty. Bits and pieces of his time in and out of consciousness were stuck in his mind, but most of the memories were hazy. He recalled a beautiful angel with a dark, fuzzy halo. A rather wild halo, really. Should halos *be* wild?

And then there were the hands. The small, graceful hands that cooled his head, fluffed his pillows, and carefully arranged and tucked his blankets. Yes, he was going to miss those hands.

He opened his eyes and she was gone. Glancing around the room frantically, Nick was inordinately relieved when he located her beside the fireplace. She pulled the rope before returning to his side.

The angel sat primly in the oversized chair and clasped her hands in her lap. She made the chair look monstrous. Why would anyone need a chair so large? It had never felt overly large before, but now it seemed excessive.

The door opened and she turned and spoke to the maid. A funny little thing with white-blonde hair and an undersized nose nodded and fled the room.

"Tilly went to fetch you some broth," the angel explained.

He nodded. His head did not hurt any longer. At least, not beyond a slight ache.

The air in the room felt different. Charged, somehow. Nick had awakened many times since the attack and let the dark-haloed angel spoon feed him, listening to her jovial, unceasing conversation. So *chatty*.

But something was different now. She was watching him closely, hesitantly. It was as though she teetered on the edge of something, but he could not quite grasp what it was. He wanted to speak and soothe her discomfort like she had done for him, but he did not think he could. At least, he did not know what he would say.

It was an odd feeling, for he had not had this problem with her before. She always seemed to fill in the gaps just fine on her own.

The door opened again, and the young maid carried a tray inside. The angel—he really needed to learn her name—picked up the spoon and eyed it warily before jutting her eyes from the soup to him and back. He wanted to offer to try and feed himself, but he couldn't get the words out. And not because he was incapable, either.

"Are you hungry?"

He nodded.

She sucked in a breath and then displayed an overly happy smile. "Very well; let us begin."

Nick waited for a moment. She seemed to wait too. Then she picked up the spoon and sped it toward him so quickly that it spilled all down the front of his shirt.

"Oh, dear! I cannot believe—well...I *can* believe. But how clumsy of me! If you'll just wait one moment." She was up and to the washbasin quickly. She brought back a dampened towel and began to blot the broth from his shirt. She had not put very much onto the spoon in the first place, so it was a rather small mess.

"Of all the times to spill soup on a patient, it had to be the first moment he was lucid," she murmured to herself.

Nick smiled to ease her discomfort. She looked up at him and colored.

"I promise you, this is the first time I have done such a clumsy thing. Well, with you at least."

"I know." His voice sounded raspy and deep and utterly unlike his normal voice. Eyes widening, his hand came up to touch his dry throat.

She placed a hand on his good arm as if she sensed his unease. "Do not worry; that is common. Once you drink some broth you should sound more like yourself."

She picked up the spoon again, bringing the bowl itself closer to Nick, and this time the liquid made it all the way to his mouth. The warm broth slid down his throat like a balm and soothed the ache in his stomach. He was suddenly ravenous, the hollow in his belly gurgling as he filled it. He drank the entire bowl and then finished off the tea.

"I know you probably want more," his nurse gently spoke, "but Dr. Mason advises that we stick to soup for now."

"Can it be anything but broth next time?"

She laughed, a musical sound which warmed his chest. He felt the answering smile push up his cheeks.

"I do not blame you for feeling so. I will talk to Cook and see what we can contrive." She gave him a wicked grin that made him feel more like a coconspirator than an invalid.

He could see her clearly now, and her real face put his dreams to shame. Her hair was in a plait around her head that gave the illusion of a halo. And it was wild. Pieces stuck out in various areas and trailed down her neck and over her brow. The effect was alluring. But that was nothing on her rich, brown eyes. They were full of intellect and depth and reminded him of a cup of chocolate.

"I should fetch the earl," she said. "He will want to see you."

She was up and gone in a heartbeat. She moved quickly for a little thing. Hadn't she told him that before? Something about running fast...but he was meant to keep it a secret because running was not a very ladylike endeavor.

Nick smiled at the memory.

The door banged open and Nick flinched.

"You are awake! Splendid!" Robert bounded before him and stopped short of barreling into the bed. He looked...*happy*. What an odd expression on the usually scowling face.

"They'll have to try harder than that if they want to take me down," Nick said. His farmer's body was tough. He hadn't lived a life of ease and leisure since returning from school, choosing to work his hands in the fields instead.

"What happened, Nicholas? Who was it?"

Nick furrowed his brows and stared into the distance. "I do not know."

Robert looked stunned. "But you were shot at from the front. Dr. Mason determined it himself."

"Yes, and the coward must have been hiding behind a patch of trees. Not the one near the bend—"

"Yes, yes." Robert waved his hand to dismiss the explanation. "I fetched you in the carriage. I saw where it happened." He stared at Nick for a long moment. "Know anyone who wants you gone?"

"Who is next in line?" Nick retorted dryly.

"No idea," Robert replied with feeling. He shook his head and let out a frustrated growl. "Anyone else? Are there any enemies in your past unrelated to the earldom?"

Nick made a show of thinking on the question, but it wasn't necessary. That is all he had thought about since the attack. At least, when he wasn't thinking about the dark-haired angel. "The girl—"

"Did she do anything funny?" Robert barked.

Nick responded slowly, his brows pulled together. "No..."

"Good." Robert nodded once, satisfied.

Nick surveyed the earl. His wild, white hair still fell to his shoulders, his gray eyes still framed by wrinkled, saggy lids. But something was different. His behavior was strange. Erratic, even. "Unless you count saving my life as *funny.*"

Robert's eyes seemed to glaze over, unfocused, so Nick gave him the time he needed to process whatever his mind was trying to wrap around. The clock beat slowly on the mantle and quiet ensued, giving Nick adequate time to study the earl. Upon closer reflection, Robert looked as if he had aged in the time Nick was unconscious. Worry lines creased his forehead, pulling his eyebrows close together so they resembled one long, furry caterpillar.

"How long have I been asleep?" Nick asked. Had it been a year and not just days?

The earl looked at him for a moment, coming back to the present. "Nearly a fortnight. The girl took care of you for the duration."

"Who is she?"

Robert suddenly looked pained. His skin took on a gray quality as if he couldn't fight to feel alive anymore and he let out a defeated breath. It was frightening; Nick had never seen the man so vulnerable. "My niece."

Nick went cold. Niece? His *niece?*

"Do not panic. She has no brothers."

Nick's cheeks grew warm. That was exactly what he had worried about. He wanted to ask if the woman had any sisters either, but instead said, "I was under the impression you have no family."

"I don't."

Nick let the thick silence sit on them for a moment. Rushing Robert was never the way to glean information or get what he wanted. He bided his time.

A few minutes passed before Robert broke the silence. "Her father is my—*was* my brother. Her mother is gone."

There was something more to tell, but Robert was shuttering his expression. He was not going to offer any more information tonight.

"Has she come to stay?" Nick asked.

"Someone fooled her. Or she is fooling me, I haven't yet decided. She claims to have received a letter signed with my name inviting her here. I sent her away, but then she..." He gestured toward Nick.

41

"She what?"

Robert growled. "She offered to nurse you until she could find other employment. Once you are better, she will be gone."

Nick's mouth dropped open. "You cannot be serious."

"I never lie."

Nick shook his head. "You cannot mean that you will force your only living relation into a domestic life when you have this enormous castle and more funds than you know what to do with. It is not right, my lord."

"Do not tell me what is right, boy," Robert growled through gritted teeth. Nick had touched on a vulnerability, to be sure. "No spawn of Patrick will live under my roof." He spat the name with disdain.

"Does she resemble him too greatly? Is it a discomfort for you?" Nick was pushing the boundaries and he knew it, but he could not stop himself. He only wished it wasn't so tiring, pressing the earl. Or that he could stand and tower over Robert. Perhaps his weakened state, lying in bed, was a benefit in this circumstance. Robert had a tendency to close up when he was feeling overpowered.

"Not in the least. She is the spitting image of her mother." Robert spoke so quietly that Nick shut his mouth, biting back the retort he had readied on the tip of his tongue.

It paid off, for Robert continued, his eyes glassy as they stared into the distance. "I could not live in a state where I must wake every day and be forced to look into that face."

"And I felt like she hardly left my bedside." Nick laughed.

Robert pierced him with a strange look. "She hasn't. She's been very attentive in her duties. I have the impression hard work is not new to her. And knowing my brother, it does not surprise me one bit."

The men were quiet, each ruminating in their own contemplative spheres. Nick had not seen Robert act this way in...*ever*. There was something about the situation that he was not sharing. And, knowing Robert, it was the key to the entire mystery.

"So she stays until I am better?" Nick asked.

"Yes."

Then I must do my best to never, ever get better.

CHAPTER 6

illy was an angel. A true, kind, generous angel. Not only had she offered to sit in with Nick when the earl was finished visiting the sickroom, the maid had left tea and a generous meal in Giulia's room for her to eat before her nap.

Giulia woke feeling rested and warm, the heavy blankets cocooning her in comfort. She padded across the cool stone floor to the table and nibbled on the lemon tart remaining on her tray. Nick's waking felt like such a burden lifted. Regardless of how the injuries were sustained, Giulia always felt a sense of responsibility toward her charges until they improved. It was displaced responsibility, and she recognized that, but it was a responsibility all the same. And she did not fight that which made her a better, more caring caregiver.

The moment her charges rounded the bend toward health she always felt such relief. Though with Nick, she felt it tenfold. She hadn't realized the tension which had gathered in her shoulders over the previous weeks or the worry that had steadily grown through his consistent bouts of foggy consciousness. He had never seemed fully awake, and it was a little frightening.

And so she had chatted incessantly, some part of her hoping that if she continued a stream of conversation, at one point he might join in.

When she had looked up this morning and seen his eyes clear and vibrant, she'd known. The tension had eased from her shoulders, but it was quickly replaced with humiliation. What must he think of her? Did he recall the things she had spoken of?

Shoving the rest of the lemon tart in her mouth, she crossed to the mirror and assessed the damage done during her nap. Giulia let out a frustrated huff and started poking pins into her coronet braid to tame a few of the wilder pieces. It was not enough for her to be cursed with frizzy, unruly hair; even in the only hairstyle she had come across that would keep it all up and away from her face, it still managed to escape and shoot out in every direction.

If only she was a man, then she could crop it short.

Giulia giggled, recalling the time she had tried to do just that. When she was nine, Ames was seventeen, and he had caught her with the scissors in the washroom of their London house. She had already hacked off a good length of hair behind one ear and was curled up on the floor clutching the hair to her heaving chest, sobbing. Ames had gently pried the hair loose and soothed her before leaving. He had returned ten minutes later with Mama Jo, a woman who lived a few houses down and took Giulia in when her father was absent for days at a time. It wasn't as if Giulia was incapable of caring for herself, but it was nice to pretend she couldn't so Mama Jo would shoo her into the matron's home and supply her with a fresh meal that Giulia did not have to prepare herself.

Mama Jo had taught Giulia how to do a coronet braid. It started on the side of her head—the side that, at the time, could still claim length—and moved around her head so the shorter pieces could be incorporated at the end. Now, eleven years later, she still supported the hairstyle, and the memories which accompanied it.

Brushing her hands down the front of her dove-gray dress, Giulia began the trek across the castle to Nick's room. She had made the journey many times over the previous weeks, and with trial and error had grown able to decipher the basic layout of the castle. It appeared the west and east wings were identical to one another, only opposite.

She did not have time for exploration as of yet, but there were areas of the castle that begged to be examined.

Reaching the large oak door that encased Nick's oversized and overly masculine room, Giulia knocked. There was a muffled beckoning on the other side of the door and she tentatively opened it.

Then she thoroughly dropped her jaw.

Nick sat in the center of the room in a large tin tub. Jack, Nick's valet, was standing above him with a bucket of water ready to dump over Nick's soapy hair. Seeing a man shirtless was not new to her, for she had assisted in repairing cuts and bruises on bare-chested men in Dr. Hendricks's care many times. And, she reminded herself, she had already seen Nick nearly shirtless when she had administered to his wound time and again. But the full effect was dazzling. He was broader than Ames, which in and of itself was shocking. And the muscles on his good arm as it hitched on the rim of the tub were as oversized and overly masculine as the room they were in.

Giulia reluctantly moved her gaze up to Nick's face and promptly clamped her mouth shut. He was grinning in a smug way that made her want to grab the bucket from Jack's hands and pour it over Nick's face herself.

Instead, she turned her focus to Jack and smiled sweetly, doing her best to appear unaffected. "When you are finished caring for the invalid, would you mind locating me? I would like to discuss his treatment plan."

Jack nodded. "Of course, Miss Pepper."

Giulia turned away but Nick's voice stopped her from closing the door. "Why wait? We can discuss it right now."

Don't take the bait. Don't *take the bait.* "You know that is highly improper."

Drat, I took the bait.

"Have you not been caring for me these last few weeks? I am sure this is nothing you have not already seen." His innocent expression was a nearly believable facade. But the rascal wasn't fooling her.

"Not in this capacity, no."

"No? In what capacity, then, did you care for me?"

Endless hours spent watching his serene face and wondering how deep his green eyes would be when he was coherent. Countless times arranging his blankets and tucking him in. Spoon-feeding him and watching his parched lips drink spoonfuls upon spoonfuls of broth. Giulia thought of the late nights when she would tell him about her adventures abroad, and the less entertaining stories that had occurred on England's soil.

They stared at one another for what felt like ages. It was a battle of wills and Giulia was caught in his deep green eyes while she strategized and sized up the enemy. Any man this attractive with an apparent flair for flirtation was dangerous.

She shifted her gaze to Jack, who was watching with interest. "Send for me when you are finished?"

He nodded and she left, clicking the door shut with force.

"What was that about?" Jack eyed his master with a look equal parts intrigue and hesitation.

"What do you mean?"

A splash came down over Nick's face and he coughed out a spray of water. He hadn't been expecting it. He brought up his good hand and wiped it over his face before looking to his valet with a wry expression.

Jack was the picture of innocence.

Nick sighed. "Just a little fun, Jack. No harm done."

"She is different," Jack warned. "She's had a tough life. Don't play with this one."

That got his hackles up. "Who said I have any intentions of *playing* with her?" Though, that didn't sound like such a bad idea. Regardless of his parentage, Nick was a perfect gentleman and he would never compromise a woman—whether she was a milkmaid or an earl's niece. But that didn't mean he had to quit teasing her.

"Don't forget who you are talking to," Jack reminded him before moving to pick up a towel. He gripped Nick's good arm and heaved him up before draping the towel over his shoulders and retrieving his dressing gown. They'd been playmates as children; Jack's father acted as bailiff for Nick's father's farm, which had put the boys in proximity. Children did not feel the constraints of status as keenly as adults.

They had grown up learning from their own fathers. Nick, how to manage his father's land, and Jack, the duties required of a bailiff. When Nick's father died and he inherited the farm, he kept Jack's father on as bailiff with the understanding that Jack would take over the role one day. When Nick had been uprooted from the life he knew and dragged to Halstead, he had offered the position of valet to Jack instead.

"Don't bother with that." Nick nodded to the dressing gown. "It is hard enough getting my arm in and out of sleeves. Let's keep to necessary clothes."

They moved through the familiar process of dressing Nick in breeches and a shirt. Once Jack had him safely deposited in his bed and propped upright on pillows, he began cleaning up the bath.

"How well do you know her, anyway?" Nick prodded.

"Better than anyone else in this house, I'd gather. She's hardly left your bedside these past weeks. And since I took care of your physical...well, I helped her."

"She didn't take meals with the others?"

"Who would she eat with?" Jack countered, gathering Nick's discarded night clothes. "She's the earl's niece so it wouldn't be proper to eat with the servants. And Lord Hart won't speak to her."

Nick grumbled. Then his stomach followed suit.

Jack must have heard the sound from across the room. "Shall I fetch your dinner?"

Nick leaned back, rubbing his eyes. He hated feeling so weak. "Yes. And fetch Robert as well."

"Fetch Robert?" Jack looked incredulous. "You want me to *fetch* an earl?"

"I need him. Send a maid if you are too scared."

Jack bristled. He muttered, "Scared, indeed," and left the room.

Nick smiled to himself while a plan formulated in his mind. Now he only needed to force himself to stay awake long enough to put the plan into action. Who knew taking a bath could be so utterly exhausting? Gaining his strength back was going to be a long and slow process. But as long as he had the beautiful, dark-haired angel to care for him, it would surely prove enjoyable.

Hmmm. Miss Pepper. Never before had he imagined his own surname would sound so enticing.

She *was* different, though. She hadn't even had the decency to blush when he had caught her staring. Weren't proper ladies supposed to blush when they were found in such an indecent situation? Weren't they supposed to blush at the mere *mention* of an indecent situation?

Nick smiled to himself. This was going to be fun, indeed.

CHAPTER 7

A commotion aroused Nick from sleep. He peeked his eyes open long enough to find a gathering of people by the door to his bedchamber whispering furiously to one another.

"We must wake him," a female voice argued, sounding put out. Ah, Miss Pepper. "He needs to eat. If he does not eat then he will not regain his strength."

"He is clearly in need of rest," Robert barked back. "His valet can sit with him and notify Cook as soon as he has awakened. Sleep is more important than food right now."

"Where is the experience you have to back up this theory, my lord?"

Well, that was saucy. Nick wanted to open his eyes and witness how red Robert's face became, but once he did, the argument would end. He kept them shut.

"I do not need credentials to prove common sense. I am a man. And I am more than twice your age."

"Ah, the 'I am older than you are, so I know best' argument. Well, my lord, I can easily run through a list of my qualifications, for there are many men I have treated in similar situations to this one and under the direction of a very wise and trained doctor. Am I not employed now to do that very thing?"

The growl emanating from Robert was low and dangerous.

Nick opened his eyes. There was no sense in prolonging the argument further. He needed to put a stop to it before Robert could request his dueling pistols.

"I believe your patient has awakened." Jack's voice broke the silence and all heads shot toward Nick.

"See what you did!" Robert nearly yelled.

Miss Pepper scoffed as she carried a tray toward Nick, setting it on the bedside table and perching on the chair beside him.

"Oh, wonderful. I am starved," Nick said for Miss Pepper's benefit as much as to end the argument. Besides, it was the truth.

She gave him a dry smile and proceeded to lift a spoon full of creamy soup to his mouth. He drank and sighed. Finally, some flavor.

Robert turned to leave, and Nick raised a hand to stop him. "I wonder if you could explain something to me, my lord."

The look Robert shot Nick was humorous. His pride had taken a few hits, but he would never show it.

"Miss Pepper has been taking her meals in here, has she not?" Nick asked.

Robert's grunt signified a yes.

"I am not sure if that would be very proper now that I am alert. A single woman taking her meals in a single man's bedchamber. What if the news spread?"

Robert seemed to think this over. He clearly was not ready to admit it, but some small part of him had to care for his niece. At the very least, he cared about the image she presented. The one of her mother.

"I will take my meals in my room," Miss Pepper offered. She must have considered this already as well.

"Oh no, that would not do," Nick responded in an exaggerated scold. "We at Halstead are much more civil-mannered than that. How would it look if we forced a guest to eat in her room? Especially when we have a grand dining room and fully equipped staff."

Robert pierced him with a glare, but he ignored it and pushed forward. "Why do you not take your meals with the earl? I am sure he would be more than gratified by your company since mine is so dismally lacking at present."

Miss Pepper glanced at the earl and shook her head, her face a rigid picture of stone. "I am not here as a guest. I couldn't possibly—"

"Nonsense, you will eat with me," the earl snapped. "Six o'clock. Don't be late."

Robert blasted from the room.

Frown lines creased Miss Pepper's brow as she pulled back and dipped the spoon into the bowl once more.

Nick's eyelids drifted shut as he took in the spoonful of delicious, creamy soup and sighed. He opened his eyes to find Miss Pepper watching him with a look of mild amusement—though he detected within her look a hint of distrust.

He flashed her a smile and waited for the reciprocating grin. Women loved his winning smiles.

Well, most women did.

This one just raised her eyebrows.

Then, she stood. What was she doing? His soup was not even half-finished.

Nick watched as she crossed to Jack and spoke to him quietly before leaving. She actually *left* the room. If Nick had not been so surprised, he would have laughed. Instead, he felt disappointed.

"The lady wants to freshen up for her dinner with the earl. Allow me." Jack's face held a suppressed smile as he picked up the spoon and brought it to Nick's mouth. What had felt intimate moments ago now dripped with awkward humiliation. Nick grabbed the spoon and shoved it into his mouth.

"I can feed myself, you half-wit."

"Go ahead."

Jack watched as Nick got through four bites before his arm slackened. "This is bloody disgracing."

"Your behavior?" Jack asked.

Nick narrowed his eyes. "My inability to feed myself." He handed

51

the spoon back to Jack without looking him in the face. "My arm feels so blasted weak."

"You lost a lot of blood, Nick. The doc said he wasn't sure if you were going to make it. It's a near miracle you did."

"And I owe it all to her, don't I?"

Jack nodded, but Nick didn't need the reassurance to know what he'd said was true. Miss Pepper had saved his life. She had stopped the bleeding and ran for help. She'd elevated him in the carriage ride. She had kept him awake until he knew he would be taken care of.

"I suppose I owe a lot to Miss Pepper."

"Yes, and you may want to start with respect."

Giulia changed into the nicer of her gray gowns and looked in the mirror, taking in every inch of her average height, frizzy hair, and plain face. She had rebraided her coronet and splashed cool water on her cheeks, but her overall appearance wasn't much different than normal. Pulling the elephant pendant from her high-necked bodice, she kissed the jeweled surface for luck before tucking it neatly away again. That habit had developed long before her father had gotten heat stroke at the sugar plantation they were observing in Africa. It was the one time the elephant had failed her.

She straightened her spine and glanced at the clock. Time to go.

This was bound to be an interesting evening. The earl was a surly and unapproachable man and had been coerced into having a dinner companion he not only didn't want, but rather despised. She could see it when she looked into his eyes. She was the embodiment of things Lord Hart hated. His brother, for one. Most likely Giulia's mother, as well. And there was something else there, something she hadn't discovered as of yet.

But she would.

Turning for the trunk at the foot of her bed, Giulia knelt on the floor before it and lifted the lid. A stack of periodicals, yellowing with age, were nestled on one side; she removed the set of gloves lying on top of them. Brushing her fingers over the worn letters that graced the cover of the top periodical, Giulia itched to open it and read her father's stories—tales full of adventure and life and deeply reminiscent of the man who wrote them.

But now was not the time. She closed the lid and drew herself up. She was scheduled to dine with the earl, and that required that she keep her wits about her.

Giulia made it to the landing, her mind floating somewhere far away from her, when a soft voice called her name. She looked up at the staircase that led to the east wing and found Jack standing at the mouth of the corridor. He began to descend, and she met him halfway.

"I am sorry to burden you," he said apologetically, "but Nick would like to see you when dinner is over."

"Oh. More flirting? Is he always so shocking?"

Jack dipped his head. "I believe he had an apology in mind."

Giulia held the valet's gaze, her own direct. "I won't put up with his behavior and I hope he has realized it. Either way, I planned to check his dressing after dinner. I haven't had a chance all day."

"I changed it when he bathed, but it could probably do with a glance from a professional." He shot her an amused glance.

She laughed again. "Do not go throwing that in my face, sir. I *am* more qualified than the earl. Though it might have been wiser to keep my mouth closed."

He contrived an innocent look that she did not believe for one second.

"I'll see you after dinner," she said. "Will you arrange his evening tea?"

Jack nodded and went back up the stairs.

Giulia trudged to the parlor where she had been told to meet the earl prior to dinner and was relieved to find it empty. She crossed to the fireplace and warmed her hands on the heat emanating from the hearth.

She could not remain here much longer, now that Nick was beginning to heal. A fortnight of searching the papers at every spare moment, and still she had not found a suitable position. Given Nick's slow recovery and the occasional fever, she had not had much time at her disposal to inquire with any of the larger houses nearby. She'd thought to ask the doctor's sister for a recommendation, but the woman had yet to visit. Anxiety built in Giulia's chest as she considered her dilemma. She would need to find something quickly if she was to secure a place to go once her duties at Halstead were complete.

Admittedly, she'd already had more time than she had previously expected. Nick's case was an odd one. He'd started out with a low fever that had hovered for a few days before advancing dangerously. She'd gotten it down though, and it had broken. But then he did not awaken as she had expected him to. Not for days and days. The doctor said it was likely the blood loss that had weakened him so.

Given Nick's demeanor, she was fairly certain no one had explained to him just how closely he had brushed death's door. Perhaps it was better if he did not know.

Heavy footsteps trod the carpet in the hallway and preceded the earl's entrance. Giulia looked to the doorway, smiling in anticipation of his arrival. She was not rewarded with an answering smile. In fact, she wasn't rewarded with a look of any kind. The earl simply walked into the room and took a chair facing away from her where he waited until Wells announced dinner. She was sure he would glance at her at that point, but apparently he planned to ignore her for the duration of the evening.

The earl made it through offering his arm to escort her into dinner, the entirety of the meal, and even a gruff 'goodnight' without once looking at Giulia's face. He had even walked her all the way to the foot of the table and deposited her there, which would have flattered most women, since it was the seat of hostess and thus a seat of honor, but Giulia knew the truth. Lord Hart was simply placing her as far away from himself as possible. Which was quite far when one considered the grand table that spanned the length of the entire gargantuan dining room. They could not have held a conversation if they'd wanted to. No, they would have had to participate in a yelling match in order to even hear one another at so great a distance. What did any man need a table that large for, anyway?

Giulia vented her frustration as she marched up the stairs and into the east wing. By the time she reached Nick's door, she was fully stomped out, but she could not get the botheration from her bones. Why was the earl so predetermined to hate her? She was not her father.

Her knuckles rapped on the door twice before she heard the "enter" from the other side.

"Is it safe?" she called.

There was muttering that she could not decipher so she pressed her ear closer to the door and then said again, "Is it safe to enter?"

She heard movement again and pressed her ear toward the door further. Drat the solid oak! It was impossible to hear through.

Suddenly Giulia felt herself falling before strong hands jutted through the open door and came around her waist, holding her up. She glanced into Jack's amused face and laughed. "I'm sorry; I could not hear. I was pressing my ear to the door."

Jack chuckled. "It is probably well that you could not." He speared a look toward the bed and the hard gaze that was trained on them from the pillows. Nick's green eyes were glaring.

Giulia placed her hands on Jack's arms and righted herself. "Thank you."

"It was my pleasure." Jack bowed. Then he spoke over his shoulder, "I will see about that tea."

Giulia waited for him to leave and promptly opened the door wide before crossing to Nick. "May I look at your injury?"

His hard glare had softened to a piercing gaze, flicking to the open doorway and back to her. His eyebrow hitched up.

"Propriety, sir."

"I see," he said in a low murmur. "You are protecting me. That is so kind of you."

She flashed him a smile. *Two can play at this game.*

"Absolutely," she drawled with dramatic flair. "We wouldn't want to tarnish your spotless reputation, now would we?"

"I am a paragon of virtue," he said, lifting his good hand to lay over his heart.

"Perhaps you ought to inform the servants of that."

Nick's brows drew together, and she held his gaze as she claimed her seat beside his bed. "What have they said about me?"

"Nothing out of the ordinary," Giulia said in a bored, airy way. "Only that you have a tendency to collect hearts. But that is neither here nor there. I wonder if you could answer a question for me?"

There was only one way she would discover the author of the letter drawing her to Halstead, and it was not through the earl himself.

"I suppose that depends upon the nature of the question."

"The earl," Giulia said without pause. "Why did he hate my father so?"

Nick stared at her.

"Has he remained alone all his life?" she pressed. "Or did he marry once? Perhaps he has close friends in Graton? Though I have seen little evidence of any connections in my fortnight here."

Nick did not open his mouth, instead watching her through curious eyes. Was the man too loyal to the earl to speak about these things?

Doing her best to swallow her disappointment, Giulia gestured to Nick's wound, rising so she might reach the dressing. Nick pulled his open shirt aside so she could have access to his shoulder. Leaning over him, she began unwrapping his bandage. She pried up the linen covering his wound and inspected the area, gratified to find the redness reduced. She closed the linen with a satisfied nod. He was healing up nicely.

"You know," he spoke quietly. Unnervingly. "I have a proposition for you."

Giulia stilled. His breath tickled her ear as he spoke and sent a ripple down her spine. If she was the type of girl to blush, she would have done so in that moment. Instead, she tried to look unaffected, think of Ames, and quickly finish wrapping Nick's shoulder.

Once she finished tying off the wrap, she stepped back and moved behind the wingback chair that sat beside his bed. Folding her arms over the top of it, she rested her chin on her arms. It was the perfect height, so she did not have to bend down at all.

"What proposition is this?"

Nick chuckled. "It would be a lot easier to speak to you if I was not forced to crane my neck. Won't you do me the honor of sitting beside me?"

She watched him for a moment like a prey leery of an attack. She was definitely wary of this man. He had a reputation, according to Tilly. Apparently he hadn't done anything *too* reckless since coming to the castle three years prior, not enough to earn him the reputation of a rake. But he supposedly left a streak of heartbreaks behind him when Robert plucked him from home and brought him to Halstead, and he only added to that list upon arriving in Devon. And with a face like that, and muscles so large and well formed...Giulia was not surprised.

Still, she was *not* going to be another one of those heartbreaks. Nor was she going to be his entertainment while he lounged and recovered.

"I will sit, but only if we set some guidelines first," she said.

"I'm listening."

"First, you must cease this inappropriate behavior. I understand from the stories I shared while you were ill that you may have deemed me a lady of low reputation, but that could not be further from the truth."

Nick had the decency to blush, pink glowing at the tips of his ears. She was testing how much he remembered and was not gratified by the response. So he had been coherent enough to hear her. And apparently, he'd paid attention.

"I'll have you know—"

He cut her off. "I would not do you the injustice of assuming anything of that nature. Your father was the son of an earl. You yourself are the granddaughter and niece of an earl. Do not mistake my reckless flirtations as a jab at your respectability. For that, at least, I am quite sorry. Please, accept my apology on the misunderstanding."

Giulia watched him for a moment longer before circling the plush chair and slowly lowering herself into the seat. "Very well. I'm listening."

CHAPTER 8

*N*ick felt a fool. He'd bungled things, surely, if Miss Pepper believed him to think so low of her. He must do what he could to right the situation. "How was dinner?"

She laughed without mirth. "Long. And boring."

He cringed. "Robert can be a bit prickly."

She raised a sleek eyebrow. "The earl can avert with the best of them."

Nick closed his eyes and pinched the bridge of his nose. Lowering his hand, he brought wary eyes to meet her. "Do not tell me he ignored you during dinner?"

"No, he did better." Leaning in, she lowered her voice. "He ignored me in the parlor, and while he escorted me to the foot of the table and then again while he took his leave."

"The foot of the table?" Nick asked. He pushed himself up on his elbow and cringed, pain lining the planes of his face as he lowered himself back onto the bed.

Miss Pepper frowned and placed a hand on his forearm. "Do not exert yourself. And it is no matter. I hadn't expected much more."

"But that table is the size of Scotland."

"I'd say larger."

Nick laughed to ease his own tension. He could feel warmth emanating from where her hand rested on his arm and he didn't want to move or call attention to it for fear she would reclaim her own space.

He ought to snap out of it, dispel the ridiculous romantic notions forming in his mind, but no one had ever made him feel this way. He'd had his share of stolen kisses and moonlit walks with a maiden or two...or ten. But none of them had ignited this internal need to know their thoughts. Not one of them had given him this warm feeling upon a simple contact. Not a single one of them had stared into his eyes and conjured a craving for a hot cup of chocolate.

Miss Pepper had been right. This was dangerous.

She must have noticed his intent stare. She quickly snatched back her hand and sat primly on the edge of the wingback chair, folding her delicate hands in her lap. "You said you had a proposition for me?"

"Yes. How do you feel about adventures?"

Apparently he had chosen the wrong approach. Her face closed up immediately.

She spoke evenly. A little too evenly. "I've had my share of them. Can't say I'm much inclined to willingly partake in another one."

Her words trailed off. If he could predict how she would have finished that sentence, it would be with *ever again*.

"Allow me to rephrase." He flashed her a smile and tried not to feel dismayed when she did not seem phased. Nick cleared his throat. "How do you feel about puzzles? Or mysteries?"

Her eyes lit up. Victory.

"Which one?" she asked.

"Hmm?"

"Which one? Puzzles or mysteries?"

He tried to pinpoint the one that had affected her. "Let's go with...mysteries?"

Her deep brown eyes lit up once more. The golden flecks hidden within shined in the candlelight and his mouth formed a smile as warmth filled his chest.

"I love a good mystery," she responded. "Would you like me to read to you?"

The offer was very tempting, and he could see how she had reached that conclusion. The enticement to forsake his scheme and pretend that a story was what he wished for all along was great. But he could not do it. He loved a good mystery himself. And without her help, this one was likely to remain unsolved.

The truth of the matter was this: Nick did not have answers to the questions Miss Pepper had asked him.

"Not entirely. Though I will never say no to a good reading." He winked and watched her sigh a little in patience. Clearing his throat, he continued. "You see, I cannot help but think there was a great reason your father was banished from Halstead."

"Banished? Whatever gave you that idea?" Her nose crinkled up in an adorable display of confusion and disgust.

Perhaps it was not yet time to reveal that Robert himself had given Nick the idea. It sounded as if Miss Pepper had been fed a different story. "Was he not?"

"No, he left of his own accord. It was my father who chose to break the connection and then Lord Hart shunned him. After that, there was no point in his returning. He never would have been welcomed."

"Not even to see his mother?"

"How could he when his mother was not alive?"

Aha! So Patrick Pepper *had* lied to his daughter. But why?

"Actually," Nick began softly. He stalled for a moment, considering the best way to break the news. Miss Pepper watched him intently and he offered a sad smile. "She only died two years ago."

"No," Miss Pepper whispered.

"I am afraid it is true."

"I don't believe you." Her eyes flashed and she stood, marching from the room before he could say anything to waylay her. His instinct was to run after her but given his current situation, he guessed he would make it to the door, perhaps the hallway given his adrenaline, before he collapsed.

He sighed. She would have to process the information and then come back to him. If she loved a good mystery as much as he thought she did, then it wouldn't take long.

Nick was full of lies. He had to be.

Giulia paced her bedroom as the ascending sun rose steadily higher, calling forth the birds that nested above her window and turning the sky a lovely pale blue. She glanced at the carpet and checked for a worn footpath, but the rug was in pristine condition. Surprising, since she had spent the entirety of last night alternating between pacing in front of the fireplace and trying—and failing—to sleep.

She paused, dropping her face into her hands.

What would Nick gain by falsifying this? The same question repeated in her mind for the thousandth time, followed quickly by: *But what would Father have gained from lying?*

It was a lot to take in.

Her stomach growled and she glanced down at her midsection. "Fine. I'll feed you."

Giulia finished dressing herself and made her way to the breakfast room before loading her plate and devouring every last bite. Her appetite had slowly returned to normal in the weeks since arriving at Halstead, but it was hard to break old habits. And when one was used to not knowing where or when their next meal would come, one always took advantage of the food present. Without hesitation.

Heavy footsteps echoed outside the door and Giulia glanced up to find the earl in the doorway, staring at her as though he had seen a ghost, his wrinkled skin pale and eyes wide. She sent him a smile and he averted his gaze before crossing to the sideboard and loading a plate of his own. She considered starting a conversation, or *trying* to start one, but the earl obviously had an aversion to her. She would probably do better to respect the distance he sought. She was a guest in his home, after all. Sort of.

She paused in the doorway and turned, speaking before she could tell herself to stop. "The gravy is superb, my lord. Never have I partaken of a finer breakfast in all my days."

She hazarded a look at the old man. He stilled above the gravy with ladle in hand, mid-spoonful. Giulia waited another few seconds before dropping a curtsy that he probably did not see and escaping to the east wing. Nick was correct. There was something odd about the earl's dislike of her, and she wanted to get to the bottom of it.

Her fist was about to connect with the door when it swung open. She jumped back to avoid a collision, but Jack had her under the elbows and righted her before she'd managed to move away.

"We really must quit meeting this way," Giulia joked.

"If you insist," Jack said with a wink. He nodded toward the bed. "He is awake."

"And decent?"

Jack lowered his voice. "That depends on what you mean by decent." He chuckled as he released her, and she scowled at him in jest before moving into the room and opening the door as wide as it could go.

"You know," Nick called across the room, "the door just may pop right off if you try to open it any further."

Giulia turned her scowl on him before crossing to his bedside. "How are you feeling this morning?"

"Better now." Nick sent her a roguish grin which she met with a stern look.

She lifted her eyebrows. "Must I remind you of our terms?"

"Must I remind you that I never doubted your reputation?"

"No?" Giulia challenged. "Yet it is acceptable for you to risk it?"

"And *that* wasn't risking it?" Nick retorted with a gesture toward the doorway.

Giulia caught his steel glare and returned it with fervor. She tried to reduce the ice in her tone when she spoke, but it was altogether impossible. "*That* was an accident. Or do you propose I make a habit of standing outside your door, lying in wait for Jack to open it so I may fall desperately into his arms?"

"Well, it sure looked as though you were enjoying yourself," he muttered.

It took her a moment to piece together what he had said, and she sighed. She came here with a specific purpose, and they were getting nowhere fast. She nodded to his shoulder. "May I?"

He sat himself up a little further and opened his shirt to give her access to the bandage. She leaned over him and peeled back the linen to check the doctor's stitches and had trouble focusing on what she was supposed to be looking for. It was nearly impossible with Nick's breath tickling the hair by her ear and his body heat reaching her torso as she leaned over him. She touched a cool finger to his warm skin to peel back the bandage further and he jumped slightly.

"Sorry," she muttered, and then began closing the bandage.

"Trust me, you have nothing to apologize for." Nick's low voice reached her gut and she shivered. Clearing her throat, she reached for the blanket around his waist and pulled it higher, out of habit.

His hand came over hers and held it in place. "I am warm enough, thank you."

Giulia nodded and retreated, wringing her hands to wipe away the feel of his contact. "Shall I fetch you some tea?"

"Some breakfast would be nice."

She regarded him for a moment and nodded. "It seems to me you should be able to stomach real food by now. You have not lost your meals since those first few days. The pea soup settled well, did it not?"

"Yes, it was lovely."

Giulia nodded before she turned to pull the rope. She hesitated on the far side of the room, feigning an interest in the fire and waited for Tilly.

She needed distance from Nick to regain her composure. He was stirring feelings within her that only one man had a right to. A man who was far away working hard for a future he was planning on sharing with her. Guilt seeped into her stomach and she scolded herself. Ames deserved better than this. He deserved complete and utter loyalty. And she planned to give it to him.

Tilly stepped inside and Giulia asked her to bring up a breakfast tray for Nick. "No more broth, Tilly. Would you inform Cook? And please make sure that while he is served solid foods, we must keep away from anything rich for today. Just in case."

Tilly bobbed a curtsy and left.

Giulia steeled herself. She was about to have a conversation with a flirtatious, attractive man that she should neither flirt with nor find attractive. Perhaps if she imagined he was covered in warts she would be able to accomplish her goal.

A small smile graced her lips as she sat in the chair across from Nick and imagined his neatly square jaw dotted with warts, his arched cheekbones pocked with bumps, his gorgeous green eyes hooded over with the malady. It was nearly working.

His face split into a glorious grin, dashing away the imaginary warts at once. "What do you find so funny?"

Well, not working nearly enough. She waved off the question and gave him one of her own. "Do you have a plan for obtaining information on what made my father flee? Or...I suppose, if there was another reason for his departure?"

"As a matter of fact, I do."

She waited patiently for him to continue, but it was fruitless. "Care to elaborate?"

"I think I would be much more inclined to talk once I have eaten."

Giulia gave him a patient look. "Very well." This man was going to be the death of her. Of all the patients she had ever assisted with, Nick was by far the most trying. He was not the first man to attempt a little flirtation with Giulia, but he was the first who was not either in her father's party and thus aware that she was off limits, or on the boat where she was constantly shadowed by the tall, dark, and leering Ames. The same Ames who insisted she wait for a betrothal—and, subsequently, the protection of his name—until he proved he could support her.

She wondered what Ames was doing at that moment, and why he had not written to her yet. In fact, why had she not received a single letter at all since arriving to Halstead? The followers of *The Adventures of Patrick Pepper and his assistant Jules* were usually more persistent than this.

CHAPTER 9

*N*ick watched Miss Pepper's face scrunch up in thought, her
adorable little nose wrinkling as though she smelled
something sour, her fine eyebrows pulled together in concentration.
Something was definitely bothering her. And he wanted to know what
it was.

He opened his mouth to ask but closed it when he heard the soft
footsteps of Tilly bringing his breakfast. He had seen the maid a thousand times since coming to Halstead, but never once had he known, or
even cared what her name was until Miss Pepper arrived. The woman
was an enigma.

She spoke to Tilly by name—which, on its own, wasn't so strange.
But Giulia addressed the maid kindly and *asked* for things instead of
relaying orders. It was bizarre for a woman of her status to treat a
servant with such regard. Giulia's thoughtfulness was evident in
everything she did, from her gentle ministrations to Nick's shoulder
to the way she treated the servants.

Yet, Nick noticed something else between the little blonde maid
and Miss Pepper. Loyalty and respect. He commended Miss Pepper for
finding that so quickly in the help, but he had a feeling she probably
commanded it everywhere she went. People liked her.

Jack certainly did, at least.

Jack.

Nick was going to have to give his valet a set down once he was out of this dratted bed and on his own two feet again. The man was insufferable. Miss Pepper was niece to the earl. She was not some lowly housemaid the valet could woo on his own time.

Nick shook his head. He wasn't being fair. Jack was more than just some valet. He was something of a friend. Distance had grown between Nick and Jack as they aged out of short coats, the chasm widening when Nick was sent off to school. But the quiet conversations and gentle support Jack offered since agreeing to become Nick's valet and come to Halstead with him were closing the gap, creating an odd bond between the men.

To speak nothing of the debt Nick owed Jack's father, who had agreed to become his steward when he left for Halstead, taking on both the responsibility of Nick's farm and tenants, but also seeing to the needs of Nick's mother and sister.

"This is wonderful, Tilly. Please set it right there. Perfect." Miss Pepper's voice cut into his ruminating, her tone carrying gratitude.

That must be it, Nick thought. *The help must appreciate being...appreciated.*

"Yes," he said to the maid. "Thank you, Tilly."

The maid and Miss Pepper both shot looks at him filled with surprise and...concern? Miss Pepper stepped forward and laid her graceful hand over his forehead, her own puckered in thought. "No fever," she muttered to herself.

Nick's fingers circled her wrist, pulling it away from his face. "Is it so very odd that I would thank Tilly for bringing me my first solid meal in years?"

"No," Miss Pepper said hesitantly. "But *years* is a bit of a stretch."

Tilly bobbed a curtsy and scooted away as quickly as she could, pulling the door shut behind her with a soft click. Bless the girl. Miss Pepper did not seem to notice.

Nick yanked her wrist softly, pulling her to sit beside him on the edge of the bed. "That smells divine," he murmured.

Miss Pepper watched him warily. "Sir, why are you holding my arm?" She spoke quietly, as if she was skirting a wild animal.

"Will you do me a favor?"

"That would depend on what you ask of me."

Ideas flooded his mind; there were so many things he could think to ask of her. He redirected his wayward thoughts to the task at hand. "I want you to call me Nick."

Her eyes grew wide as surprise etched her face. "But we hardly know one another."

"I don't know about that," Nick countered. Her hand had fallen slack in his and he started drawing circles on the underside of her wrist with his thumb. "You've told me quite a bit about yourself. Except, oddly enough, for your name."

She watched him. She said nothing, but she did not pull her hand away either. He continued. "I feel as if I know you quite well, actually. And we've told each other things in confidence, if you will recall. Surely that makes us something like friends."

"In regard to?"

He leaned forward and lowered his voice. "How very fast you can run, of course."

She let out a light laugh, but it wasn't much. It certainly wasn't enough. She was being polite.

"And," he continued, "we are business partners."

She arched a brow.

"Our quest to uncover the mystery involving your father's history with Halstead."

"Oh."

"Yes. You see? I have multiple valid points." He had made an effort to word their project in a way that would keep her interested. He'd nearly flinched when he'd said 'quest' and hoped it would not make her pull back. She hadn't, thank heavens, but she also hadn't yet agreed.

"There is one thing you have not considered, I fear," she said as she pulled her hand away and laid it in her lap. She was still sitting on the edge of his bed, her hip pressed against his side and warming him from the inside out.

"And what is that?"

"That perhaps I am not at liberty to allow the use of my given name."

This he had not expected. He stilled for a moment but recovered quickly. "A name is not a promise, Miss Pepper."

"Oh, I am fairly certain I know exactly why *you* feel that way, sir."

"What are you implying?" He tried not to feel affronted, but it was difficult to keep any of the offense he felt from leaking into his tone.

"I have heard of your reputation and the pitiful women who fall for your charm only to be left heartbroken and alone. I value myself too much for that. I am worth more than a few stolen kisses." She delivered her speech with a calm surety that told Nick she wasn't judging him. She wasn't speaking from atop her high, spiritual mount. No, it was worse. She was calmly explaining why she was worth more than the likes of him.

And she was right.

"I commend you, but that does not speak to whether or not you are free, as you mentioned." He swallowed. "Is there a man in your life? Are you promised?"

She stilled. Rising, she sat on the chair beside the bed, leaving a chill in the void. Apparently, that had been the wrong thing to say.

"I am not betrothed, no."

Nick waited for her to say more, but her lips were pinched in a thin line, her eyes unwilling to meet his gaze. He tried for a lighter tone. "If nothing else, we are cousins. Might that be reason for some familiarity?"

"Only distantly, I am told. Though I could not get a clear answer from the servants about just how we are related."

"We are both descendants of Albert Pepper," Nick explained. "The fourth Earl of Hart."

"That is distant, indeed," she said, eyebrows raised. "My uncle is the seventh earl, is he not?"

Nick nodded. He had one last point in his favor. "And besides," he said, doing his best to sound nonchalant, "you have not called me Mr. Pepper once, and I think I understand why. I am offering you an alternative. We do not have to discuss it further."

The ghostly pallor of Miss Pepper's skin proved that Nick was correct. She must not appreciate calling him by the name her father had claimed. In all her time beside him, he had never once been called by name. Unless one counted the nickname…

"Of course," he persevered, "you can always continue to call me *Danger*."

She dropped her chin. "How can you remember that?" She sounded embarrassed, but she did not regain the color in her face. How could one have *such* control over their features?

"As I said, I remember a lot of things you told me when I was recovering. They are quite jumbled, to be frank. But I remember them, nonetheless."

"Very well, Nick. I can see you will not relent. But you must understand this in no way signifies anything great."

He grinned. Success. "Of course, Miss Pepper."

She chuckled and began to cut the ham on his plate. He salivated just thinking about it. "Do I not deserve the same courtesy?"

She snorted. It made him want to make her laugh again.

"You are relentless," she said.

"I am persistent," he countered.

"There is a difference?" She cocked an eyebrow. Then she brought the fork to his mouth and fed him a large bite of tender, juicy ham. He groaned in ecstasy. Broth had *nothing* on real food, on the feeling of something solid filling his stomach. He had missed this.

He also knew himself capable of feeding himself this ham, but he would not give that away yet. The longer he appeared to need Miss Pepper, the longer she stayed at Halstead.

Miss Pepper laughed and shook her head while she prepared another bite. "Julia."

He perked up, coming out of his euphoria.

She gave him a stern look. "But my name begins with a 'G'. G-I-U-L-I-A. None of this British *Julia* nonsense."

"Italian?" he asked.

"Yes."

He took another bite and chewed while he watched her prepare a forkful and smother it in gravy. She was fantastic. "But you are British, yes?"

She glanced up at him with offense so fierce he nearly choked on his ham.

"I am *half* British, yes. And half of me is Italian."

Nick decided not to push the issue. It appeared to be a tender one. He put his hands up in mock surrender. "Very well, Giulia."

She smiled to herself while she fed him another bite.

He had not felt this satisfied in a long, long time.

CHAPTER 10

*G*iulia spent the better part of the morning listening to Nick's plan to help her win over the earl. Of course, he did not present it that way. According to him, the plan outlined how they would solve the mystery. But Giulia was clever. She could tell he was skirting his true motivations. She had no idea what Nick had to gain by repairing the relationship between Giulia and her uncle, but he *did* have a reason, even if he kept it to himself. She wanted to figure out *his* motivations nearly as much as she wanted to learn the truth behind her father and uncle's relationship, so she went along with Nick's orchestrations.

They may have had different reasons for wanting to know the truth about the past, but they had a common goal, and their best chance of figuring it out required they worked together. As soon as Giulia had recovered from the impact of finding out about her father's dishonesty regarding her grandmother's death, she was determined to discover why. If the woman had wanted nothing to do with Giulia, then Father would have told her that. He always valued her *levelheaded intellect*, as he so kindly phrased it, and he had always been honest with her—or so she thought.

Father had never tried to hide the truth about her mother leaving.

He'd never laid any blame at Giulia's door either, though she conjured enough of that herself. Losing a mother at four years old would do that to a girl. Particularly when her mother walked out without a backward glance.

Giulia had to get her mind back on track. Her blood was beginning to heat and if it started to simmer, then it was a quick jump straight to boil.

She glanced at the man sitting up in the oversized four-poster bed and watched as he focused on the writing desk on his lap. He was taking notes so they could have all of their information gathered in one place.

Standing, Giulia leaned over Nick and read what he had written so far to make sure he hadn't forgotten anything. She skimmed the left column where he'd penned his version of history—things he had learned from the earl or other members of the household. Even Giulia's grandmother, the dowager countess, Lady Hart herself.

It took every ounce of willpower to not beg more details about Lady Hart. What was she like? Did she have kind eyes? Did her sons take after her, or did they more closely resemble their father? Had Lady Hart even known that Giulia existed?

But Giulia was afraid of the answers, much like she was afraid to open Father's journal. That piece of information she had thus far kept from Nick. She was positive that if she brought it up, he would demand they read it for the sake of the mystery.

Giulia almost regretted betraying her love of a good mystery.

Almost, but not quite.

"Resemblance to my mother?" Giulia paraphrased the note she read on Nick's paper. "What has that to do with anything?"

"Robert mentioned it. He said he could never live in a house where he had to look at your face every day and see her."

Well, that was news. Giulia moved back to her chair and reclined in it. But only so slightly. "So he must have traveled to Italy with my father. That is where they met and married."

Nick glanced up at her. "They married in Italy?"

73

"Yes. They spent the early years of their marriage living with my mother's family. They moved to London right before I was born."

"Do you know what brought them here?"

"Father was proud of his heritage. I may have spent half of my life traveling around the world, but we always came home. He never said as much, but I can only assume Italy was a stepping stone in their journey and never where he wanted to spend the rest of his life."

Whether or not her mother knew that was a different story, and Giulia had often thought that perhaps Father had not made his intentions clear before the marriage. He had a tendency to dive in head first on every adventure, fully submerging himself in the culture and the customs of whatever country he was visiting. He could have led her mother on without realizing he was doing so.

Jack stepped into the room, followed closely by Dr. Mason.

Giulia saw Nick covertly cover his list with a blank piece of parchment as she turned to greet the newcomers. "Good day, Dr. Mason." She held up her hands in mock surrender. "Now please, do not be angry with me—"

"Miss Pepper," he said solemnly. "I could never be angry with you."

"That is rather convenient," she said, maintaining an amused smile, "for I disregarded your advice."

His red eyebrows raised in surprise as his head dipped slightly. "Well, was it very terrible advice?"

Giulia chuckled. "No, I would say it was quite sound...at the time."

A twinkle lit his eye. She studied his fine, angular jaw and high cheekbones. His auburn hair was just the right amount of disheveled and he carried his doctor's bag with a level of nonchalance that made him all the more appealing. Nothing like those high and mighty London doctors who carried their bags like a badge of honor and praise, yet hardly touched their patients.

"Well," she began, clearing her throat, "I have started our patient on a diet of solid, bland foods. He has done so well with the broth and soups that I went against your advice and tested bread and ham." She specifically left the gravy out. He had not asked for an inventory, anyway, so she was not lying.

"I can see that our patient is looking much better today, so I must thank you for taking the initiative. I applaud your judgement in this circumstance."

"But," Giulia finished for the doctor, "I should heed you in the future?"

"It is most likely your safest course of action."

"Of course." Giulia smiled at Dr. Mason. His kind rebuke was heard and received. Although, she really *had* been right in this situation. She did know what she was doing.

"Now, Miss Pepper, I brought along my sister and she has been shown into the drawing room. She awaits your company, if it would please you."

"Of course, Dr. Mason." Giulia curtseyed and left. Nick didn't look too pleased, but he was about to be poked and prodded in a very uncomfortable manner, so perhaps it was to be expected.

Giulia, on the other hand, could not have been happier. She was about to meet a friend. Or, at least, she hoped that was the case.

Giulia had not wished to be out of mourning and back into wearing at least a smidgen of color more than she did in this moment. She looked at the woman seated across from her and was dumbfounded by her beauty.

Dr. Mason's sister looked to be within a year or two of Giulia's own age, and she had the most glorious red hair framing a perfect heart-shaped face and luminescent pale blue eyes. Her pale skin was not marred by a single freckle. The entire ensemble was set off to perfection by a crisp, black gown. It made Giulia's dove gray wilt in comparison and fully shamed her into a loss of speech—an entirely foreign feeling.

"Do you plan to stay long in Devon?" Amelia Fawn asked in a musical voice. Was she absolutely perfect in every way?

"I am not sure at the present. I have been looking for a position in the papers but have not had much luck as of yet."

Mrs. Fawn's slender red eyebrows rose a fraction. "Allow me to know if there is anything I may do to assist you in the search. I have lived in Graton for most of my life. If you would like, I can make some inquiries on your behalf."

"Yes, I would appreciate that very much. I would love to do something in the realm of teaching, whether as a governess or teaching assistant. I have sufficient experience."

Mrs. Fawn nodded her head. "Do you have a time frame in mind?"

With Nick still abed, it was impossible to know. He seemed to be healing more every day, but his was a slow-moving process. And she had agreed to stay as long as he needed her. "Not particularly, no. But I would guess within the next few weeks, or perhaps a month."

Silence stretched for a moment and Giulia swallowed hard. Mrs. Fawn's beauty was intimidating enough, but to add kindness, too? Her serenity was lovely, but also made it difficult to decipher if her kindness was truly good, or if there was an ulterior motive at play. Giulia wanted to believe the woman was genuine, but that did not keep her from holding her guard in place.

"I can see how that might make things difficult," Giulia laughed lightly. "Perhaps it is best to hold off at present. I am entirely at the disposal of my invalid."

Mrs. Fawn perked up. "*Your* invalid?"

"Oh, this is uncomfortable." Giulia shifted in her seat while she tried to figure a way out of her verbal blunder. "I only meant that my sole focus at Halstead Manor is to assist restoring Nicholas Pepper to health. Your brother did not tell you?"

"He did." Mrs. Fawn seemed to physically deflate a fraction. "I only wondered if you had a particular relationship with Mr. Pepper by the way you phrased it. The man has a bit of a reputation and I was preparing to warn you most strongly."

Giulia nodded. "I have heard as much from the servants, but do not fear. I am in no danger of losing my heart to him."

"Be that as it may, you ought to be cautious. Mr. Pepper has a tendency to flirt most outrageously with little intent to pursue the situation."

She spoke like a woman with experience in the matter. Before Giulia could inquire further, however, Mrs. Fawn continued. "Are you allowed time away from the invalid?"

"I would imagine so. He is recovering nicely. And he does have a rather attentive valet."

"Splendid." Mrs. Fawn clapped her hands together and leaned forward slightly, lowering her voice. "I would like to extend an invitation to tea, then. There are a few local ladies who would love to make your acquaintance. And I assume you would not mind a break from this entirely male household."

"Yes, I suppose a break would be nice," Giulia said hesitantly. She had never spent much time around women though, and tea with a few local ladies was almost frightening.

Surely it was not a large gathering, she thought, surveying Mrs. Fawn's black mourning gown. It had thrown her off guard when she first entered the room for it was unusual to pay calls when one was in mourning. Now she was hosting a tea? Perhaps Graton had a different set of etiquette than the rest of England.

"Does Thursday suit?" Mrs. Fawn looked the picture of poise.

"Thursday suits."

Mrs. Fawn's smile grew. She appeared pleased, and it made her all the more remarkable. It was an overwhelming experience being on this end of that magnitude of beauty.

Dr. Mason entered the room and glanced from Giulia to his sister, a smile playing on his lips.

"It was so pleasant to meet you," Mrs. Fawn cooed as she rose. "I look forward to Thursday."

"As do I."

They said their farewells and Giulia approached the tall windows that lined the front wall, watching the siblings climb into a phaeton. She returned to the seating area, lowering herself into a cream upholstered chair and allowing her mind to wander to Ames.

What would he think of these niceties? Of the plush drawing

room, and Giulia entertaining a caller as though she was the lady of the house? He likely would have laughed, loudly and with great disrespect. He would have told Giulia to cease putting on airs and behave like the humble maiden her father had raised her to be.

And then he might have asked why in all of her time at Halstead, Giulia had yet to tell another soul of his existence. She swallowed the bile rising in her throat and wrapped her arms around her midsection. She'd never been in a situation such as this before. How did one explain a relationship such as theirs? He was part of her—her other half. For as long as she could remember, he was a part of her life and a permanent fixture in her day-to-day.

Now that he was *not* so intricately sewn into her daily life, she'd had a chance to breathe, to see the type of person she was when she was on her own. In a way, it was liberating.

She scowled and rose. Just thinking those words felt like the deepest betrayal. She would push these new independent thoughts from her mind. She must. Ames was the one. He was perfect for her. No one—*no one* understood her like he did. And they were going to be married. He was hard at work providing a living for her. He was following his dreams so they could follow theirs together. Right?

She shook her head and made it halfway up the stairs before she turned and followed her feet to the earl's study. Before she gave heed to her actions, her fist was lightly knocking on the heavy door.

A gruff "Enter!" brought her hand to the doorknob and she watched it turn as her feet carried her inside the study. She took three steady footsteps into the room and halted, clasping her hands before her. The earl looked surprised to see her, but that was to be expected. His eyes held a touch of guarded vulnerability that she hadn't seen before; she smiled sweetly, hoping it meant a lull in his typical, crotchety behavior.

"Has any mail been delivered in my father's name? If so, I would like it to be given to me so I may continue his correspondence. I apologize if that may be uncomfortable for you, but you need not be concerned; it is expected. The people who write to my father—his readers—are expecting a response, and I do not wish to disappoint them."

There was a pause as she held the earl's gaze.

Lord Hart cleared his throat and fidgeted with his neckcloth. "Very well. I will see that they are delivered to your chamber." He nodded and the steel returned to his eyes. She bowed her head and left the room before racing up the west wing stairs and into her own room where she flopped onto the plush bed. That had been exhilarating.

CHAPTER 11

When Giulia reached her room after another silent dinner, there were letters stacked in columns on her writing desk. Funny, the earl hadn't mentioned them that evening. Of course, he hadn't mentioned *anything* at dinner, so that was not really a surprise. She had hoped the few encounters they'd had would cause Lord Hart to soften up enough to at least *glance* at her this evening. But her hope had been in vain.

She lowered herself onto the chair and began sifting through the mail, searching for one scrawl in particular. She got to the end of the first pile and frowned. At least there were two more piles. Sifting through the second column, Giulia noted the same handwriting a few times. It was the oddest thing; the wax was sealed with the image of a rooster. A very familiar rooster, though she could not place where she knew it from.

Abandoning her quest for a letter from Ames, she plucked a rooster-sealed missive from the pile and ran her thumb under the wax before unfolding the paper. It was short, but she jumped to the bottom to read the signature before finishing the note.

How could this be? She went cold all over as her hand absentmindedly fished the elephant from her bodice before putting it to her lips.

She pursed them into a kiss but did not move the elephant away, as if she could siphon courage from the object.

The elephant dropped from her fingers and she scattered the piles of letters in a frenzy, pulling out the offending missives containing the rooster-sealed wax until she had a neat pile before her. Three. There were three more unopened letters sealed with the rooster and directed to her. Not to Father, but to her. How had they been thrown into the lot with the rest? Surely the servants knew that her mail could be delivered.

She was still alive.

Giulia's fingers hovered over the rooster as a memory came unbidden to her mind. An unfinished cross stitch secured in a hoop, the image of a rooster—*this* rooster—in its center and a name half-stitched above the animal. Now that she could see the rooster before her so clearly, her mind filled in the blank. Cattaneo.

Her mother's family name.

Father had thrown the cross stitch into the fire with no uncertain rage when Giulia had found it and presented it to him nearly a year after her mother had left. She recalled being hurt by the action and had gone to retrieve the last memento of her mother when Father had picked her up and tossed her in bed, growling that *that woman* was no longer welcome in the Pepper family and neither were her things. The next day Father had apologized, but his temper was forever etched on her brain. Not that it needed to be. In all of her subsequent fifteen years she had never seen evidence of it again.

Still, she had never fully moved on from the guilt she felt regarding her mother's departure. If her mother had loved her, she would have stayed, wouldn't she?

And now, this.

Her finger broke seal after seal until all four letters were opened, read, reread, and then lined up in chronological order.

"My Darling Giulia—"

"...sorry to hear of your father's passing..."

"If you would be so kind as to help me."

That was the fudge. Sixteen years of silence and now her condolences were riddled with pleas for a favor. Giulia's stomach soured and she pushed away from the desk. Her eye caught on the fallen notes scattering the floor and she bent to retrieve them. It only took a moment to gather and sort the remaining letters and discover that nothing had come from Ames.

Plopping on the edge of her seat, Giulia huffed a breath, blowing a stray hair out of her face. She had been gone from London for weeks now. Was Ames not wondering how she fared, at the very least? How her uncle received her? No, he probably wasn't. He was under the same illusion as she that the earl had invited her to Halstead.

The room grew unbearably stuffy and her pulse raced as anxiety clenched her stomach. The last month had turned her world upside down, then sideways, and then kicked her in the stomach for good measure. And that was not counting the grief she continued to struggle with over losing her father nearly nine months ago.

She grew angry at her situation. She should be Mrs. Giulia Ames right now, far away from this horrid castle and grouchy uncle and too-attractive invalid.

Nick. Her throat went dry. A wry laugh slipped out and she sunk onto the floor, covering her face in her hands. She could not help that he was the most attractive man she had ever seen. She had no control over her rapidly beating pulse whenever he was within an arm's reach. And she *really* could not help the overwhelming guilt that clouded her whenever she had such thoughts.

Ames should be with her. She wouldn't be thinking of other men if Ames was present. His lack of correspondence wasn't helping the situation, particularly when he had to be the person forwarding the letters to Halstead Manor; her father's readership knew of her new direction at her uncle's home, but her mother did not. She had directed her letters to the London house.

Giulia gathered the rooster-sealed letters before folding them as one and leaving the room. Her feet led her through the dark corridors and over the landing of the main staircase toward Nick's room of their own volition. She had not intended to go there but felt as if she was watching her feet move instead of telling them where to go. The disconnect was disconcerting.

Her fist paused above the door and she let out a whoosh of breath before knocking ever so lightly. A moment later the door swung softly open and Jack stood on the other side.

"Is he awake?" she asked.

"Yes." Jack hesitated momentarily, his gaze flicking to her eyes before he stepped aside.

"Would you stay?" Giulia asked.

Jack smiled knowingly. Not only was the hour late, but she had no nursing business to complete at this time and if she and Nick were discovered alone it would be bad for both of their reputations.

"Of course." Jack let her in and closed the door behind her. She crossed the room, watching Nick's curious gaze as it flitted from her to the stack of letters in her hand.

She raised the letters and sighed. "I have received a clue." She fanned them. "Or four."

His interest deepened and he patted the bed beside him. Giulia shook her head and settled into the maroon wingback next to the bed.

She noticed Jack take a seat in the other wingback that sat beside the fire. Odd. A servant would never take such liberties, especially when the master was inhabiting the room. Although, Jack had never acted like a submissive servant. She had long suspected that there was more there than a simple servant/master relationship, and it made her respect Nick a little more for his compassion.

"May I?" Nick gestured to the letters. They were glued to her hands and she felt an odd reluctance to let them go. The whole concept was still surreal. The reality of her name written in her mother's loopy hand had yet to truly settle.

"Perhaps," Nick spoke softly, seeming to sense the magnitude of the situation, "you can begin by telling me what those are."

That sounded even worse. *Verbalize* something she could not even force herself to wrap her head around? No, thank you. She straightened her spine and thrust the letters forward.

Nick took them tentatively before settling against his headboard and perusing the words. Giulia watched as his eyebrows did a dance with each new letter. They seemed to rise higher and higher before falling and drawing together, only to rise again. When he finished, he laid the folded papers in his lap and looked at her with a softness in his eyes and a smile slightly turning his lips. Was it pity?

She hardened. "I do not know what you are thinking, Nicholas Pepper, but I can tell you right this instant to stop your pitying and get to work helping me piece this together. This is a business arrangement. Enough of your soft gazes."

He only deepened his look of concern and she shot to her feet, glaring.

Nick's hands came up in surrender. "Very well, you have my word. No more soft gazes."

"Then tell me what you think of this," Giulia said.

"I thought you hadn't heard from your mother since she left you."

"I haven't," she whispered, her gaze stuck on the pile of letters in his lap.

Nick's arched brows rose again. "Well, this is quite a bit of correspondence all of a sudden. And rather desperate sounding, too."

Giulia chewed on her lip. "That is what I thought as well. I can honestly say I have no idea what she is referring to. Father wasn't one for souvenirs. We packed light and traveled light, and if you looked at our home you would see there is no great evidence of our trips abroad. Of course, I have gathered a collection of my own over the years, but it is small and there is no jeweled key. I would know. I had to go through all of my father's things before vacating the house."

"Perhaps it was left in your mother's things?" Nick offered. "She wrote that your father refused to return 'her key,' so perhaps it was something she had left behind unintentionally."

"No, if she left it behind then it is long gone. He disposed of everything that belonged to her immediately." An image flashed in her mind of the rooster cross stitch burning in the fire, the flames licking the rooster's tail feathers as a young Giulia watched on in horror.

"Then maybe it was not her key," Nick said hesitantly. "Maybe she simply wants something your father would not give to her. She did wait until he died to approach you."

"The owner of the key is rather irrelevant at this point. Never have I seen anything like she described. A jeweled key? She simply expects me to know what she is referring to, but I do not." Giulia scoffed. "As if we have been in contact for the last sixteen years." She threw her arms up in frustration and then buried her face in her hands.

Raising her head, she scoffed again when she saw Nick's face etched in sorrow.

Giulia pointed a finger at him. "I meant what I said, Nick. No pity, please, or I will solve this on my own."

He smiled guiltily. "Has your father ever talked about a key?"

"No, never."

They sat in thought, and both jumped slightly when Jack's voice broke the silence. "It is getting late; maybe your detective work would benefit from a good night's sleep and a refreshed mind."

Giulia nodded. "You are right, Jack. I don't know what I was thinking, coming here tonight. I should have saved it for morning." She shuddered and gave Nick a weak smile, holding out her hand for the letters. He put his own in it instead, squeezing her fingers.

"Do you mind if I keep these tonight? I will go over them again and see if there is something we may have missed."

Giulia relented. "Very well." She pulled her hand reluctantly from his firm, sustaining grip and clasped her hands to dispel the overwhelming absence she felt.

"Goodnight, Nick." She turned toward the door that Jack held open for her and stopped to place a hand on his arm. "Goodnight, Jack." He smiled at her and closed the door behind her. The dark hallway felt cool and empty and made her feel small.

Giulia wrapped her arms around her waist and began the trek to the west wing. She had not felt this lonely in months. And what she truly wanted, the strong arms of her father wrapped around her and comforting away her sorrows, she could never have again. A renewed sense of anger at Ames for sending her away filled her body. *Why* had he not reached out to her? Was one simple letter so much to ask?

She stopped dead in her tracks. She had earlier determined that she needed to tell Nick about Ames and shut the door on any fluttering feelings she was beginning to have. Their late-night meeting would have been the perfect opportunity. Why had she not?

Once again, she'd failed to speak the truth. Groaning, she continued toward her room. She would tell him tomorrow. All she had to do was picture Ames's loving face, his dark hair falling over his forehead, an appreciative look in his eyes. Ames may not possess Nick's classic good looks, but he was handsome to her.

Would it have hurt for him to protect her with a betrothal? Why had he been so adamant about waiting for that? The wedding, she understood. Or, at least, she tried to understand. But waiting for the betrothal as well?

That, she did not understand at all.

CHAPTER 12

The sun rose far too early and Nick groaned. He hadn't gotten much sleep, thanks to his healing shoulder. His entire body felt stiff and he craved a good, sweaty battle of fisticuffs. Or even a large pile of wood to chop. Really, anything he could do to overwork his arms and give himself the overwhelming feeling of satisfaction he received when he worked his muscles good and hard.

But, no. That was not to be. Not for a long while, according to Dr. Mason. The bullet did a number on his shoulder, and while it was healing nicely, he would not regain full use of his arm or even full rotation of his shoulder for a couple of months. *Months.*

He turned onto his good arm and lay sideways while he watched the sun rise. The letters stacked on the bedside table caught his attention and he grew even more solemn.

Poor Giulia; as if she needed more heartache. And that wretched mother of hers. There was obviously something of value related to that key. Given the description, 'jeweled,' it could very well be the key itself that was valuable. And the woman's plea to Giulia to name a date and place and she would travel to England to retrieve it? That was the largest clue, to be sure.

One did not cross an ocean for a mere trinket. Particularly when she had waited for its owner's demise to claim what she believed to be hers.

Nick wanted to burn the letters. If only he could erase Giulia's problems so easily.

He stilled at the thought. He had only known the girl for a week, *weeks* if one counted his semi-lucid bouts of listening to the stories of her unconventional life. Where had this sudden overprotectiveness come from?

She was alone, that was why. Her father was gone, and she had no one in the world whom she could rely on. That *must* be the reason for his sudden need to protect her. That, and her tiny, delicate frame. It just begged to be protected. And the way she straightened her back like she was preparing for battle. That, too. He wanted to obliterate any need for her to ever fight a battle again.

Now, if only he could get Robert to come around a little faster. If he could convince Robert of her worth then he need not concern himself with defending her. Robert could do that in spades. The man was immensely loyal when he chose to be. It begged the question: why had Giulia not ignited his paternal instinct already? Really. The man had sat her at the foot of the table. The *foot* of the table, for pity's sake!

Nick groaned. A reconciliation was going to be more difficult than he had anticipated. Had he really been so naive as to assume that he could suggest shared dinners and the two would fall into a relationship? Of course it had been that easy for him when he came to Halstead, but he was the heir. Robert wanted to mold and craft him, and Nick had submitted willingly. Well, semi-willingly.

Perhaps he ought to include his valet in his scheme. Jack, the lucky man. Did he notice how Giulia placed a hand on his arm when they talked? Did he even notice that she was doing it? Nick noticed, that was for certain. The little waif.

Speak of the devil.

"You are awake," Jack said with his characteristic cheerfulness as he entered the room with the large tin tub. "Care for a bath?"

"Food. I would prefer food."

Jack nodded and placed the tub on the rug near the fire before stoking the flames.

"How does your shoulder fare?"

Nick groaned as he forced himself into a sitting position. "I've been better."

"Would you like me to call up Miss Pepper? Maybe she can cut your ham for you again."

"Yes, why don't you do that," Nick said, his tone even.

Jack chuckled to himself as he walked out of the room and Nick felt an immediate rush of envy flood his body. What he wouldn't give to be walking down those stairs himself. To fill a plate at the sideboard in the breakfast room all alone. To eat in silence. An uncharacteristic malaise settled over him and he let out a breath in one long, slow whirl. He needed to find a way to pass the days quicker. Giulia was not coming to him as often as she had before, and he could only do so much detective work from the comforts of his room.

But if he rose and left his bedchamber, her time at Halstead would be at an end.

A knock sounded at the door and he ignored the disappointment he felt when Robert came in.

"Good morning, my lord."

Robert grunted and sat in the wingback chair beside his bed. Giulia's chair. Somehow the piece of furniture did not look so monstrous with the earl filling its cushions.

"I've had my men scouring the land and they may have found something connected to your attack."

That piqued his interest. "Yes?"

"There was a bag left behind in the woods where the scoundrel hid. It contained mostly the remnants of food from the imbecile's meal, but there was a ticket, too. A ticket into Graton from London."

"Well, that's a lead," Nick retorted.

"It's a start. But the odd thing was the date. The ticket was three months old," Robert said with a meaningful look. "Wells sent Briggs's kid to town to question Jolly."

Nick groaned, and to his surprise, Robert laughed. "I know you aren't too fond of him, but if anyone has information, Jolly will."

"I know, I know."

"Well," Robert clapped his hands down on his knees in preparation to stand, "Just keeping you updated, my boy."

"Robert?"

The earl halted halfway up and raised one gray bushy eyebrow at Nick.

"Have you considered just giving your niece the benefit of the doubt?"

Robert continued to rise, his face contorting into a scowl.

Nick hurried to continue, "From what I can tell, she knows nothing about whatever rift there was between you and your brother. She thinks he left of his own accord."

Robert's face grew dark and Nick threw caution to the wind. It couldn't make things any worse, that was apparent. "Robert, she did not even know your mother was alive all these years. Her father told her she was dead."

The earl stilled. When he turned, his face was red with rage and Nick swallowed. He'd been mistaken. Apparently he *could* make it worse.

The earl spoke, his words slow and ominous. "Why don't you stay out of my affairs, Nick?"

"I think you're throwing away a chance here."

"A chance at what?" Robert yelled, his round cheeks glowing red; they looked all the brighter against the white of his hair. "You expect me to give Patrick's brat a home here?"

"No, Robert," Nick said calmly. "I expect you to recognize it as a chance to have a family yourself. To have a relationship with the one person on this earth you can claim as a close blood relation—not a third cousin, but a niece. The one person who will pass down *your* Pepper genes. Maybe not in the earldom, but you can still give her a life here. You can still give yourself something, Robert. No one else is here to claim her; do you see that? She has no one else. Don't pass this chance up."

There was a deadly silence and Nick held his breath. Robert growled, shooting Nick one final look before stomping from the room. But he did not yell again. He did not counter Nick or argue with him. That had to be a good sign, right?

This was how Robert worked. The man needed time for Nick's words to settle and then he would come to his own conclusion regarding his niece. Nick could only hope he had planted the right seed.

The next few days passed slowly for Giulia. She spent her mealtimes with the silent earl, and the in-betweens with Nick. They had yet to discuss the rooster-sealed letters in much more detail, and she was grateful for that. She had also yet to tell Nick about Ames, which was a problem of its own.

But the opportunity had not presented itself for such a conversation. She felt so conceited coming right out with it. She knew better than to believe that Nick's flirtation meant he had designs on her. And while she certainly found him attractive, she had no designs on him. In fact, he only caused her to miss Ames all the more. She longed to fall into Ames's strong embrace and have his large and capable arms come around her, giving her the protection and love she desired. Of course, a simple letter would probably accomplish the same thing, but that was asking too much. Naturally. Who had the time to sit and write a letter to the love of their life? Certainly not Ames. No, he was far too busy.

Giulia put down the quill she was sharpening before she accidentally slipped and cut herself and let out a breath. *Easy there, Giulia, he really is busy. Busy setting up a life for you, you ungrateful girl.*

Returning her attention to the letters on her desk, Giulia completed three responses to her father's admirers before she put away the ink and readied herself for the day. The periodical which published Father's stories had printed a short letter to readers, informing them of Patrick Pepper's untimely demise, and doubling the letters sent her way. Notes condoling his loss and begging to know what happened to Jules poured into Halstead.

Giulia was of half a mind to pen a note to her father's publisher, begging them to cease forwarding the letters. But she could not find it in her heart to ignore those people who fell so deeply in love with the stories which had shaped her life.

For now, at least, she would reply to as many as she could. Especially while Lord Hart was around to frank them for her.

The one note she had not replied to was the missive from Mrs. Fawn, reiterating her invitation to tea that very day. Giulia still found it odd that the woman was hosting a tea while in mourning, but who was she to judge? Perhaps Mrs. Fawn did not miss her husband. Maybe it had been a marriage of convenience.

Giulia shook her head. It was not her business to judge Mrs. Fawn's social practices. Drawing herself up, she studied herself in the mirror. Her coronet braid was about as tamed as she could manage, her dove gray dress clean, but plain. She pulled the elephant pendant out from the high neckline to kiss and replaced it with a finesse gained through habit.

Nerves prickled her stomach and caused butterflies to flutter throughout her body. Mrs. Fawn was intimidating enough, but to have tea with her friends? What had Giulia been thinking, agreeing to such a scheme? She stared at her own plain appearance and straightened her shoulders, garnering confidence from her elephant kiss and the knowledge that she had plenty to contribute to any conversation.

She was the granddaughter of an earl. She had every reason to hold her head high.

And she did so as she traveled the length of the castle toward the invalid's room.

Nick was wide awake when she entered his chamber and approached the bed, the remnants of his breakfast sitting on the tray and pushed out of the way. "May I check your bandage?" she asked.

He smiled at her and began unfastening his shirt. She glanced away to give him some semblance of privacy and then spoke to alleviate some of the tension she felt. "I will be seeing Dr. Mason today. I thought I should bring him an updated account of your injury."

Nick's brows knit together slightly. "You are going somewhere?"

"Yes," Giulia responded, a little annoyed. "Do not look so surprised."

"Well I *am* surprised. I was unaware you knew anyone around here."

"Not that it is any concern of yours, Nicholas Pepper," she said with a playful edge, "but I happened to meet Dr. Mason's sister last time he called, and she has invited me to tea."

"Ah, yes; I remember the fatally beautiful Mrs. Fawn."

Giulia tried not to be jealous. Truly, she did. But it was not altogether possible, perhaps, for one to control every last emotion one felt.

"Be wary of those ladies," Nick warned. He dropped his voice. "They are admirable, but a bit eccentric."

Giulia reared her head back in surprise. "How did you know I was meeting Mrs. Fawn's friends?"

"Because," Nick replied smugly, "they are inseparable."

Giulia ignored his warning and leaned down to undo his bandage. She could feel his eyes boring into the side of her face as she checked his injury, lifting the dressing and noting the healing skin. It looked good. It actually looked really, really good. She was surprised at how quickly his shoulder was healing. Given the state of his injury, it was odd that he still felt weak enough to remain in bed.

"Well, the ham must possess magic," Giulia joked as she replaced his bandage. "I cannot think of another reason why you would be healing so quickly. Your progress is truly incredible."

"That, or I can thank my magnificent caregiver."

"I will pass it on to Dr. Mason. I hope I am able to catch him at his home. I may as well save him a trip out here."

"Yes," Nick said dryly, "how very thoughtful of you."

She threw him a quizzical glance. "Did you want to see him?"

"Not as badly as he wants to see you."

Giulia huffed. "Nick! How dare you insinuate such a thing." She gave him her best glare while he refastened his shirt, smirking. It was infuriating, and entirely distracting.

"That was no insinuation, Giulia. Simple observation could tell you that."

"Well," she said, holding his gaze. It was time. She'd nearly told him once before, but now she simply had to be out with it. The flapping of nonexistent wings in her stomach made her feel as though she walked across a precarious bridge. She was surprised when her voice sounded steady. "I'll have you know that *if* that is the case, he will be sorely disappointed."

"Is that so?" Nick looked smug.

"Yes." A brief pause highlighted her hesitation, but she lifted her chin. "I am already spoken for."

Nick's face fell momentarily, but he quickly righted it. The breath of silence did not last long. "You said you were not betrothed though."

"Betrothed, no. But spoken for just the same."

Nick raised an eyebrow as if to question her reasoning.

"We had reason to wait, not that I owe you an explanation."

"Very well; when do we get to meet the lucky man?"

"Probably never," Giulia said over her shoulder as she walked toward the door, escaping as quickly as she could. "Have a good day, Nick. I will see you this evening."

"Don't forget my warning," he called after her. "Be on your guard."

Giulia shook her head as she walked out. The man was infuriating. He was also her ticket to staying at Halstead for the time being. For that, and that alone, she was grateful for him.

But that wasn't the whole of it, was it? Not truly. If it was, why would she feel such unease in her gut?

CHAPTER 13

*G*iulia stood outside of the large house and gulped. Now *this* was a manor. And somehow, much more intimidating than her uncle's castle. On the other side of the door sat the beautiful Mrs. Fawn and who knew how many of her friends.

What had Giulia agreed to? She shuddered in the chilly air, pulling her cloak tighter about her shoulders and willing her stomach to cease rolling. She ran a finger along the chain of her necklace for luck and straightened her spine. Pushing her shoulders back, she crossed the gravel drive and knocked on the door.

A stately butler opened the door and ushered her into an elegant foyer, and Giulia did her best to raise her jaw from the floor. Never had she seen a corridor so exquisitely decorated. Nearly everything was white and trimmed in gold edging, from the crisp walls with gilded moldings, to the fabulous chandelier above the door. Even the white marble floor was impeccable; Giulia feared her shoes, dusty from the gravel drive, would mar its pristine condition.

She followed the butler into a drawing room—after checking the bottom of her feet and graciously finding them passably clean—and was awed once more by the exquisite, tasteful decor. She'd seen ornate palaces in India and attended lavish balls in Barbados, but none she found more beautiful than the simple, elegant design of a British drawing room. Lavender silk hung on the walls and butter yellow, upholstered furniture dotted the floor. The large, ornate fireplace took up the majority of one wall and tall, framed windows covered another, letting in extensive sunlight.

Mrs. Fawn, dressed in black and just as striking as Giulia remembered her, rose and pulled Giulia into the center of the room to present her to the two women seated on the settee.

"Miss Pepper, I am so glad you made it," Mrs. Fawn said, her smile earnest and her voice soft. "Come, you must meet my friends. This is Hattie Green, and Mabel Sheffield."

Giulia smiled at the women in turn and was subsequently overwhelmed by the amount of beauty in the room. Each of them was different, and each was breathtaking. She felt small in comparison. If only she could sink into the elegant sofa Mrs. Fawn led her to and fade into the cushions.

Miss Green delivered the most dazzling grin. She tilted her freckled face, revealing a small, upturned nose that spoke of mischief-making and a cleverness in the woman's eyes that led Giulia to believe she ought not to cross this one.

Miss Sheffield was, in comparison, an Amazonian. She stood to welcome Giulia, towering in both her height and demeanor. She appeared strong and confident, yet slender and dignified. Her thick, dark hair was piled high on her head and her gown was an exquisite shade of green that brought out the deeper hues of her navy-violet eyes.

For a moment Giulia was dumbstruck. She could easily see how Nick had labeled them as a pack. Standing together, they appeared as if they could slay with a look. Alone they were beautiful, together appeared unstoppable.

Giulia's courage flagged and she lowered herself into a seat opposite the friends. She hated herself for thinking it, but she couldn't help but wonder what fatal flaw each of these women possessed. How else were three women such as these yet unmarried?

Mrs. Fawn's situation was understandable—she, a widow—but the others? There had to be a reason. And it had nothing to do with their location, for according to Tilly, Graton saw its share of social activities.

"Miss Pepper, we are so very glad to meet you." Miss Green leaned forward as she spoke as though she was imparting a secret. "We have been looking forward to this tea with immense anticipation."

We? They even spoke for each other. Giulia accepted the cup of tea Mrs. Fawn offered and took a sip before responding. "As have I." *Really, Pepper, is that the best you could do?* "Thank you, Mrs. Fawn, for extending the invitation."

"We do not stand on ceremony here," Mrs. Fawn said at once, shaking her head as she continued to prepare tea for the others. "Please call me Amelia. Mrs. Fawn sounds so old, does it not?"

It was a blessed thing the women were so relaxed. Giulia was used to the less strict lifestyle of the ships and savage towns of the West Indies and South America. Referring to the women by their Christian names ought not to be a challenge.

"You must be starved for entertainment," Mabel interjected before Giulia had the chance to answer. "Being all alone at Halstead as you are, I mean."

"She's not alone, Mae," Hattie interjected with a telling glance. "She has Mr. Pepper there."

"Oh, I forgot," Mabel said with amusement. "Not that I envy you *too* much in that regard. He is nice to look at, but he is such a flirt, is he not?"

"Yes, he is that." Giulia sipped her tea again and nibbled on a ginger biscuit.

Amelia raised a hand, tucking a stray red curl into her coiffure. "He is far more pleasant now than when he first arrived at Halstead."

Hattie scoffed. "Who was first? Was it I?"

"No," Mabel said, shaking her head. She sipped her tea before lowering the cup on her lap, wrapped in both hands. "Amelia was first. *Then* you."

"Just before I married Mr. King," Amelia agreed. "I believe I met Mr. Pepper at the Assemblies. He cut a dashing figure and did not seem to care one whit for my engagement; he was quite determined to convince me to go out driving with him. With looks like that, one is bound to have a conceited disposition."

Giulia couldn't believe what she was hearing. If that was a rule, then she had to be in a room full of conceited women. And they seemed just the opposite to her.

"But you *did* go out driving with him," Mabel recalled.

Amelia's eyes widened, her eyebrows lifting. "And he very nearly kissed me, the cad."

Giulia's stomach grew hollow despite the tea she was sipping.

"He would have kissed me, too," Hattie said, "had I not ducked under his arm and escaped his embrace in the maze at the Goulding's garden party."

Both Amelia and Hattie turned to face Mabel. "He did kiss me," she said, letting out a long sigh. "Though he only made it to my cheek. It only took two months for the man to work his way through all three of us. Before he ceased his attentions."

"To say nothing for the women he likely left behind," Hattie added. "And the others here."

Giulia swallowed. "There were others?"

Amelia lifted one shoulder in a dainty shrug. "I cannot be certain. But the man has a slippery tongue. I believe him to be harmless—the old earl saw to that, I have heard—but I cannot think Mr. Pepper knows how to converse with a woman without some degree of flirtation."

Giulia certainly knew that to be the case for her. The man was likely bored from the confinement to his chamber. And Giulia was naught but a source to break the tedium.

"Have you found any luck in searching for a position?" Amelia asked, her head tilting to the side.

"Not yet. For now, I am at the disposal of the earl."

"Ah yes," Hattie said ominously, "the irritable earl."

Giulia chuckled. Hattie was not wrong. But Mabel shot her friend a warning look.

"What?" Hattie asked innocently. "I only speak the truth."

Amelia shook her head. "That, no one would deny."

"Now, you must tell us," Hattie continued, heedless of Mabel's raised eyebrows. "Is Lord Hart so very crotchety behind closed doors? Or is it for the benefit of the public?"

"Honestly, I would not be the right person to ask." Giulia's gaze flicked between three sets of expectant eyes while she considered how much she should divulge. She felt she could trust them, though. Something about their easy manners and kind eyes inspired confidence in Giulia. "My uncle and I have not exactly forged a relationship yet. I spend most of my time tending to the heir."

Mabel spoke softly. "Amelia did tell us you were nursing Mr. Pepper after his injury. You are the one who found him, were you not? Was that very traumatic?"

"It was a bit of a nuisance. But no, I would not say traumatic. It is not so very new to me, you see. I have done my share of nursing."

"But you cannot be more than eighteen!" Hattie exclaimed.

Giulia pretended to bristle. "I am twenty, thank you kindly."

Mabel nodded sagely. "Oh yes, such advanced years to be sure."

Giulia smiled, fingering the rim of her tea cup as she responded. "I prefer to think I have experience beyond my years. I have spent more than half my life traveling abroad; tending gunshot wounds is only the beginning of my experience." Silence filled the room and she hazarded a look to find, once again, three sets of eyes fixed on her. They were not, however, looks full of sympathy or disgust as she was used to receiving, but merely interest. It buoyed her.

She cleared her throat and continued. "My father believed that adventure was the flavor of life. We had a home in London, but Father would contrive the desire to visit a new place and would not stop until he had traveled there and fully experienced the culture. And he did not like to pick the more civilized locales, so I spent most of my childhood on a boat, or in another country tending to my father."

She smiled, hoping she wasn't boring the women with her story. But they each watched her, engaged. "There were occasions when the natives would not be too thrilled to have such curious interlopers. Or one of our party would catch an ailment specific to the locale. I became very good at figuring out who to see in a village or what to do to fix whatever the ailment was. And then when my father died, Ames found us passage home under the chaperonage of a seasoned doctor and his wife, so I assisted Dr. Hendricks on the journey and learned a lot."

"Your upbringing sounds so romantic," Hattie said with a dreamy quality to her gaze.

"It sounds romantic, maybe. In reality, it was not." Giulia's shoulders were heavy from the sullen mood she'd brought to the room. She delivered a bright smile. "Needless to say, I am happy to remain in England for the rest of my days."

"Who is Ames?" Amelia questioned.

"Oh, did I mention him?" Giulia hesitated. "He worked for my father. He has been sort of our man-of-all-work. He began as a footman in our home and worked his way up. But really, my father always considered him family."

Amelia moved to the seat beside Giulia and took her hand. "I am so sorry for your grief. Losing a parent is a very difficult trial."

Giulia smiled. "Yes but losing a parent *and* a spouse would be unbearable. I cannot imagine what you are going through."

Surprise flickered in Amelia's eyes and behind her, Hattie snorted. "You think losing one is a trial? Imagine losing three."

"Three parents?"

"Three spouses," Amelia responded, her voice dry, though she did not appear as amused as her friend. Her smile was tight, with fine lines fanning beside her eyes.

Giulia couldn't contain her shock. Was that why they were unwed? The three women had *each* lost a husband?

"I think we have confused our guest." Hattie giggled.

"It is not so very interesting." Amelia squeezed Giulia's hand once before releasing. "But it is why I have been dubbed the *Black Widow*." She cast her gaze to the ceiling.

Mabel nodded. "Yes, that and your propensity for wearing the color black."

Giulia looked at them each in turn, confused.

"It was all me," Amelia explained. "I have lost three husbands."

Giulia stared at the beautiful, regal woman as the words soaked in. One woman had married and buried husbands thrice. It was such an outrageous claim for one so young that Giulia stared, open-mouthed at Amelia and did something most unbecoming.

She laughed.

And then, much to her surprise, the other women joined in. Laughter floated about the room, touching each soul and then dying out nearly as quickly as it had come on.

Giulia pulled a handkerchief from her sleeve and wiped her eyes, unsure if she felt more relief or embarrassment. But the gentle looks on each woman's face was a testament of their acceptance.

The shared mirth had somehow bonded her to these ladies. She felt comfortable, which was foreign to her. She was not used to having friends. At least, not females her own age who spoke English. It was a welcome experience and she suddenly found that she did not want it to end, ever.

Mabel looked pointedly at Hattie with an eyebrow raised and then at Amelia. Amelia nodded and Hattie simply lifted her shoulders in a shrug. "Very well, it's decided," Mabel announced triumphantly. "We would like to invite you to our literary society."

"Your literary society?" Giulia was more than a little confused. She had never heard of such a thing.

"Yes; we choose a book and we all read it, and then every Thursday we meet in our loft and discuss it."

"Loft?"

"Yes," Mabel said, nodding for emphasis, "our loft. It is in the old barn on the edge of Hattie's property, so it lines the border between Green House and Halstead Manor."

"I did not know anyone lived so close."

"Well," Hattie said, screwing up her nose, "close is relative. Do you ride? Because on horseback it really is not so far."

"I do." Giulia shifted slightly in her seat. She had never ridden sidesaddle, but how very different could it be?

"Would you like to join us next Thursday?" Amelia asked eagerly.

Giulia looked from one lady to another, wanting so badly to be admitted and accepted into their group, but nervous at the prospect. What if she came to care for these women and then had to leave suddenly? Her position was temporary, and she had not had any luck finding employment worth pursuing in the papers.

It would not be so different from what she had endured her entire life, but this time she desperately didn't want their association to end. Alas, how could she argue with the patterns of life? She had never stayed in one place long enough to make friends she could keep, and this was no different. She would just enjoy this camaraderie while she had it and then when it was over, that was that.

She gave the group an encouraging smile. "I do not know if I have time to read an entire book in one week."

"Oh, that is irrelevant," Hattie said, swatting the air as though shoving away Giulia's concern.

Mabel grinned. "We hardly ever actually read the books; that is just our excuse for getting together."

"I see," Giulia said, even though she did not. If they did not read the books, then why not just gather for tea or some other activity?

"You may not now," Amelia said, "but you will, come Thursday."

Giulia stayed and spoke with the women for another half-hour, finding herself at ease with their varying personalities. She discovered that Amelia and Hattie were both three and twenty, and Mabel was two years their senior, all three approaching spinsterhood quickly by England Society's standards. She did not discover anything further about Amelia's three deceased husbands, or why Hattie and Mabel remained single, but those were things she might learn over time, perhaps.

Dr. Mason was out for the duration of her visit, so Giulia left Amelia with a message for him regarding Nick and said farewell to her new friends.

The words were sweet, and she felt giddy at the revelation.

Giulia Pepper now had friends.

CHAPTER 14

"She already retired for the evening," Jack said, bending to retrieve a book that had fallen off of the table next to Nick's bed.

"But she has not come in to check on me." Nick was aware of how pouty he sounded, but he was used to saying goodnight to his dark-haired angel. And he was used to her wanting to say goodnight to him.

He caught a look of irritation crossing over Jack's face as the valet turned away to tend the fire. "Is there something wrong, Jack?"

The man glanced over his shoulder, an impassive expression falling over his face. "Of course not, sir."

Nick did not believe him. What could be the trouble though? "News from home?" Nick pressed.

Jack returned his attention to the fire. "All is well at your farm, I am told. My father wrote me just last week." There was an element of discord in Jack's tone, but Nick could not quite put his finger on the cause. Or on what the man's displeasure could mean.

Jack continued. "But Miss Pepper has caused quite a stir downstairs. Apparently she gave the earl a set down during dinner and stomped from the room."

Nick choked on his tea, nearly spitting it across his blanket. "And you waited until now to share this with me?"

Jack crossed the room, his gaze falling to the tea cup in Nick's hand. "Well, you didn't ask before."

Nick pushed his lips into a flat line. "Do you know what it was that bothered her?"

"Denny told me she got upset that the earl would not look at her. According to him, Miss Pepper told Lord Hart that if she was to be treated like she had the plague, then she would just as soon eat in the confinement of her room."

Nick groaned. That was not the way to win Robert's approval. The old man was as stubborn as a mule. Perhaps Giulia's tea with the women earlier in the day did not go very well. Nick formed a wry smile. He could only imagine what nonsense those women had filled Giulia's head with. Had they poisoned her against Nick? Was *that* why she had not come to bid him a good evening? Surely those women recognized that the man he had been on arriving at Halstead was not the man he was today.

He shook his head. Not that it mattered what Giulia thought. The woman was as good as engaged. What had she said? Oh, right. She was *spoken for*. Nick's only thought was that if he had spoken for Giulia, he would not have let her go. He would have secured a ring on her finger as soon as the banns could be read.

Not that he ever thought along those lines, of course.

He did recognize that one day he would need to marry. If not, the earldom would be passed on to who-knows-what type of miscreant. The title had come to him, hadn't it? And he was a farmer's son. A gentleman farmer, of course. But a farmer, nonetheless.

Now, to contrive a way to convince Giulia to ignore the stories Mrs. Fawn and her friends likely fed her—that would take some finesse. It was a good thing he was blessed with a quick wit and a tongue to match.

"Do you need anything?" Jack asked as he stood poised near the door, his back straight and Nick's dirty clothing hanging over his arm to be laundered.

"No, I will see you in the morning."

Jack's mouth was firm, his jaw tight as he nodded and left the room.

Nick blew out his candle and lay back in bed, the moonlight streaming through the window and lighting the chair Giulia usually sat in. He watched the empty space for so long he could imagine her filling it, her smile lighting up the depths of her chocolate eyes, and her wild hair streaming in every direction. She had seen more countries, cultures, and people than any one person could dream of experiencing. Yet, for her, it had been a burden. She never said as much, but Nick could tell.

Whether she knew it or not, she was searching for a home. And if he had anything to do with it, he was going to give her one. In Robert.

Hours crawled by and sleep evaded him. Nick sat up slowly and swung his legs over the side of the bed. Using the bedpost for support, he hoisted himself to a standing position and remained there until he felt balanced. Jack had been helping him get up and walk around a few times a day since he'd first awoken, and now that he was regaining his strength, Nick was grateful the injury was entirely on his shoulder and in no way affected his ability to walk. Still, the longer Giulia did not see him up and moving around, the better.

He planned to stretch his invalid status for as long as he could, though he would be glad if the doctor was no longer part of his treatment plan. His stomach soured with the image of Dr. Mason and Giulia discussing him. Mason had come to phrase their shared interest as *our* patient and Giulia went right along with him. Of course the man did not truly value her opinion on anything medical, he was simply humoring her.

But Nick would not let her down by making the doctor's flaws clear. No, Giulia could figure that out on her own. She clearly did not see Mason the same way that he saw her.

She couldn't possibly, for her heart was spoken for.

Unless she had created a fictional man to guard herself. Nick shook his head, his mouth forming an amused smile. That was the most likely scenario. The man who had spoken for Giulia's heart probably did not exist. He couldn't. How could any man have allowed Giulia to travel to Halstead so utterly alone? Not a very smart fellow at all, this fictional intended of hers.

And besides, if she really had an intended, she would have mentioned him right away, wouldn't she? Any lovesick girl would, that was for certain.

Nick smirked, comforted by his theory. He would go along with her little story for now, if it made her feel safer. At least until he could prove to her that he was no longer the cad he used to be.

His stomach rumbled. Holding onto the bed post for support, he stared at the bedroom door. He could make it down to the kitchen on his own, surely. He was tired, but he could walk.

Nick reached for his dressing gown at the end of the bed and threw it over his good shoulder, letting it drape over his injured side. He made it through the door, snatched a candle on his way out, and trudged down the hall, steeling himself for the stairs. He was surprised by how quickly he felt fatigued. It made him want to hit something, but that would be counterproductive. It was hard to accomplish any level of exercise when one was doing one's best to appear an invalid.

Instead, he continued to balance a candle in one hand and leaned on the railing with his good arm. He followed the stairs down to the small door hidden in an alcove off of the foyer that he knew would take him into the kitchen.

Easing the door open, a faint glow came from downstairs, giving him pause. Was it early enough for the servants to begin breakfast preparations?

Nick sighed in relief. What a blessing. Now he could eat a real meal.

The bustling noise of servants at work was absent, however, as he descended the servants' stairs. Eerie quiet met him instead, and his reservations grew as he got closer to the kitchen.

When he reached the floor, he stopped short. Giulia sat at the wooden work table in the center of the room, her mouth full and half of a lemon tart suspended in her hand. Her wide-eyed innocence pierced his heart. And, my, was she beautiful. Her hair, out of its usual confines, trailed over her shoulder in a loose braid; he could see why she always secured it the way she did, for her hair was a wild mass of frizz.

"Fancy meeting you here," Nick muttered, affecting a weakened gait as he crossed to the table and leaned against the back of a chair as though he could not stand without its support.

Giulia glanced away sheepishly and resumed chewing her pilfered sweet. She set down the other half of her tart and wiped her hands on a rag. When she turned her gaze back on him it was full of censure. "What are you thinking, Nick? It is not a good idea for you to be up and traipsing about by yourself in the middle of the night."

"And it is safe for you?"

She shot him a look that told him exactly what she thought about that.

He raised his hand in surrender and then gestured to the chair beside her.

Giulia stood to pull the chair out for him, but he didn't miss her huff of exasperation. She moved to the teapot and began stoking the small fire she must have laid. "Tea should only take a few minutes," she called over her shoulder as she set the water to boil. Raising an eyebrow, she continued, "That is what you have risked your life for, is it not?"

Nick chuckled. "My, aren't we into theatrics in the middle of the night?"

Giulia reclaimed her chair beside Nick's and continued nibbling her lemon tart. His mouth watered as he eyed the treat. "There aren't any more of those around, are there?"

Giulia smiled. "Perhaps."

They stared at one another for a moment, Giulia eyeing Nick with a gleam of mischief in her eyes.

"And may I have one?" he asked.

"That depends," she said matter-of-factly. "It is mine; if I share it with you, what will I get in return?"

His pulse began to race. What could he give her, indeed? His blood heated and his hands itched to move toward her. To pick up her hand, to pull her into his arms. Well, *arm*. To taste the tang of lemon on her lips.

She seemed to notice the shift in the atmosphere and her eyes darted to his mouth. Once, not too long ago, that was the only sign he would have needed to pounce. Now, he could not bring himself to close the distance. Not like this. No, it was too risky. She wanted him to, that much was apparent. But *she* needed to know that she wanted to kiss him. He felt the familiar stealth of a hunter, carefully sizing up his prey. Yet, it was different this time. She was different.

Giulia cleared her throat loudly and shot to her feet. She returned with another tart and placed it in front of Nick before scooting her chair a little farther away and sitting again.

He bit into the tart and savored the sour flavor on his tongue. "This was yours, you say?"

"Yes, but it must be our little secret. I was quite hungry when I first arrived at Halstead and took to coming down here in the night for something to eat. I was caught a few times, so now Cook leaves these for me and no one knows about them except us. When I empty the plate, she simply replenishes them." She shrugged. "That was my last one, so enjoy it."

"Trust me, I am."

Giulia glanced around the dim kitchen as if searching for something to do. She must have found it because she shot to her feet again. Ah, the tea. He watched as she prepared a cup for him and refilled her own. She returned to the table and set his cup on the surface before turning to nurse her own beverage.

"I did not see you tonight."

Giulia smiled guiltily. "You must have heard why. I am sure it is all around the castle by now."

"You mean how you yelled at the earl until you were blue in the face?"

The blood drained from her face, her words escaping as hardly more than a whisper. "That is what is being said?"

"No." Nick chuckled, reaching forward and squeezing her hand to reassure her. "I did not hear much, I swear to you. I only heard that you refused to eat with Robert if he was going to ignore you."

Giulia sat up straighter. "That, I did. And rightfully so. In this house I am more servant than guest and if the earl would like to treat me as a servant then I will eat like one. Well," she looked away and then back at Nick, "as near to one as I can. I would not be accepted down here at mealtimes, I am afraid, though I do not blame them. I wouldn't want to make anyone uncomfortable."

"No, only the earl."

She smiled to herself and Nick suddenly felt the need to know the secrets of her mind and, if he could, her heart. She raised an eyebrow at him. "He had it coming."

He chuckled. "You are one of a kind, Giulia."

Her face sobered and he felt the strings pull on his heart. Squeezing her fingers, he spoke softly. "What is it?"

"Oh, nothing." She laughed awkwardly and shook her head. "My father used to say that to me. Only, he would say, 'You are one of a kind, Jules, the only jewels I need.'"

"Jules?"

"He insisted I go by Jules after my mother left. I think he was trying to erase every bit of Italian from me that he could. Coming to Halstead and being known as Giulia...well, it is a first for me." She laughed dryly. "Perhaps I've grown bitter toward my father's name for me because it is how he wrote of me in his periodical."

Nick reared back. "What periodical?"

Her eyebrows drew together. *"The Adventures of Patrick Pepper and His Assistant, Jules.* You've not heard of it? There were many jests over my name and the jewels that happened to litter his adventure stories."

"I see." Though, he really did not. How had he not heard of this?

"The periodicals were how he funded our adventurous lifestyle. We would go on a grand trip and he would gain experience to write into stories, printed as periodicals. It was a cycle, traveling until he tired of it and then returning to London where he would write until he tired of that." She sighed. "Father always felt antsy, you see. He was never happy settling in one place for very long. And it was a good thing, as far as his profession was concerned. It gave him plenty to write about."

"But it must have been hard for you, never staying in one place for long. Never having a home."

She looked surprised at that. "But I did have a home. Home does not have to be a particular building, Nick. What is that anyway but wood or stone? I had my home in another person, in my father's heart. He may have been eccentric, but *he* was my home."

"And now your home is gone," he whispered. It was all coming together now. "Was it just the two of you on all of these grand adventures?"

She laughed awkwardly. "Um, well, no. Father would hire the occasional servant to accompany us, or when we would arrive at our destination, but most of the time it was Father, me, and Ames."

"Ames?" Nick pictured a big, brawny man with gray hair and a bristling beard, ready for adventure.

Giulia looked away. "Yes, Ames."

There was a lot of weight in the name when it left her lips. This was clearly a man of significance. "Who is he?"

"My intended."

The lemon tart soured in Nick's stomach. So, perhaps no beard. And most likely not gray, either. A tightness pulled in his chest and he tried to speak as though he was unbothered. "Where is Ames, then?"

"In London." She sipped her tea before looking back to Nick. "He is building his wood crafting business and then he will send for me. He makes the most beautiful furniture you have ever seen, Nick. I have no doubt he will do well."

"And you miss him." It was not a question, for Nick could see the truth in her face, in the way she spoke about this man.

"Yes," she said quietly.

Nick had been wrong. Giulia was not pretending to have someone waiting for her in order to push him away. For some reason, that rankled more. Giulia truly was unattainable.

Nick downed the rest of his tea and stood. The blood rushed from his head and he swayed as little black dots outlined the edges of his vision. Two small hands slid around his waist, steadying him, and the warmth they brought was more fulfilling than the tea he had just finished.

"Let me help you upstairs."

He did not argue with her. He braced himself on the back of his chair and Giulia released him to rinse their tea cups and extinguish the fire. She picked up Nick's candle after pocketing her own unlit one and put an arm around his waist.

"Lean on me," she said. "I am much stronger than I look."

Nick glanced down at her form in the soft light and smiled. The top of her head barely reached his shoulder. Small, indeed. He wrapped his arm around her and began to ascend the stairs. It was a blessed thing he was merely affecting the need for assistance—had he truly needed help, he had a hard time believing this little slip of a woman would be sufficient.

"How was tea with the fine women of Graton?" Nick asked to ease the awkwardness. The words no sooner left his mouth than he wished to recall them. Perhaps it was not the time to reiterate whatever they had said to her today.

"It was lovely." Giulia said, the smile evident in her voice. "*They* were lovely. You could have warned me, you know."

"I thought I did."

"Not about their prowess, about their beauty. I could not even speak when I met them, I was so overcome. I felt so out of place."

Nick stopped as they reached the main floor and closed the door to the kitchen behind them. "What do you mean, out of place?"

She swatted a hand as if to push the conversation away with air and resumed her position as his walking support.

"Giulia, you cannot mean that you were out of place among them in regard to your beauty."

"I was not begging for compliments, Nick," she said crisply. "It was merely an observation."

"Well it was an inaccurate one, I can assure you."

"You are not going to make me believe you are so blind," Giulia countered. "They are among the most beautiful women I have ever seen."

"I am not arguing on their merits, Giulia, but your skewed ideas of your own. You fit right in with those women. You could be their leader."

Silence stretched as they finished climbing the stairs, pausing periodically for Nick to pretend to regain his breath, before completing the trek to his room. Giulia helped him inside and he did not complain or try to send her away. He wanted her to think he needed the help; it would keep her around longer, and he was not ready to let her leave.

She set the candle on the table beside his bed and cast him a stern look. "Do not try that again until you have regained more of your strength, please. What if no one was down there to help you back up?"

"Then I would have spent a very uncomfortable night on the kitchen floor."

Giulia shook her head, an endearing smile gracing her lips. "Goodnight, Nick."

He stopped her from leaving with a hand to her arm. "Giulia, I meant what I said. You are very beautiful. More so, in fact, than any of those women."

"I told you, Nick, I am immune to your clever charms. I have Ames."

He held her arm for a moment longer, searching her eyes for a grain of affection before letting it go. He watched her light her own candle with his flame and then walk from the room, closing the door behind her.

How would he get her to see that he was simply speaking the truth? He meant every single word.

CHAPTER 15

*G*iulia took advantage of Jack's offer to relieve her from Nick's bedside and spent the morning exploring the castle. Wandering the empty halls of the west wing, she considered her outburst the previous evening at the earl's dinner table. She had half-expected a servant to come to her in the night and escort her off of the property, but no one ever came. She had waited up so long that her missed dinner and scattered nerves forced her down to the kitchen to relieve her empty stomach.

She hadn't expected a visitor. She'd gone down to the kitchen at night often and never once had she run into another soul—not after being caught by the cook, at least.

Shaking her head, she sighed. Nick was a tease. He relied on his handsome smile to ease tensions. And it worked very well. Only, she could not let him see that. It took all of her strength to remain unaffected when Nick released the full effect of his charisma on her. She did her best to conjure Ames's countenance in her mind, but his distance—literally and figuratively, she had *still* yet to receive a letter—was making that increasingly difficult.

Why hadn't he written her? It was easy to be cross at him for not reaching out to her when she really needed support. It was equally difficult to remind herself that Ames could not read her mind, and therefore had no idea how much she felt like she needed him. But really, how hard could it be to write a letter, particularly when one said they would?

Giulia traced her finger along a tapestry covering the length of the corridor. More mail arrived every day from Patrick Pepper's adoring fans offering their condolences and sorrow over losing the famed adventurist; the letters included many, many inquiries on whether *Jules* was going to continue in his stead. She had gotten rather adept at quick, gracious responses that snuffed that flame before it could get out of hand. Never in a hundred lifetimes would she continue to write her father's adventure stories.

Her responses to the fans' inquiries were quick, but the letters were arriving with increasing speed and she was getting behind. But what could she do? Giulia owed these fans her livelihood. They deserved a response for their support and kindness, no matter how little the letters did to alleviate Ames's absence.

She reached the end of the corridor and an alcove appeared before her with a curved, wooden door. Out of all of the thick, oak doors that littered the castle, this one was unique. It looked to be original to the building, which had to be hundreds of years old, with its splintering wood and iron supports. The iron lock appeared broken, and anticipation skittered through her veins. Regardless of her disdain for the adventures that took precedence in her lifetime, the thrill of a mystery was ingrained deep in her blood—whether or not she cared to admit it.

Giulia wrapped her fingers around the cold, iron ring that stood in place of a doorknob and pulled. The heavy hinges creaked from years of neglect as the door came forward a fraction before halting.

It appeared unlocked, only stuck. Giulia furrowed her brows and braced both of her hands on the ring, getting a good grip before pulling with all of her strength. The door inched forward. Light poured from the crack and cold air snaked through, running up her arms and driving chills down her flesh.

Giulia paused, leaning her hands on her knees and waiting for her breathing to slow before trying again. But it was to no avail. The door simply would not budge another inch. She peeked her head through the gap to find stairs that led up and turned out of sight. A spiral staircase could only mean one thing; this was the entrance to one of the four towers dotting the castle's corners. Excitement coursed through her body and she took hold of the iron ring, rallied her strength, and yanked one more time; slowly the door inched open until finally, a space opened up wide enough for Giulia to slip through.

A chill permeated her bones. She shuddered but did not hesitate to ascend the stairs; they seemed to go on forever, confirming her suspicion that she was climbing to the top of one of the towers that squared the castle.

Disappointment filled her when she reached the top of the stairs to find another heavy door with a large padlock in place.

Giulia deflated. "Well, drat."

Now she *really* missed Ames and his ability to pick a lock. Oh, who was she kidding? She missed all of him. She let out a sigh and yanked on the door for good measure. Naturally, the lock did not evaporate, and the door did not budge.

Putting her hands on her hips, she glared at the offending object before spinning on her heel and bouncing down the stairs. Well, that adventure had been a dead end. *For now.*

Once she got to the end of the hallway, she hesitated. Turning right would lead her directly to her bedroom and the mound of unanswered letters that begged for her attention. She could picture the steadily growing mountain of correspondence piling up on her desk, and her shoulders fell a little.

But her outburst with her uncle still haunted her mind; she would respond to the letters, but first, she needed to apologize.

Making her way to the earl's study, Giulia swallowed the lump that gathered in her throat. She closed her eyes for a moment, tilting her face toward the ceiling and trying to figure out what she would say. She pulled out her elephant and kissed it before slipping it back into her gown and knocking on the door.

A moment went by and nothing happened. She knocked again, but the silence endured. Turning, Giulia huffed. Was everything destined to be a dead end this morning?

Wells turned the corner and stopped short, his white eyebrows hitching in surprise. "Is there something I can do for you, Miss Pepper?"

"No, thank you, Wells." Giulia darted a glance behind the older man, but the earl did not appear. She let out a frustrated breath. "I was only looking for Lord Hart."

"He can be found in the stables, Miss Pepper."

"Oh," she said in surprise. "I did not know he rides." She shook her head; of course he did. He was a gentleman, after all.

Wells's mouth twitched in a suppressed smile. "Yes, Miss Pepper, he quite enjoys it as well."

"It is only that I have never seen him outside. The only place I thought he ventured beyond the dining room was his study."

"Of late, yes, that seems to be the case." Wells leaned in and lowered his voice. "Of course, when he has trouble working through a problem he tends to do his best thinking on horseback."

"I see. And..." Giulia appraised the older man for a moment before proceeding. "Do I happen to be today's problem?"

"That, I cannot say." Wells straightened and returned to his formal role, loyalty keeping him silent. But his knowing look gave her all of the information she needed.

"Thank you, Wells," Giulia said over her shoulder as she slipped past him toward the front door. The biting cold hit her like a wall, and she sucked in a fortifying breath before continuing on around the back of the castle. She needed to speak to the earl before she lost her nerve. The autumn air was crisp and reviving. She pulled in a deep breath and let it cleanse her. A glance at the sky told her that rain was on its way. If the earl was not back from his ride already then surely he would be soon. The clouds looked menacing and far too close.

She trekked behind the castle and across a field cut low and well maintained. It had become obvious that the earl did not shirk his duties. He might be a hermit in some sense of the word, but he thoroughly cared for the grounds and castle, and if that was any sign, most likely his tenants and lands as well. Even the west wing, which appeared to be unused for the most part, was clean and dust free.

Halfway to the stable entrance, Giulia halted. The earl strode out of the large open doors and directly toward her. He was watching the oncoming storm with an equally alarming expression on his wrinkled features and she thought that perhaps confronting the man head on was not the wisest course of action.

Lord Hart glanced down before she could retreat and found her staring. He stopped a few yards in front of her and scowled. His cool gray eyes were lit from the sunlight and sent her back to the last time she had looked into her father's lifeless eyes. She faltered, losing her ability to speak. She missed her father so much, it physically hurt.

Looking into *his* eyes on the face of her uncle was an odd combination of pain and pleasure that she simultaneously shied away from and wished she could hold onto all in the same breath. The earl cleared his throat and pulled her out of her reverie.

"Right," she said, straightening her spine. It gave her another inch or so of height; she would take all the help she could get. "Good day, Uncle. I wanted to apologize for my outburst last evening. It was disrespectful, and as a guest at your table I should not have raised my voice in such a way." She swallowed. "I merely request some notice if you are going to choose to send me away."

He grunted and began to walk past her.

"My lord," she called, "while I enjoy the grunts you so often deliver in lieu of words, I must request a response at this time."

He paused and turned to face her slowly, his long white hair fluttering slightly in the wind. She clenched her hands into fists, her nails biting into the flesh of her palms as she held her tongue.

"Nicholas has not recovered fully," he said.

Giulia stood still, waiting for the earl to continue, but her waiting was in vain. "And I take that to mean that you do not wish me gone yet?"

There was a flicker of something in his scowl, and she wondered if it was caused by amusement or irritation. "You may take my words any way you wish. You have made an agreement and I expect you to fulfill your side of the bargain."

"Very well, my lord. And shall I take my dinners in my room?" she challenged.

He held her gaze. "You regret what you have said so I see no need to prolong this ordeal. You may continue to take your meals in the dining room."

"You misunderstood. I do not regret what I said, only my delivery."

"Oh?" The earl faced her fully, his gaze flicking over her with haughty arrogance.

She forced her shoulders back even farther and tilted her chin up. "I think I have been punished enough for your dislike of my father, who, I must remind you, I am not. And I refuse to continue eating in a room where I am cast into exile at the end of a table the size of Scotland and utterly ignored."

The earl scrutinized her face, another twitch marring his own. She would have assumed it to be irritation, yet he was not shaking, turning red, or any of the other signs that showed concealed anger. "You will continue to eat in the dining room," he announced before turning and fleeing to the castle, his stride long and quick.

As a person who had been given an inordinate amount of independence for the majority of her life, Giulia was not one to take demands easily. She bristled at the authority Lord Hart delivered, but something in her gut told her not to fight him on this.

He had looked at her face. He'd actually looked into her eyes. In her opinion, that was progress.

CHAPTER 16

"Are you being forced to leave at first light?" Nick asked as Giulia entered his bedchamber. She shot him a dry look but did not do him the courtesy of responding. Instead, she cornered Jack in his customary seat near the fire and discussed something with him for far too long. Well, it was only a moment, but their heads bent so close together made the hair on the back of Nick's neck bristle.

Why was he so completely jealous of Jack? It was ridiculous. He had never been jealous of another man a day in his life.

Giulia approached him and lowered herself into the overstuffed wingback chair beside his bed. "I have good news." Her smile was contagious, and he could not help answering with one of his own. She looked very pleased with herself.

"And do you care to share it with me today, or must I wait until your departure at first light?"

Giulia sighed, sitting back in the chair. "I am not going anywhere yet. And I am to continue eating meals with the earl."

"That is wonderful news." Nick grinned. If Robert would endure an outburst like that and then invite the guest back, there was some thawing occurring. Perhaps the earl had simply needed her to stand up to him.

"That is not good news at all, Nick. I don't want to continue eating that way. Lord Hart is rude, belittling, and conceited—"

"If that is not your news, then what is?"

She eyed him for a moment, obviously displeased by being cut off. "I found us another mystery." Her eyes gleamed and he was instantly aware of a desire to present her with new mysteries as often as he could.

"But we have not solved our first one yet."

"Yes, but I do not see what more we can do about that. We have exhausted all of our avenues of information." She glanced away for a moment and it was obvious she was keeping something from him. He had thought it once or twice before, but now it was clear. She was avoiding something.

"Very well," Nick said, trying to keep her talking. "Do not keep me in suspense."

She leaned forward, a customary action when one wished to discuss secrets and mysteries, despite how alone they might be or how much the others around them could not care at all about the matter they were discussing. Jack certainly did not.

"I have found an abandoned door. The lock was broken so I was able to get inside; I found a staircase that led to the top of a tower and, you'll never guess…"

He waited for a moment before realizing that she expected a guess. "No, I will not."

"You are no fun. It was another door! Only this time, it was locked, and I could not get in." The slightest pout tilted her lips and her chocolate eyes glittered.

He must make a note to request a hot cup of chocolate one of these mornings.

"Where was this door?" he asked, amused by her eagerness.

"At the top of the tower in the west wing. I would ask if you have seen it, but the door to the stairs was so old and forgotten, I could hardly wrench it open. The hinges were terribly rusty."

"So tell me, Giulia, what is so mysterious about this particular set of doors?"

"Well," she said, pulling her legs up under her and tucking her gown around her feet, "they were old. Completely different than the rest of the doors in this ancient place. They could even be original to the castle."

Jack stepped up behind Giulia and began gathering the items from Nick's tea, setting them on the tray.

"How is that so mysterious?" Nick asked, ignoring his valet. "The Pepper men have been notorious for the immaculate maintenance of this castle. It is a point of pride for them, and many features in the building are original to the castle. Half of the tapestries, I imagine, and the grand chandelier that greets you at the front door are only part of it."

"Perhaps," Giulia agreed, "but none of the *doors* are."

He gazed at her for a moment and decided to bite the bait. She was going somewhere with this, he just could not guess where. "And why is that so fascinating?"

"Because of that Pepper pride. Everything in this castle is pristine and well cared for, even the west wing, which has not had much use at all in the last few decades. According to my sources, at least."

"That is correct."

She leaned closer still. "Then why would the earl care so particularly for the grounds and the building and keep the dust away, yet ignore this one dilapidated door? Unless he wished to hide whatever was behind it."

She had a point there.

The sound of metal hitting stone rent the air as Jack dropped the tea tray, the implements hitting the floor and crashing loudly.

"Gads, man," Nick yelled, his hand clutching his rapidly beating heart. "Are you trying to kill me?"

Jack's head came up, his narrowed gaze resting on Nick.

Nick waved a dismissive hand. "Just clean it up."

Giulia chuckled, her breathing coming in quick spurts. "Where was I?"

"The door." Nick's mouth curled into a slow smile.

She grinned back at him. "I am right, aren't I? The earl must be hiding something."

"He could be. But, as you said, the door is locked."

"I know." Giulia furrowed her brows and the adorable pout returned to her lips. He felt a rush of warmth and longing flow through his body.

She sighed. "If only Ames was here."

The warmth in Nick's veins quickly vanished. "Whatever for?"

"He is very talented at picking locks."

Nick raised his eyebrows. What type of man was this?

She cast her gaze to the ceiling, expelling a slow breath. "Step down from your high tower, Nicholas Pepper. It came in handy a time or two on our—"

"Adventures?"

"I was going to say *voyages*," she replied dryly.

He chuckled. "Perhaps you should take me to the door."

Giulia shook her head dismissively. "It is not possible."

"Whyever not?"

She lifted one shoulder in a dainty shrug. "Too many stairs."

"I do not need to climb them." And besides, he was perfectly able to do so. He simply would have to take many breaks, pretending to find the steps tricky. He couldn't have her knowing how much better he felt. He locked her eyes in his determined gaze. "I would like to see the door."

"Yes, but to get to the door, we need to go down a set of stairs to the landing, then up another set to the west wing, and I fear that it will tire you before we even reach the tower and the other set of stairs waiting there."

He could manage it...but, what if he didn't have to? Nick watched Jack pick up the remnants of the tray and leave the room before turning back to Giulia and lowering his voice. "Well, if that is all that concerns you, then I believe I have a solution to our problem."

Giulia could not help but smile at the childish grin that spread across Nick's face. His lips curved in a tantalizing line and his emerald eyes glittered in playful anticipation. She sighed in a long-suffering manner. "I am afraid to ask."

"No questions, Giulia. Just help me with my dressing gown."

She sucked in a breath. "Perhaps Jack would be better suited..." One quick glance around the room proved that the man had slipped out at some point. She swallowed.

"Relax, Jules, I am fully dressed. I just want to ward off the chill and putting my arm in a coat at this point is still painful." He gestured to the sling on his arm for emphasis.

Her heart hammered in her chest. Nick had used her father's nickname for her, but it did not bother her. It had rolled so easily from his tongue that she found that she rather enjoyed it. A peace settled over her heart like a balm, and she relented. "Very well." She trudged toward his dressing gown and helped him into the sleeve before tying it around his waist to keep the gown from slipping off of his shoulder. He looked much the same as he had when they'd shared a midnight lemon tart; just as handsome, just as...tantalizing. She forced her gaze away, moving toward the door.

"Good idea. Close the door, will you?"

Giulia spun around to find Nick standing beside the fireplace. "What do you mean, close the door? Are we not venturing to the west wing?"

"You shall see." The impish grin spread on his face, deepening crease marks on the sides of his mouth.

Giulia did as he bid and crossed back to him slowly. "What are you not telling me, Nick Pepper?"

"Does that ever feel strange to you, Jules?"

She paused, frowning. "Do you mean how you use a nickname that I have expressly explained I am trying to escape?"

"No," he said, smiling down at her. His voice softened, sending a shiver down her spine. "I don't recall you disliking your nickname. In fact, I rather thought you missed being called by it. I was referring to how you call me by your own surname."

"It is your surname as well."

"Yes, exactly."

He stood there, leaning against the mantle with one ankle crossed over the other in flawless ease. She expected a smirk, but mere curiosity shone on his face and she released a bit of the pent-up energy coiling in her lungs.

She leaned against the mantle facing him, crossing her own arms in a slight mirror to his. "It is strange, I admit. But we are cousins after all, so it is not all that bizarre. In fact…" She hesitated. Perhaps he did not want this in depth of an answer. Nick continued to look at her expectantly, so she continued. "In fact, it helps me to trust you, I believe. You are family, and I can almost picture you as the brother I did not get to have when I consider you as 'Nicholas Pepper' and not just 'Nick.'"

His eyes widened in surprise and he faltered against the mantle before righting himself and standing up straight. He cleared his throat and gestured to the bookcase that sat against the wall behind Giulia. "Shall we?"

Giulia raised an eyebrow. "It is a very nice bookcase."

Nick leaned over her and placed his hand on the medallion that took residence on the top corner of the fireplace before turning it in a quarter circle. A soft sound popped behind her and Giulia turned and gasped, her hand flying up to cover her mouth. The bookcase had opened, actually *opened* beside the fireplace and a small dark crack appeared between the bookcase and the stone wall it sat against. Nick picked up the candle that he had apparently lit from the mantle and stepped around Giulia to the opening in the wall.

He leaned down and whispered near her ear. "After you, Jules."

Excitement skittered through her body and she tried to suppress a grin. "A secret passageway? An actual secret passageway?"

"The very thing."

Giulia placed her hand in the opening and pulled the bookcase aside. It swiveled outward and she stepped into the dark corridor. Nick followed closely behind her, closing the covert door most of the way but leaving a finger's width of a crack, presumably for them to get back into his room when they were finished.

Shadows bounced along the narrow corridor from the small candle's flame, casting warm light over Nick's face. "Would you like me to lead?" he offered.

Giulia took the candle from his hand and shook her head. Nick hardly fit as it was; there was no way he would be able to slide past her without covering himself in cobwebs. The flames lit his sharp features and made his eyes look darker. She whispered, because to speak loudly in a secret passageway seemed to break some code of adventurers. "I will lead, just tell me where to go."

"Straight." Nick nodded ahead. "If we do not veer off at all then this path will lead us directly to the west wing."

Giulia turned and began walking, her hand trailing along the cool stone until she snagged a silky spiderweb and jumped. Her free hand flew to her chest as she willed it to calm and Nick's warm hand came to rest on her shoulder. "Are you frightened?" he asked from behind her.

"No, it was only a spiderweb."

Nick chuckled a deep, throaty sound. "I should have warned you."

She turned her head back slightly, her chin brushing against his knuckles. "I should have assumed."

They passed along a few openings that led further into the castle, and one staircase that led up before coming to the end of the corridor. It was shorter than she had anticipated, and she stopped at the wall. "How do we...?"

Nick leaned over her, reaching for something in the dark corner, when a click sounded, and the wall opened a fraction. She could feel his heart beating against her back and her own breath stalled. When he moved back, Giulia pushed on the door, but it did not budge. "It's not opening," she whispered.

Nick drew closer, his breath tickling the hair beside her ear and sending a wave of chills down her neck. "This one does not swing, it slides."

He proceeded to push the door aside until it slid into the dark.

Giulia moved to exit but bumped into a heavy, threaded wall, like a carpet. Or perhaps a tapestry. She pushed it away from the wall and slid behind it until she exited into a bedchamber. At first she thought it was her own, but the colors were wrong. Nick followed her, still grinning. "See? No stairs."

"No stairs, indeed." Giulia moved toward the door. "Where are we, anyway?"

"I believe this is the west wing."

She shot him a wry look and led him into the corridor. Giulia laughed dryly, shooting Nick an exasperated look. "*Of course* the secret passageway would empty into the room next to mine instead of my own. Heaven forbid an adventure actually goes my way for once."

Nick shot a look at her bedroom door and she grabbed his hand, swinging him around and pulling him in the opposite direction. "Come, the tower is this way."

He chuckled but did not resist. "What did you mean?" he asked. "Do things not usually go your way?"

Giulia smiled to herself. "How else would I have gained extensive knowledge about nursing? I, of course, hardly ever got ill or hurt, but everyone around me seemed to attract ailments or injuries constantly." She released Nick's hand and fingered the chain to her jeweled elephant. "Which meant, naturally, that I have spent far too much time in the sick room instead of on the adventures. When we visited Brazil, the hired help my father brought along contracted a deadly spider bite on our second day in the Amazon. I spent the duration of the trip tending to him until his death while my father and Ames explored the jungle. By the time the man died, Father was ready to return to London."

She stopped as they reached the door to the tower and gazed at it, unseeing. "He really should have named that one *The Adventures of Patrick Pepper and his Assistant Ames,* but I doubt his readers would have appreciated the change." Giulia laughed and turned to face Nick, ignoring the pity in his eyes. "In truth, he should have named most of the stories after Ames, but people liked reading about the delicate little girl and how her father heroically saved her from one scrape or another. I imagine it wouldn't have been received quite the same way if he was saving another man."

"A man?"

"Yes. Ames." Giulia moved toward the door and picked up the iron ring before letting it drop, the clanging ringing in the small alcove.

A puzzled look crossed Nick's brow. "How old is Ames?"

"Eight and twenty. It is not so very old, you know. He is only eight years my senior."

There was a pregnant silence between them, and Giulia wanted to push it away. "Would you like to see the stairs?"

Nick's mouth formed a smile, unveiling the crease beside his mouth. "Absolutely."

Giulia slipped through the door and waited. She turned and poked her head through the door to where Nick was standing with his brow raised. "Are you coming?"

"Through that tiny crack, you mean?"

She stepped back into the hall and surveyed the space. Even if Nick's arm was not trapped in a sling, he could hardly fit through the space. "The hinges are rusted shut; this is the best I could do."

Nick stepped toward the door and wrapped his fingers around the handle in a firm grip before pulling. He got it open another finger's width before Giulia clutched his hand to stop him. "We can come back when you are better. There is no sense in you spending all of your strength on this. It's frivolous."

Nick gently moved her aside and pulled again. "I am not dead yet." He slid the door another hand's length and turned to her with a gleam in his eye.

Giulia looked heavenward and slowly released a breath. "You are incorrigible."

They slipped through the door one at a time and paused, shoulder to shoulder at the base of a set of curved, stone stairs. Light shone through the arrow holes that lined the staircase and glittered on the dust mites they'd disturbed. She faced Nick, noting the way the sun rays lit his golden hair. "Perhaps we should tackle the stairs another time."

"Yes," Nick muttered, his deep eyes locked on hers. "Perhaps we shall." His hand came up, cupping her cheek while his eyes locked on hers. His thumb trailed the line of her jaw, causing her body to still except for the butterfly wings that flapped within her heart.

Her new friends had warned her about this. They had told her of Nick's vile attempts to steal a kiss from each of them, all within his first month of knowing them. His intent gaze and soft, stroking fingers did not mean anything more than a man doing his best to conquer another lady.

Giulia placed her hand over his and held it still. She intended to remove it right away, but the feel of his fingers underneath hers caused her traitorous heart to leap. She held Nick's gaze, reading a look within his eyes that spoke of anticipation. They stood close, hidden in the small, dim space, locked in time. A desire to forget Amelia's warnings overcame her. No one would know...

But Giulia would. And she would not allow herself to be conquered by such a clever flirt. She pulled his hand away from her face and reluctantly stepped toward the door.

It was not lost on her that regardless of his motives, Nick stirred a feeling deep within her which Ames had never invited. Ames had given her butterflies, but he had never made her feel warm all over in this way. He had never made her heart gallop or robbed her of breath.

No, she could not compare them. It was not a safe thing to do.

Nick followed her in silence as they made their way back to his chamber. Giulia busied herself with plumping Nick's pillows and helping him back into bed, successfully avoiding eye contact.

"Do you think," Giulia said matter-of-factly, her voice hoarse, "that the earl is hiding something beyond that locked door at the top of the tower? As I think more upon it, I'm not sure he is. It is quite apparent the door has not been in use for some time. Perhaps Lord Hart does not even know about it. The alcove does hide the door quite well."

"I considered that. But unlike the door, it is rather difficult to hide the tower. I am sure that in his sixty years of life he has, at one point, been apprised of whatever is at the top. As far as whether or not he is hiding something,"—Nick leaned back on his pillows and closed his eyes—"I doubt it. At least, he is not hiding anything of value, for the room has not been accessed in years if that rusty door is any sign."

"Yes." Giulia nodded, her brow furrowed. "I suppose I agree."

Giulia stood behind the wingback chair and folded her hands over the top. Anxiety made her feel skittish and she knew the desire to be up and doing something with her hands. She'd had entirely enough adventure for one morning. "If you will excuse me, I will fetch a fresh pot of tea. Would you like a new book as well?"

"Not right now, thank you." Nick kept his eyes closed as he spoke, and she hesitated.

"Would you like me to wait on tea?"

"No," he murmured, "tea sounds lovely." He still did not move, and she paused, drinking in the sight of his relaxed face. There was no flirtation lining his eyes, no quirk of his mouth as he lay still on the bed; it was refreshing. She found herself smiling at him, but quickly wiped it from her mouth.

This man was wreaking havoc on her nerves, and she needed to get a handle on them right away.

CHAPTER 17

Giulia descended the stairs for dinner dressed in a plain, gray gown, her hair freshly plaited and her cheeks pinkened from a round of pinching to bring them some life. She was nearly out of mourning, but it didn't signify. She could not afford to replace either of her gowns, no matter how somber she looked.

Not that Lord Hart *ever* looked at her. Was she prepared for another evening of being ignored and banished to the far end of the table? Was this really much better than going to the poor house? She paused on the staircase, her hand gripping the rail as her eyes fluttered shut.

What a foolish thought. This situation was without a doubt better than going to the poor house. Forget dignity; she was receiving substantial, hot meals twice a day, tea whenever she wished, and lemon tarts nearly every night after the household fell asleep. She had hardly eaten this well nor this consistently in her entire life. Not that she and her father had *always* been poor, but as Giulia was the sole person in charge of making dinner for a good portion of the time, and she herself had no training in the kitchen, they had gotten by on very basic recipes. And whenever funds had begun to diminish during their various excursions, so had the food.

She continued toward the parlor and straightened her shoulders. She would get through these ridiculous dinners for two reasons. First, because it was food, hot, delicious, and plentiful; second, because her father would have expected it of her.

She was surprised when she arrived at the parlor to find the earl standing near the fireplace. He had never arrived before her for dinner and she found it disconcerting. Was she late? A glance at the mantle clock told her that she was on time, as usual. She slipped into the room and crossed to the chair she usually occupied, hoping her uncle would not notice her.

Lord Hart turned and faced her. Well, so much for staying invisible. She tried to swallow the dryness that came to her throat when his pale eyes pierced her. His gaze was unrelenting, and she found herself wishing he would return to aloofness. This direct attention was disconcerting.

Rising, Giulia delivered a curtsy and the earl acknowledged it with a slight nod.

Something had shifted between them, and she was unsure how she felt about it.

Before she was called upon to speak, Wells came to the rescue with the announcement that dinner was ready. The earl offered his customary arm and she took it, averting his gaze as he led her into the dining room. Instead of turning left at the table, however, to guide her to its foot, Lord Hart shocked her by turning toward the head. He rounded it and deposited her in the chair to the right of his own. Surprise halted her speech and a quick glance down at the end of the table proved that her usual place setting was absent. This was not a decision made in the moment; the earl had planned it.

A footman with jet black hair and a Grecian nose set a soup bowl before her and she waited, unsure of how to proceed. The earl was watching her closely and it set her on edge. She sat in the high-backed chair patiently and hoped he would dive into his soup and leave her to the solemn invisibility she was used to.

The silence stretched. She could hear a clock ticking somewhere behind her and she wondered what would happen if she simply stood and moved her bowl down to the end of the table and resumed her customary seat.

Another glance at the earl was telling. The man was poised, spoon in hand, waiting for her. Well, maybe not *her* exactly but he was waiting for something, and she had no idea what else it could be. She shifted in her seat to squarely face him. Maybe he wanted to make up for all of the time he had refused to look at her in the past, all at once.

"My lord, is there something I may do for you?" She heard herself speak and wondered when her brain had decided to address the man. The words seemed to do the job, no matter how unintentional her break of the soundless barrier between them might have been.

The earl blinked a few times, his gray eyes clearing. "Nicholas is healing well, I believe."

So he wanted to talk, did he? "Yes, quite well. He is slowly regaining his full strength—he still grows quite winded when exerting himself—but his shoulder looks quite good."

"He is a Pepper man, after all." The earl preened as if he was the reason Nick was doing so well and Giulia bit back the comment that teetered on the edge of her tongue about how she was a Pepper as well and *that* did not seem to have any bearing with the earl.

They ate their soup in silence and moved throughout the meal with spurts of polite conversation littering the calm lulls of eating. Inane conversation was hardly more enjoyable than the pure silence she was used to. If this was how dinner was going to be then Giulia would gladly resume their previous positions. Had she truly asked for this?

It was disconcerting having her father's eyes trained so avidly on her—particularly when they belonged to her uncle. She could feel the earl's unrelenting gaze through all of dinner.

The meal came to a close and Giulia excused herself, claiming a need to check on Nick. The earl bid her goodnight, his steel gray eyes scanning her own as if he studied a book written in a language he did not understand. She felt stripped and guarded at the same time and the prickles sticking her skin only intensified as she turned her back and fled.

In his bedchamber, Nick was seated in the wingback chair that had remained beside the fire. A tray full of empty dishes and glasses sat on a table beside him and he held a book in his hands.

"You have graduated from the bed, I see."

"Yes." Nick placed a finger in the book before peeling his gaze from it and shooting her a smile. "I have found that I feel much more digni-fied eating my dinner in a chair than I do propped up in bed."

Giulia crossed to the fire and lowered herself on the footstool just paces away from Nick. "And the aspect of feeding yourself with your own fork has nothing to do with that added dignity, I am sure."

His smile turned impish. "I would gladly sacrifice my dignity if you wanted to continue to feed me."

She waved a hand to push away his flirtation and then leaned forward, her chin resting on her knuckles. "I had a very interesting evening."

Nick's eyebrows rose and he set his book on the table beside his dinner tray, giving her his full attention.

"We..." She thought for a moment about her evening. It was strange for more than one reason. "We danced, actually."

Nick's eyebrows hitched up so high they disappeared under the blond strands that fell over his forehead. "You *danced*? With the earl?"

"In a manner of speaking, yes."

He nodded in understanding and leaned forward on his own hands. Though she doubted that he really understood at all. "He looked at me tonight."

"Oh?"

"Yes, he looked at me *and* sat me beside him at the table."

"He did, did he?"

"Yes. He looked at me, he sat me beside him at the table instead of far away in no man's land, and..."

Nick looked at her expectantly and she dragged the moment on a little further. There was nothing as satisfying as dangling the expectation of a piece of information before Nick, especially when it was obvious that he really wanted to know what it was.

"And...he talked to me."

"About?"

"Oh, this and that." Giulia waved her hands around before clasping them in her lap. "Basic things, really. Inane conversation. But—"

"Not normal," Nick finished for her.

"No." Giulia smiled at her mystery-solving partner. "Not normal at all."

"I think we have another piece to the puzzle. Or, perhaps," Nick said, sitting back in his chair and crossing his ankles, his hands folding over his chest, "another step toward softening up our informant."

"How do you mean?"

"Well, if he is willing to speak with you, perhaps he can explain what happened between your father and the rest of the Pepper family himself."

"Yes, perhaps."

She turned toward the fire and watched the glowing embers fade between red and black. She could easily cut out the earl and simply read her father's journal, but there was no guarantee that he mentioned anything about his family within its pages. Besides, reading it would be too difficult. The idea alone caused her pulse to quicken.

She *had* tried to read the journal, numerous times. The farthest she had gotten was opening the cover and examining the beautiful charcoal drawing of Halstead Manor. The manor that was, in all actuality, a castle.

"You're hiding something." Nick's deep voice cut through her reverie and caused Giulia to flinch.

"What makes you say that?" she asked.

He studied her. "I can tell."

She stared at the man. He had the strangest ability to read her, and whether or not she wanted to admit it aloud, he was usually correct. That day when he had offered her use of his given name, he'd known somehow that she could not bring herself to say Mr. Pepper aloud, for that had been her father's name and it would have tasted bitter on her tongue. When Nick called her Jules, she had reveled in hearing the name her father had given her.

Originally, going by Giulia seemed like the right thing to do, it was what she was known by outside of her father's world. Yet somehow pushing away *Jules* was not as triumphant as she'd expected. She began to feel like she was pushing away her father as well. She enjoyed hearing her given name, but she had missed Jules and Nick had somehow sensed that. Just as he could tell she was keeping the journal from him.

She searched his deep green eyes and focused on their pure, forest-like hues. How much could she trust the man? In matters of the heart, she was sure he was a careless flirt, stealing kisses and playing with women's feelings as though they mattered little. But in regard to *this*, Giulia had the odd sense that the man could be trusted. It was unclear exactly how she knew, but she felt the truth of it in her chest.

Regardless of how much she trusted him, however, she was not ready to delve into the stories and truths and hand-drawn pictures that filled her father's journal. The bitter reality nettled her like an unexpected bee sting. The truth was that she was afraid of what she would find. If her father had lied about his own mother being alive for most of Giulia's life, what else had he kept from her?

"It is nothing," she said with a laugh, trying to lighten the thick mood that settled over them, her gaze trained firmly on the embers blanketing the hearth.

"I'm not sure I agree with that," Nick said softly. "It is clearly troublesome for you, and I would not call that nothing."

His soft tone melted her resolve and she glanced at him, giving in as she locked in on his caring face. He was not pitying her, and she loved that.

She let out a soft sigh. "I have my father's journal. I am uncertain if it can answer any of our questions, but it is a resource we have yet to examine."

Nick's face softened further. "I take that to mean that you have not yet read it."

"No." She looked down at her hands and watched her fingers play with the skirt of her gown. "I have not."

"Would you like me to?"

She glanced up, surprised. That was a course of action she had not considered. If Nick read through it first, then he could tell her if there was any information pertaining to his history with his brother. And if there was none, she could wait until she was ready to read it herself. To see her father's scrawl and touch pages he had carefully scribed was a pain she could postpone a little while longer.

She froze mid-thought. Would allowing Nick to read Father's journal be a betrayal? She searched the man seated before her for any sign of malintent but struggled to find any. Nicholas Pepper was family, after all. He was the future earl and her Father's cousin, albeit in a distant way. But it was not as if he was a complete stranger.

"That may be a good idea, yes." Once she had answered, she could feel her shoulders sag from a weight relieved. The journal had sat in the drawer in the table beside her bed for the duration of her time at Halstead, and in the corner of her trunk prior to that for eight months, all the while mocking and taunting and pulling her in. It was a constant reminder of something left unfinished, yet it was something she had no desire to even begin.

Guilt warred with a low buzz of anxiety every time she eyed the holding place of the book, one of the very few things that Father had specifically left to her. He'd even expressed a desire, in his final few hours, that she commit to read it cover to cover. She had promised she would, and naturally she would one day fulfill that promise, but that day was not today. It was not going to be anytime soon.

"You know," Nick said slowly as he leaned forward, his head tilting in consideration, "we can go through the journal together if that would be easier for you."

She shot to her feet and swiftly moved toward the door, clutching her hands before her. "No," she called over her shoulder, "you may read it. I have far too much to do anyway."

She did not turn back to see his reaction, but instead picked up speed. By the time she reached the west wing she was running.

You know, Ames, she thought, as she made her way into her room and toward the drawer that held her father's journal, *a letter would be awfully nice right about now.*

CHAPTER 18

*T*he rest of the week passed in a slow, steady rhythm that began to feel as familiar as it felt comfortable. Giulia saw to Nick's meals and checked his shoulder daily, helping him to stretch his muscles and regain his strength. She walked with him and Jack around the east wing, slowly adding stairs to their route until they could complete the exercise without Jack's assistance.

She continued to respond to her father's mail, the letters flowing in with equal speed and the pile remaining a steady mound. Giulia watched the incoming post with anticipation for anything from Ames, or anything postmarked from Italy, though she was less ready to admit that aloud.

And she completely and utterly ignored any of Nick's attempts to discuss the things that he was learning as he read her father's journal.

Giulia had become adept at sidestepping conversation regarding her past or any of the conversations he wanted to bring up regarding her father's stories. She would simply ask, "Is it about my grandmother?" or "Does it pertain to our mystery?" and more often than not, Nick's face would give her the answer she desired, and the topic would be dropped. On the occasion that he pushed the matter, she would ignore him, and if that proved futile she would simply leave. Despite his growing strength, she was still faster than him.

"Must you go visit your friends today? I was hoping we could venture outside." Nick whined as he lounged in the wingback chair beside his fire while Giulia tied on her serviceable straw bonnet. She was preparing to attend her first literary society meeting, and felt uncomfortable in her plum riding habit, one of the few articles of clothing she still owned that was neither serviceable nor gray. It felt like a betrayal to her mourning, but the color was dark, and Tilly assured her that outside of those inside Halstead, and the ladies she was going to visit, she was unlikely to come across anyone else. And it was not as if she could ride without a habit.

"You still may," Giulia said. "I am sure Jack would be happy to escort you outside."

"You know what I mean."

"No, I really do not," Giulia corrected. "I am hardly any help on the stairs as it is. Jack will be happy to help you get outside. Though where you plan to go is a mystery to me. There is nothing around for miles."

Nick slumped, his pout making him look like a child who had not gotten his way.

Giulia delivered an exasperated sigh. "My goodness, Nicholas Pepper, quit your pouting. I am going out for tea and I will not be gone long. Now run along and find Jack and he will play with you; just be careful not to fall into the moat."

He shot her a wry look before pulling himself to his full height. When he towered over her like that, he really was quite intimidating, but she would never let him know it. She patted his arm twice and spun away, clutching the long end of her skirts as she sauntered out of the room, pretending to be the adult when she was nearly half the size of the man she belittled.

A low chuckle followed her into the hall, and she smiled to herself.

A groom by the name of Baker with a nearly bald head that belied his younger years accompanied her on horseback across the earl's land and to the edge of the property.

When she had described her destination the day before, the groom had seemed to know precisely which unused barn on the Green's land she was referring to and offered to lead her there instead of drawing a map as she had requested. Now she was beyond grateful for that offer, for she was certain she would have gotten lost had she ventured out on her own. There were trees scattered here and there which all looked the same, and for all she knew, they were traveling in a large circle.

Baker kept his horse beside hers. "If you go by road, there is a turn up the lane from Halstead. Follow that and it will lead directly to the property line that meets with the Greens' land," Baker explained, gesturing behind them to the direction of Halstead. Or, at least, that is what she thought he was pointing to. "And from there it is a direct left until you reach the barn. That is the long way around though and would take at least twice as long."

"That is useful to know, thank you. I doubt I could travel this way again without getting mercilessly lost."

Baker smiled at her. "Anytime, Miss Pepper. Will you be wanting me to wait to escort you home then?"

She thought for a moment before shaking her head. "That is unnecessary, Baker. I can follow directions well enough. And I don't mind the longer route. I've missed riding horses." She ran her hand along the mare's chestnut-colored neck and felt the warm rumbling skin beneath her gloved fingers.

A large, looming barn appeared before them and took Giulia by surprise. It was old and weathered and appeared to be in complete disarray. It nearly looked as if it was going to topple over and she was suddenly fearful as she pictured the loft inside where the bevy of swans—she had begun to think of the graceful women as such—had told her their weekly Literary Society meetings took place. She gulped, offering a nervous laugh and a side glance at Baker, who continued forward as if nothing was amiss. The man must have thought she was crazy when she requested directions to this barn. He was a good, obedient servant, that was for certain.

Jumping down from the horse, she handed her reins to Baker and approached the door. Before she could knock, however, it swung forward, and Giulia jumped back to avoid being hit. Mabel grinned, casting her an apologetic look before taking the reins from Baker and dismissing him. The groom looked at Giulia for confirmation and she offered him a shrug before following Mabel and the earl's horse into the barn. It closed behind her and she spun to find Amelia bolting the door. It was dim on the ground level, but there was light pouring from high above, over the edge of a large loft. Connecting the ground to the loft was a ladder that looked solid and secure and...new. In fact, the entire floor of the loft looked new. Or, at least, newly reinforced. It gave her a measure of comfort and she let out a slow breath of relief.

"You needn't have worried," Amelia said as she secured Giulia's mare in a stall. She strung her arm through Giulia's and led her toward the ladder. "We would not have led you into a dangerous situation."

Giulia smiled sheepishly and ducked her head. "I only worried when I saw the state of the barn."

"And rightfully so!" Hattie called down from the loft. "If Mae didn't fall through and break her leg a few years ago we would never have gone to the trouble to reinforce the loft and it would be a very dangerous place, indeed."

Giulia gasped. "She fell through? All the way to the ground?"

"Yes." Amelia nodded. "We had to meet in her bedroom for months while that wretched leg healed."

"And what an inconvenience it was for you, wasn't it?" Mabel said dryly as she walked toward them from the stalls where four horses were locked in and happily munching on hay.

"*Such* an inconvenience." Amelia chuckled as she climbed the ladder.

Mabel crossed the barn, a slight limp marring her elegant stroll. How had Giulia missed it before? Somehow Mabel's tall stature seemed to overshadow the limp, her grace and poise making it seem small and insignificant.

Giulia followed Amelia, who looked dashing in her elegant black riding habit, up the ladder and gasped when she reached the top. High above the dismal decay of the barn floor with its pathetic stalls, dirt floors, and haphazard door was an oasis of color, comfort, and beauty. The loft was about one-third the length of the overall barn, which was still larger than Nick's oversized bedroom. It was littered with rugs of various styles and colors, with two sofas in the center of the floor facing each other, and quilts strewn about in careless disarray; light flooded the scene from the large open barn door on the wall of the loft. Paintings dotted the walls in such magnitude that hardly any of the actual barn walls showed through, and oversized pillows were gathered in piles near the edge of the sofas in what looked like a makeshift bed.

The space was wide, open, and bright, yet cozy and comfortable in a way that enveloped Giulia in a warm hug. She admired the women who had put this space together and felt honored to be invited into what was obviously a sanctuary of theirs.

A soft nudge on her boot reminded her that she was still perched at the top of the ladder and she continued the rest of the way into the loft, followed closely by Mabel.

"This is..." Giulia faltered, she did not know how to put into words what she felt about this place. She knew that most of the words that came to mind would not do it justice.

"Pretty spectacular, isn't it?" Mabel whispered as she passed Giulia and dropped onto one of the sofas, resting her feet on a patched-up ottoman that sat in the middle of the seating area. She reached across the cushions and gathered the blankets, folding them into an orderly pile. "Though it is a bit of a mess today, Hattie. Did you arrive early and take a nap?"

"It was like this when we arrived," Amelia said, sitting opposite her friend and pulling her feet under her. She leaned against the back of the sofa and pulled a yellow and green quilt from Mabel's neat pile, laying it over her lap.

Hattie stood by the open doorway and stretched her hands high above her head. She turned to Giulia and gestured for her to join her.

The loft was high above the ground and from the open door, Giulia could see for miles. The crisp air was biting but the sun was bright and glorious and lit the world in a joyful way. "It is beautiful."

"It is," Hattie agreed. "And you can see Halstead Manor from here as well. Look over there."

Giulia looked where Hattie pointed and saw the tops of the towers peeking out from over the trees. The splendor of the castle made pride swell in her chest. That was the home of her ancestors. "It is so strange that a castle would be called a manor," she said, more to herself than to Hattie. "You'd think the Pepper pride would have caused them to name it correctly."

"It is the Pepper pride that is keeping the name as it is," Hattie returned.

"What do you mean?" Giulia turned and followed Hattie to the sofas. Hattie lowered herself onto the pile of pillows and lay propped up on the arrangement, pulling a quilt onto her lap as well. Giulia sat on the edge of the sofa and faced Hattie.

"Well, when the castle was being built, the family who owned it submitted information to the King describing the 'manor' they were constructing. They bribed the necessary officials, encouraging a blind eye, then built a small manor in the front of the property while hiding the castle as far back as they could."

"Whatever for?"

"To save from paying more taxes, of course." Amelia shrugged.

Giulia laughed out loud and then sobered when she saw that they were entirely serious. "Whatever happened to the actual manor?"

"It was only a front, and it eventually fell apart. It has not been around for hundreds of years."

"And the king never discovered that there was actually a castle?"

"Oh, it was discovered. One can't keep a castle hidden, regardless of how hard one tries." Hattie laughed. "And the taxes were paid. But the Lord Hart at the time was given the title of earl for bravery in the wars. He'd previously been a viscount. And he was so proud of his grandfather for getting away with the whole charade that he dubbed his castle Halstead Manor and no earl since has wanted to change it."

"They are an awfully prideful group, the Pepper men," Mabel interjected. "Proud to be British, and proud of their ability to fool the British government. It is all very childish."

Hattie snorted. "Childish. That is not limited just to *Pepper* men, surely."

"No," Amelia said with a laugh, "not just the Pepper men. But it is a trait both sexes can claim on occasion."

Giulia thought back to Nick's pouting earlier and smiled in agreement.

"Well *that* is a knowing smile, Miss Pepper," Mabel said facetiously. "Do tell."

She laughed awkwardly and shook her head.

"Do you have a beau?" Hattie asked, her eyes holding a dreamy gaze.

Giulia nodded. "Yes, I suppose you could say that."

All at once, the three women leaned forward eagerly. Three sets of eyes trained on Giulia and she chuckled awkwardly. "It is not so romantic."

"Who is he?" Hattie asked.

"Ames. Well, Gerald Ames to be precise. But his Christian name doesn't suit at all. He's been called Ames his whole life."

"You mentioned him at our tea," Mabel said. "He is your father's man of all work, yes? Where is he now?" Mabel lay on her side with her head propped up by her elbow, taking up the entire sofa with her long body spread out.

"Ames is in London, building a business making furniture. He wanted to be sure he could provide for me before we marry."

"You are engaged!" Hattie's head shot up.

"No, not exactly."

"Then promised?"

Giulia paused for a moment, wondering what to say. A solemn wind passed over the group and Amelia moved beside her and took Giulia's hand in her own. "To be honest, I am not sure," Giulia whispered. She thought back to their conversation when Ames had produced the letter from her uncle—the forged letter, she now knew, though she'd yet to discover *who* forged it—and then how he'd obtained a ticket for her to travel to Halstead. He had packed her belongings and given her such a lingering kiss on her forehead, that she knew he was saying something more than she had been able to read at the time.

Sympathetic eyes trained on her and she laughed mirthlessly. "Do forgive me. I am not usually such dismal company."

Amelia squeezed her hand and pulled another quilt from the floor, this one a beautiful combination of pinks and whites. Hattie scooted closer on her pillow bed and leaned against the edge of the sofa where Giulia was sitting. Mabel sat up, clutching a pillow to her stomach and giving her full attention to Giulia. For the first time in her life, Giulia felt like the center of attention in a good way. The circle of arms, open ears, and sympathetic gazes did not feel like pity, it felt like concern, and she found herself spilling the contents of her own worries easily.

"I've known Ames most of my life. He is older than I am, but we always felt like siblings. That is, until we got older. When I turned fifteen Ames gave me a kiss for my birthday, and it was all downhill from there. I fell for him instantly." She smiled at the memory. They had been on a ship traveling back to London at the time and Ames had pulled her from the sick room where she was helping to care for a sick passenger and his son who had taken ill. The kiss had left her light-headed and giddy and she'd been ready to commit to that man's kisses for the rest of her life. Since then, he'd cared about her, protected her, and had known her better than nearly anyone else.

"When my father died," she continued, "he left everything to Ames, surely in the hope that we would marry and share the inheritance. We traveled back to London under the chaperonage of a doctor. When we arrived in England, however, I received a letter inviting me to Halstead and Ames wanted me to go. He was not ready to wed and told me he needed to be sure he could support a family before taking a wife."

No one said anything, and Giulia continued, quietly. "I have not received word from Ames since I left London." She sucked in a breath and focused on her lap. "And I cannot help but wonder why he has not reached out to me. If his woodworking business is failing, I would not push him away. Though I highly doubt that will be the case. Either way, I cannot account for his silence."

"Do you believe he has planned on taking your father's inheritance all for himself? Leaving you nothing?" Mabel looked affronted.

"It wasn't much to take. And he earned it, after all. I am sure Ames assumed I would be accepted at Halstead with open arms and cared for by the earl."

How could he believe otherwise? Ames couldn't know that the invitation was falsified.

Mabel was mollified. "And you have been."

"Well, open arms may be a stretch, but I *am* being cared for."

Hattie looked up, sorrow etched on her face. "Have you considered writing to him? He might be very busy. Perhaps he has not had a moment to think about it."

"It is an option," Giulia said, shrugging. "But I cannot bring myself to reach out to him first. It is childish, perhaps, but I wonder if his regard for me is flagging. I am afraid to write to him for fear that he will return a letter breaking our connection for good."

Three kind faces tilted toward Giulia and she chuckled a little to ease the tension. She'd brought with her a melancholy that weighed down the room. Smiling, she said, "He does care for me a little, at least. He made sure I had a chaperone on the ship home—she was a respectable doctor's wife—and then again, in London, before he sent me here."

"He was looking out for your best interests," Mabel conceded.

"Yes, he always was good at that," Giulia agreed.

"Well, you need not fear for your future, Giulia, for you have friends now," Hattie said as she reached up and clasped Giulia's free hand tightly in her own.

"Yes," Mabel agreed as she stood and crossed to a table along the far wall that Giulia had not noticed before. She returned with a small box. "Now, shall we drown away those sorrows in a time-honored tradition?" She cocked an eyebrow and presented the box, opening the lid to reveal an abundance of red and white striped sweets.

"Peppermint." Hattie reached up and took one before settling into her pillows again and savoring her treat. Her head turned away slightly, and Giulia noticed what was keeping her hair up in its elegant sweep—a charcoal writing pencil. That was an odd hair accessory, to be sure.

"It appears we are missing a good number of them," Mabel said, eyeing the box of peppermints.

"Perhaps a groom has found our stash and stopped in for an afternoon sweet," Hattie said, grinning.

"The same groom who made a mess of the blankets, perhaps," Amelia added. "Hiding away for an afternoon nap."

The women sat around in comfortable nonchalance, passing the sweets around and lounging in unladylike comfort for the better part of the hour. Hattie griped about the incompetence of her neighbors, and how she kept finding their animals on her own property. Mabel entertained them with an anecdote about her young sister, and then Amelia turned the conversation toward her brother and his new baby. It took a minute for Giulia to realize that Amelia was not talking about Dr. Andrew Mason, but their older brother, Frederick, recently married and now a father. He lived in London with his wife and Amelia had received a vivid account of the birth from her sister-in-law, which the ladies all laughed over until they could not laugh any longer.

"Oh dear, look at the sun," Amelia said with a sigh.

"We better head home," Mabel agreed.

"Thank you for inviting me. I can scarcely recall a more enjoyable afternoon in quite some time." Giulia looked at each of their faces, cataloguing the images for future reference.

"I hope you will grow used to it," Hattie said as she stood and shook out her skirts. "We look forward to seeing you again next Thursday."

"Same time, same place." Mabel smiled as she moved to put away the peppermint box.

Giulia could not believe she was being grafted into this group and their comfortable literary society. "Every week?"

"Yes," Amelia said, grinning, "every week. As any respectable literary society would do."

Hattie scoffed. "Literary society, indeed."

"Well it's a step up from our old name," Amelia said with a grin.

Hattie laughed, covering her face with both hands. "Oh, do not say it!"

Mabel chuckled from where she was closing the door, cutting out the sunlight and shrouding them in the dim light that peeked through the slats of the barn walls.

"Now you *must* share," Giulia said.

"The Ugly Duckling Society," Amelia said dryly.

"Oh heavens!" Giulia laughed. "That could not be more inaccurate."

Amelia swatted a hand through the air. "We all had sort of an awkward childhood. My red hair was untamable, Hattie hated her freckles—"

"Still do!" Hattie shouted.

Amelia shot Hattie a stern look and continued, "And Mabel felt like a giant."

Mabel crossed to the ladder and began descending. She did not add *still do* as well, but it was obvious in her expression that she felt the same as Hattie about her insecurity.

"To be fair, we did all look rather awkward as girls," Hattie added. "And we chose the name hoping we'd live the fairy tale and outgrow our uncomfortable traits."

"We decided to change the name a few years ago." Amelia's voice grew distant and Hattie crossed to her before squeezing her shoulders and then descending from the loft.

"That is ironic," Giulia said as she followed them down the ladder. "I've lately thought of you as *The Swans*, even before I heard that story."

Mabel laughed from somewhere below them. "I like that!"

"Should we pick a new book for next week?" Amelia asked as she moved toward her own horse. Each of the ladies were collecting their horses and leading them out of the barn, Giulia following suit.

"How about *The Taming of the Shrew*?" Mabel offered.

"No, I have not finished *Emma* yet!" Hattie said, stricken. "I am only halfway through."

"Fine; *Emma* will remain for now."

Giulia led her horse outside to a mounting block that was situated beside the barn. "I thought you did not actually read the books?"

"*We* do not, usually. But Hattie does," Mabel explained. "And we change them frequently enough to keep up the facade."

"As if anyone actually believes we discuss books." Hattie snorted.

Mabel gave Hattie a pointed look. "I am sure they believe *you* do."

The ladies all mounted their horses and guided them in different directions.

"Until next week!" Hattie called as she urged her horse and took off. They each bid farewell and moved away in four different directions, and Giulia found herself already looking forward to the following meeting of the Literary Society.

CHAPTER 19

*N*ick put down the leather-bound journal and rubbed his eyes with the palms of his hands. Patrick Pepper was one of a kind, that was certain. Who else in their right mind would traipse across oceans and continents to satisfy mere curiosities? For that seemed to be all the man thought about. He was curious, *endlessly* curious about other countries. Their customs, their weather, the way people dressed or cooked or spoke. Patrick Pepper wondered about it all. And then, he satisfied his fascinations and wrote about them.

Nick had yet to discover where *The Adventures of Patrick Pepper and his Assistant Jules* had been published. He could not ask Giulia, of course, for she obviously did not want the stories read. And Robert was a brick wall when it came to inquiries regarding Patrick. The earl did not seem to shrink away from the topic any longer as if he was being burned by a fire that only he could see or feel, but he was steadfast in his refusal to discuss it.

Giulia, however, was not as forbidden a topic as she had been previously. Robert still refrained from speaking about her, but he did not dissuade Nick from sharing the odd anecdote about her. In fact, Nick had found more and more ways of sneaking Giulia into his conversations with the earl, and even found the old man struggling to refrain from commenting himself lately.

If Giulia's information was correct, then Robert was holding conversations with her at dinner now. What started out as mere polite chatter had slowly developed over the week into basic debates about various neutral topics such as the upkeep of the castle or the best meal to feed an invalid based on their stage of healing. Robert himself did not give away any hints of softening toward his niece, but Nick sensed the man's resolve dissolving.

Whatever had changed Robert's mind, it must have had something to do with Giulia's outburst the week before, and Nick could do nothing but wonder *why* it had had any impact on the earl.

Much as he could do nothing but wonder precisely what Giulia was doing at that very moment. She had gone to visit with the local ladies earlier, but that had been hours ago, and she should be home by now. The sun had already begun its descent and the sky was dimming quickly.

Nick slipped the book under the pillow beside his own that went unused and hoisted himself from the bed. His strength was nearly fully returned to him and he felt good using his muscles once again.

He feigned more exhaustion than he felt, but only to prolong his invalid status for Giulia's sake. And for Robert, if he was being honest. The man might be warming up to his niece, but Nick wouldn't put it past the earl to force her out now due to his own misguided pride if Nick showed just how recovered he really was.

An uneasiness spread through him and he crossed over to the rope and gave it a tug before moving to the window to scan the horizon. His window faced the wrong direction to watch for her arrival, but he had a clear shot of the stables, which appeared busy for some reason. The door opened behind him and he heard Jack enter.

"Has Giulia come back yet?" he asked.

"No," Jack said in a strained voice.

Nick spun around. "What is it?"

Jack looked uncomfortable. "It may be nothing."

Nick felt his stomach drop to his feet. He froze in place, focusing on his valet. "*What* may be nothing?"

"Well…"

Nick crossed the room in three large steps and took Jack by the coat with his good hand. The fear in his gut was reflected in his servant's eyes and he knew it was most definitely *not* nothing.

Jack placed his hands over Nick's. "Her horse has returned."

Nick struggled to swallow. "Just her horse?"

"Yes…without her." Jack hurried to add, "It may be nothing, and Baker is already gone in search of her. A few more grooms are saddling now to join in the search; they are going to fan out between here and the Green's old barn. Baker believes she may have gotten lost returning, but they are going to check the roads just in case."

Nick released Jack's coat and took a step back. "I must go help."

"No." Jack straightened to his full height and stood firm. "You will be no help in your condition. I know you are healing fast, but you are hardly fit for horseback."

"But Robert?"

"Yes, the earl has been informed."

"Informed?" Nick yelled. "He has been informed? And what in blazes does he plan to actually do about it?" His chest was heaving in all of his fury and he wanted to storm the earl's study and pound some sense into the man.

Jack remained calm. "He is out searching as well."

Well, that sobered Nick quickly. He sank into his chair and dropped his face into his hand. He could sense Jack approaching him and wanted to utter an apology but knew the man could sense it. They understood one another in that way.

"I will go out as well," Jack said.

"Yes, you should," Nick agreed.

"Let me help you downstairs first. Then you can be there when she gets back."

Nick waved him away. "No, I can make it fine on my own."

"Very well." Jack turned to leave but Nick grabbed his arm and he stopped, looking over his shoulder.

"Just find her."

Jack nodded once at his master before he turned and ran out the door. Nick dropped to his knees and prayed.

Time passed slowly as Nick paced before the parlor windows, which had a clear shot of the front drive. He stopped occasionally to scan the road before resuming his pacing, shaking his head and trying not to consider the darkness outside or the hours since Jack had sped off to join in the search. Where could she be?

Nick was utterly miserable. He hadn't known Giulia for long. It couldn't have been too much over a month. Maybe six weeks. How had he grown to care so much? He was riddled with anxiety at the fear of history repeating itself. A missing person, a horse returned without its rider…this was how the evening had gone when he had been shot. Or so he had been told.

There were far too many similarities between that horrible night, and this evening for Nick to feel at ease.

He plopped down in a chair and pinched the bridge of his nose, squeezing his eyes shut. He should be out there. He should be searching with the others. He was a man of action, and all of this sitting around and waiting was not good for his anxiety. What could possibly have happened? If only he had been more diligent in discovering the man who had shot *him*, perhaps this could have been prevented and Giulia would be home and safe and not out in the world somewhere, possibly hurt or…or worse.

He swallowed hard and shot to his feet. The blood drained from his head in the movement, causing him to waver. He lowered himself back onto the chair and waited for the black spots that littered the edges of his vision to disappear.

A deep breath and firm grips on the arms of the chair helped to slow his heart rate. There was no sense in jumping to conclusions. Giulia could have just as easily fallen from her horse, or even gotten down for one reason or another, and then lost the steed. Perhaps she had lost her horse, and then taken off in the wrong direction, thinking she was going toward Halstead but heading the opposite way instead. She could easily be lost. Not hurt, just lost. That would explain why it was taking so blasted long for the men to find her.

"Ugh!" Nick yelled. He was going to drive himself crazy with all of this conjecture.

A light bobbed in the distance, reflecting on the window and Nick shot up to examine it. It appeared to be a lantern coming down the road. More lights came around the lane bend, following closely behind the first lantern, lighting the path more fully and revealing men on horses. The search party was returning.

Nick ran to the front door, throwing it open as the group neared the drawbridge. He scanned the horses until he found what he was looking for and relief flowed through his veins like a warm bath, filling his body and sheltering him in peace.

She was alive.

Giulia sat sideways behind Robert on his oversized black steed, her tiny arms holding on to his round waist. She was not smiling, but aside from that she appeared to be unhurt. He approached and went to lift his arms to pull her down when his hurt arm snagged halfway up, sending shooting pains down his chest. Cursing, he rubbed his shoulder.

Dr. Mason approached, reaching up for her and pulling her from Robert's horse, his hands lingering around her waist. Resentment filled Nick's body as he stepped back to make room for Robert to alight and watched Mason lead Giulia toward the house with an arm around her shoulders.

"She is unhurt?" Nick murmured to Robert as the older man tossed his reins to a groom and they fell in step behind Giulia and Mason.

"Yes," the earl replied.

"Where was she found?"

"On the Green's property line, just much farther south. She was nearly to the main road."

Nick waited for more information as they followed Giulia across the drawbridge, but Robert was not forthcoming. He pulled on Robert's sleeve, forcing the earl to stop and spin, and growl.

"What happened?" Nick asked.

Robert looked away into the darkness which had swallowed his land, his gaze sweeping the horizon before speaking. "We don't know. She was heading back to the lane so she would not get lost trying to find Halstead and a loud bang scared the horse. She lost control."

"A *bang?*" Nick could feel his temperature cool as fear rippled down his neck.

"A gunshot. She did not say as much, but it was obvious based on her description."

It was Nick's turn to look away. He would never forgive himself if this was the same scum who had targeted him.

"It is not your fault, Nick," Robert said with uncharacteristic softness. "She is well, anyway."

"Did she fall from the horse?"

"Yes, but as I said, she is unhurt." Robert scrubbed a hand over his face. "She is skilled on horseback, and apparently was taught how to fall."

Nick nodded in understanding, but that did not ease the guilt. "We need to find him." He was surprised by the steel in his own voice.

"I have sent out every man I could spare to do another search. Though if there was anyone to find I think we would have found him on our first search."

"Who would target Giulia? Who would target me?" Nick shook his head in wonder as they continued toward the house. "I have never had an enemy in my life."

"But now you are the future earl."

"As I have been for the last three years. Still, no enemies. My father had no brothers. I do not even know who would be next in line for the earldom."

"You can think of no one who would want to harm you?" Robert questioned.

"Not enough to try and kill me. I do not get along perfectly with everyone, naturally, but to try and shoot me? No, I can think of no one that hates me that much."

"We need to discover who is next in line behind you. You don't have any male cousins?"

"No, none."

Robert shook his head and held the door open while Nick stepped through it. "I am going to my study. Check on Giulia."

Nick turned. "Why not check on her yourself?"

Robert shook his head as he continued toward his study. "I am satisfied. I am going to take care of a little business before I eat."

Nick watched the earl disappear down the hall and shook his head. The man cared, that much was obvious. Too bad the Pepper pride was getting in the way or Robert could enjoy a relationship with Giulia. They would get along splendidly if their walls were down, Nick was sure.

Nick turned toward the parlor where he had spent the last hour pacing and anticipation quickened his steps. Crossing the threshold, he pulled up short, his gaze riveted by the woman's wild hair and intelligent gaze. He relaxed at once, watching her. She was here. She was well, and she was whole.

Mason stood near the fireplace, one arm leaning against the mantle while the other rested on his hip. Giulia poured a glass of amber liquid and handed it to the doctor. She smiled at Nick before crossing toward him. She was abnormally pale, and as Nick let her lead him to the settee, he realized that she was taking care of him, when it was she who should be cared for. She had just been thrown from a horse, for pity's sake!

He lowered himself onto the sofa and was exceedingly satisfied when she sat beside him. "How are you feeling?" she asked, concern pulling her brows together.

Nick laughed. "Me? I am fine; do not worry over me." His gaze swept over her again, reliving his relief that she was unharmed. He turned to Mason, who had taken a seat in a cream-colored armchair across from them. "What do you think, doc? Is she truly well?"

Mason nodded. "Appears unharmed to me. Although," he turned his attention to Giulia, "you will most likely be sore tomorrow. No one walks away from a fall like that without any repercussions."

"Yes," she nodded, "it is not my first time being thrown. I know what to expect." Giulia stood and addressed the men at the same time. "I must go and change for dinner; I am covered in dirt. Please tell the earl not to wait for me." She smiled at them both and then left the room.

Nick was dazed. He had spent an hour pacing, worrying, stressing over the horrible possibilities, only for her to return fully well. She did not seem rattled in the least. Could she be putting on a brave face, or had Robert blown things out of proportion?

He faced Mason. "Now," he said evenly, "tell me. Must we be worried?"

Mason's dark red eyebrows were pulled together, but he did not look concerned, simply mystified. "She appears well, physically. Until we know the culprit, however, there is no way to know exactly what to expect. Was this a strange, random occurrence? Someone poaching on the earl's land that shot too close to Miss Pepper's horse? Or has someone set out to hurt the Peppers?" He eyed Nick, who raised his hands in innocence.

"I just told Lord Hart the same thing that I will tell you," Nick said. "Aside from whomever may be next in line for the earldom, I can think of no person who would want me gone. I have no enemies that I know of."

Mason's eyes glazed over, and he nodded in understanding. "Well," he said, standing, "I better be off. My sister will want to know that Miss Pepper is safe."

Nick stood, bowing his head. Mason returned the nod before eyeing his bad shoulder. "You should be healed by now, but Miss Pepper treated you as though you were still an invalid."

"I am well," Nick replied, saying no more.

Mason studied him, but Nick did not want to explain the ruse or his wish to keep the woman around longer. He led the way to the front door, walking Mason out.

As soon as the door closed behind the doctor, Nick turned for the earl's study. They were going to figure this out. Now that Giulia was involved—*if* Giulia was involved—the stakes had risen heavily. This would not go unanswered.

CHAPTER 20

$\mathcal{G}$iulia closed her door and turned the lock before leaning against it and sliding to the floor, lowering her forehead onto her knees. She wrapped her hands around her legs as tears rolled down her cheeks.

She was shaken—completely and utterly rattled. She felt like she had seen a ghost. Except *this* being was fully alive and well and holding a gun. Sixteen years may have passed, but no amount of time could erase the face of one's mother. No, that was an image that was burned into her brain, regardless of whether or not she cared to remember.

Her tears slowed and she raised her face, wiping her cheeks with the sleeve of her riding habit. She pulled in a slow, shaky breath before releasing it just as slowly. Maybe she had not seen what she thought she had. Perhaps her mother was simply in the area and happened to be standing in the trees along her uncle's property just before a gunshot rang through the air.

Another convulsion shook her frame and she shivered. She should go downstairs immediately and tell the earl what she saw. She should tell *someone*, she knew that much. But how exactly was she supposed to do that? When Dr. Mason had found her and asked what had happened, she wanted to explain it then, but she could not find the words. It seemed too absurd.

Giulia shook her head and scoffed quietly. It *was* absurd. Her mother? It could not have been her mother. Her mother lived in Italy.

Giulia got to her feet and began removing her soiled dress. No amount of wariness diminished the reality of her situation. She knew what she saw. It was unbelievable, but that did not change that it had happened. And the earl would want to know.

Taking off her dress, she folded it over a chair in front of her vanity and pulled on her other gray gown. She needed to examine the letters her mother had sent. What had the woman wanted? A key, wasn't it? If she could discover more about this key, then she might know what her mother had crossed an ocean for.

Perhaps she would need to swallow her hesitancy and read through her father's journal sooner than later. She could skim it for any mention of a key without really delving in.

And then there was Ames. Was he in danger too? Thinking of the dark-haired man who had owned her heart for the last five years, she felt a new pang of hurt. How could he leave her alone when she needed him so dearly?

Her eyes slid shut. Unless, of course, Ames no longer cared for her. Why else would he fail to write to her?

The revelations and possibilities hit her like a bag of bricks. One after the other. She felt bruised and broken, lost and grasping for something solid to cling to.

She wiped her eyes. A thorough evaluation of her face in the mirror showed that she was no worse for the wear, and she steeled herself to return downstairs for dinner. If she was going to get through this evening without falling apart, then she would have to remain neutral. It had worked when they found her stumbling through the dark along the fence, and it could work again.

Giulia left her room, practicing her neutral face as she walked down the hall. She would have to stay alert and prepared if she was going to fool Nick. She had succeeded earlier, which had been shocking. He could usually read her so well. And what was he about, running outside? Either he'd had a rapid and miraculous recovery, or he had been hiding how well he was truly feeling from her for quite some time.

She was no longer surprised to enter the parlor and find the earl waiting for her prior to dinner, but tonight there was another man standing beside him and Giulia sucked in her breath. Nick, standing tall and elegant in his evening clothes, looked powerful and composed. His sling was absent, replaced by a well-cut black coat covering a crisp ivory waistcoat. Shirt-points of a reasonable height—but not so tall as to be dangerous to his cheeks—were surrounded by an expertly tied cravat, and his blond hair had been dampened and combed into a neat style.

The man was handsome in shirtsleeves and a dressing gown as an invalid. In full dinner dress he was a force to be reckoned with. She suddenly wished she did have an engagement with Ames to force her thoughts away from Nick.

There was no agreement, no secret engagement holding her back. Ames had not written to her once since she had left him, even while he'd taken care to forward the letters from her mother.

Giulia went cold all over, the sensation as uncomfortable as it was foreign. Her father had always taught her to face her fears, to look strangers square in the eye and not back down from discomfort. She was raised to be proud, strong, and independent, yet she had held onto this image of Ames building a life for her, Ames protecting her, Ames taking care of her.

Well, Ames was not here.

A barely audible scoff escaped her lips as she discovered that she had turned into exactly what her father had raised her *not* to be. She squared her shoulders and approached the men, desperate and deter-mined to pass herself off as unaffected. Unaffected by the discovery that Ames did not care for her, by the fact that she had seen her mother, that she had been shot at by someone—potentially *by* her mother—and that Nick, the biggest flirt in all of Devon, looked unfairly dapper this evening.

Nick and the earl were enveloped in a deep conversation and Giulia paused, watching them. She could not hear what they were saying but found their closeness and camaraderie interesting. It appeared that the earl was not opposed to close relationships as a rule, for he clearly shared one with Nick. Lord Hart was just opposed to a close relationship with her, specifically.

"Dinner is ready," Wells announced before stepping out of the room. Nick and the earl both looked up, their gazes simultaneously landing on Giulia. She smiled at the sour-faced earl and took his offered arm before walking into the dining room with Nick on their heels. Lord Hart took his customary seat at the head of the table, with Giulia on one side and Nick on the other.

"Perhaps it is best if you do not leave the castle again," Lord Hart said into his bowl. Giulia wondered which of them he was speaking to before he glanced at her and continued, "At least until we have apprehended Nicholas's attacker, or have a better idea about who is after him."

Giulia nodded. Did they think that the shot today was meant for Nick and not her? She had tried to describe a bang that could be interpreted as a multitude of things, but apparently she had not fooled the earl. "If you think that is best."

She felt suspended, as though she was floating above the table. Nick was nearly healed—in truth, he looked perfectly well this evening —but Lord Hart was not going to make her leave yet. She did not quite know what to think about the situation.

"I do," he grunted.

"I agree," Nick said. "As long as we are unsure who is orchestrating these attacks, it may not be safe for any of us outside of these walls."

She looked into his concerned eyes and yearned to tell him the truth, to explain that she knew exactly who was behind the gunshot. But the words would not come. Was it a displaced sense of loyalty keeping her mouth shut, or had she simply not come to terms with the truth herself yet?

Either way, words would not form in her mouth and she merely nodded again. It was a far cry from her usual demeanor, and she needed to rectify it quickly or Nick would surely figure out that something was amiss.

"I was able to see a lot of your property, my lord," she said to her uncle, "on my impromptu journey. That is, I was able to see quite a bit before the horse let me go. And I must say, this is such a beautiful land. The Green's property gave me a wide view of the surrounding area and I cannot think of a more peaceful place than the English countryside."

"Nowhere more peaceful than this?" Nick cocked an eyebrow. "And this comes from our world traveler."

"I am hardly a voice of authority on the matter, but I can speak for myself, and I wholeheartedly believe that. Even this old, stony castle is immensely peaceful in its own odd way. I have yet to find a place where I was able to feel comfortable so quickly. And it has nothing to do with the bedroom I have been appointed." She took a bite of her potatoes and then continued. "My lord, you have the most magnificent home. I have scarcely lived in such luxury and I must say I am getting used to it. When I leave here I must be sure to find a position in a similar household, for I do not think I can ever sleep on a bed that is not made from feathers again."

The earl looked up and then shot a glance to Nick before clearing his throat. "Actually, I wanted to speak to you about that."

Giulia paused, lowering her fork.

Lord Hart gestured to his heir. "Nicholas is healing well enough and I believe he has ceased the need for a nurse. But there is another way in which I can employ your assistance before you make your departure."

This was news. "In what capacity?"

"I have the need for a feminine eye, if you will."

Intriguing. She glanced to Nick, but he looked as shocked as she was.

"You see," Lord Hart began, "I am going to host a ball for Nicholas, and I could use your help in the planning and the execution of the event. We have not held anything remotely like a ball since my mother was here to oversee it, and I have found that I do not know the first thing about hosting such an event."

Giulia was stunned. "I have never planned a ball before, my lord."

He waved a hand as if that was inconsequential. "Yes, well, we have a housekeeper for the technicalities."

Then what did Lord Hart need *Giulia* for? She looked at Nick and he lifted his shoulders in a shrug.

"I would be happy to help," she said. Particularly when it meant she could remain at Halstead longer. "But is it not unwise to open the castle with such a threat hanging over us?"

The earl shot her a determined look. "Halstead is impenetrable. Only our trusted guests will be admitted. We will be safe."

His logic was sound, but for the minor issue that he did not know *who* the threat was. But who was Giulia to argue with the earl? "Very good, my lord. What is the occasion for the ball?"

"Nicholas is to be married."

A spray of food hit the table, followed shortly by a round of coughing. "I am *what*?" Nick yelled.

"It is time for you to marry," the earl said easily between bites of food, not the least perturbed. He appeared not to notice the food that now littered the table in front of Nick, nor the shock on his heir's face.

"And have you already chosen the bride as well, Robert, or is this ball in anticipation of my becoming engaged?"

"No need for hysterics, my boy. The ball is for you to meet eligible ladies from which you may choose a wife for yourself."

"I see, and when am I to make this choice?"

Lord Hart turned to Nick. "Would the end of the night be too much to ask?"

Giulia looked from one man to the other. Nick stared, his mouth hung slack as if it was, indeed, far too much to ask. The earl returned to his dinner.

Nick cleared his throat. He looked prepared to fight and Giulia stepped in before daggers could be thrown. "When is the ball to take place, my lord?"

"A fortnight from tomorrow will suffice."

"Very well. That sounds doable, doesn't it, Nick?"

Nick grunted as he stabbed his meat and began sawing with vigor.

"I have a guest list prepared," Lord Hart said. "Nicholas may add to it, and we can meet tomorrow to go over the logistics." He speared Giulia with a look, his eyes widening under their bushy eyebrows. "But then I expect you to take charge."

"That sounds agreeable, my lord."

Lord Hart grunted in return and resumed eating. He was a savvy opponent, to be sure, and Giulia was glad that in this particular moment he was not *her* opponent. She smiled at the furious man who sat across from her and felt gratitude at the turn of events that had taken place.

She no longer had to nurse Nick, and she had a reason to stay on for a few more weeks. If nothing else, that would give her time to find a position. And, hopefully, to figure out what to do about her mother's recent reappearance in her life.

CHAPTER 21

"*N*ick, wait," Giulia called out as she followed the man up the staircase.

He paused on the landing and turned around, a wry smile turning up the corners of his lips as he massaged his injured shoulder. "Come to rub it in, have you?"

Giulia shot him her most innocent expression. "Whatever could you mean?"

He dropped his hand from his shoulder, groaning. "Since coming here, I knew Robert would need me to marry—the earldom requires it. I only did not expect it so soon."

"Soon? Have you not been here for years?" Giulia caught his surprise and softened her tone. "I can only assume Lord Hart would like to secure the line. Particularly after the danger you've faced of late."

"Yes. He needs another heir in case my attacker succeeds in offing me." He smiled wryly.

"There is no need to be vulgar. You cannot fault the earl for wanting to be sure the line is secure. I imagine his pride took enough of a beating when he had to track you down."

Hurt flashed in Nick's eyes and Giulia realized the slight she had inadvertently delivered. She hurried to correct it. "I am not belittling your background, Nick. I do not even know enough of your background to do so. I only meant that the Pepper pride runs deep, and the earl probably did not relish having to search the distant branches of the family tree for the next earl instead of supplying one of his own."

"What did you need, Giulia?" Nick asked quietly, void of emotion.

She swallowed the lump in her throat and looked away. She'd made things worse, and Nick wanted to be away from her. That stung. "I was hoping to get my father's, um..." She cleared her throat and started again. "I would like the journal back."

He eyed her for a moment, and she could feel his stare burning into her eyes while she avoided his. "Very well. It does belong to you; I could not refuse if I wanted to."

"Do you want to refuse?" she asked, confused.

"I am interested in finishing it, of course. But if you do not want me to then I must respect that."

"No, it is not that—"

He turned away. "Allow me to fetch it right now."

"No!" She surprised herself at her vehemence and Nick spun, shooting her a look full of concern and confusion. "I will get it from you another time. Goodnight." She turned toward the west staircase and fled before he could say another word.

She would read the journal. She had to read it if she was going to figure out what this key was that her mother was seeking. But she did not want to begin right away, and she did not want to sleep with the journal taunting her. Nick could have it for one more night.

Giulia's heart raced as she locked her door and moved toward the writing desk that sat perched against the wall, overlooking the window and the dark world beyond. The moon peeked out from the top edge of the window and pulled a smile from her. In her own strange way, she had always been attracted to the moon. In a sense, she viewed it as a surrogate mother. Regardless of what continent she was on, or if she was not on any continent at all, the moon was the same everywhere.

She had her best discussions and revelations when speaking with the moon, and it seemed to always be there when she needed it. Like the night she had found Nick, and the clouds had cleared so the moon could shine down and light the way for Giulia. And like now, when she needed to analyze her mother's letters, she could pull strength from the giant, beautiful light in the dark sky.

She pushed aside the piles of correspondence that had come in earlier that day and pulled the top drawer open of the writing desk before removing the four rooster-stamped letters that had traveled all the way from Italy to London, and then on to Halstead. One at a time she smoothed them out on the surface of the desk until they were spread before her in chronological order. The first one had arrived six months prior, and the subsequent three only weeks after that. Each one spoke of the key that was jeweled and belonged to Giulia's mother, yet her father had refused to return it. And each one sounded more and more desperate.

Then, there was that familiar name. The name she had not heard very often spoken aloud, but so familiar to Giulia that she felt a kinship when reading the signature. *Lily Cattaneo.* Apparently Lily had dropped "Pepper" from her name altogether.

A thought occurred to Giulia and she froze in fear. She pulled out a fresh sheet of paper and ink from the drawer, laying the items carefully on the desk. Dipping her quill in the ink, she tapped it lightly, staring at the blank page and wondering what to write. She would as soon not write a single word, but she could not leave Ames unwarned.

Not when there was a chance that the key was in his possession.

Giulia drew herself up, glancing to the moon through the window and drawing courage from its bright edifice. She could do this. She *had* to.

Dipping the pen to replenish its ink, she wrote to Ames. Once she began, it became all too easy to describe the trials facing her. Without too much unnecessary detail, she wrote of the situation she had discovered Nick in upon her arrival at Halstead, of the letters written by her mother, and the concern she had that the key was somewhere in Ames's belongings, and that her mother would surmise the same thing and come after him.

When the letter was completed, Giulia leaned back in her seat, reading over her words once more. She sounded impassive, a friend relaying information. She could only hope Ames would reply at once. Before she could think better of it, Giulia dipped her pen once more and added a final question. *How do things fare with your woodworking shop?*

She inhaled a deep, cleansing breath and penned the direction on the front before sealing it. However Ames responded to her letter, at least now she would know where they stood.

Before she could consciously think about what she was doing, she stood to take the letter to Wells. The clock slowed her down, however, and she lowered herself into her chair as it chimed a ridiculously late hour. Drained and tired as she was, she hardly noticed the knocking sound that came from somewhere in the distance.

She was pulled from her exhaustive reverie when the knock came again, and she realized it was coming from her door. She pulled it open, however, and found that no one was there. A quick step into the hall revealed that no one was anywhere near her door.

The knocking came again, and she startled, shivers running down her neck. The knock had come from within her room. Easing her door closed, Giulia slid the bolt into place and waited, her heart slamming into her breastbone and her breath coming in short, quick spurts.

It came again and she followed the muffled knocking to the far wall, running her hand along the tapestry. Silence reigned, and Giulia held her breath, hoping the silence remained.

She was not the least bit surprised, however, when the knocking sounded one more time directly behind the tapestry.

Easing it away from the wall, she felt her hand along the cool stone and found the break that signified the possibility of a doorway. Her hand hovered over the potential doorway before hitting it in response. Silence engulfed her as she waited; she could only hope she was communicating with Nick.

She heard the clicking and knew that whoever was on the other side of the secret doorway was turning the mechanism that would unlatch the false wall and open it enough that they could slide it aside. Fear prickled the back of her neck when she considered the possibility of her covert visitor being Lily Cattaneo.

The click reverberated in the quiet room and Giulia held her breath. She wanted to move away but found herself paralyzed in place as she watched the wall slowly move aside. The candlelight coming from the secret passageway illuminated the hand that was pushing the door aside and she let out a breath of relief when she recognized it.

"Good heavens, Nick. You frightened me!"

His head popped through the space and he cocked an eyebrow. "Whatever did I do to frighten you?"

"You know," she said as she pushed the tapestry aside and let him into her room. "All of this talk about attackers and staying within the castle walls, and then I receive a late-night visitor through a secret passageway."

His mouth tilted into an amused smile, his eyes glittering from the firelight. In shirtsleeves and breeches, his hair tousled and the shadow of a beard grazing his jaw, he looked handsome and relaxed. "Your life sounds like a gothic novel."

"Far too much like a gothic novel, to be sure."

Nick leaned against the wall with one hand propped behind his back, the other holding a candle. A grin on his face was evidence of his amusement.

"May I ask what you are doing here?"

"I brought the journal." He pulled it out from behind his back and reached forward to give it to her.

She stepped away instinctively. "I told you I would get it from you tomorrow."

"Yes, you did say that." He moved to set it on the writing desk and turned to face her again, compassion darkening his eyes. "And you were a little too anxious, I might add. What is causing you such distress, Jules?"

So she hadn't fooled him after all. "What gives you reason to believe I am in distress?" she asked, her voice strained.

He gestured to the letters on the writing desk. "You are reading your mother's letters? And now you want your father's journal?" He looked from the desk to Giulia, his brows hitched together in confusion. "What are you not telling me?"

Giulia froze.

His eyes narrowed, piercing through her and pinning her against the wall. She tried to think of a way out but nothing believable presented itself. She scrambled for something to say but could see in his gaze that he sensed her struggle. She had never felt so vulnerable and exposed before, and her feelings conflicted with the desire to pour everything out and into Nick's listening ears. She craved the release that would come from telling him everything, but no matter how much she wanted to, she could not get her mouth to open.

Giulia stared at the man, watching herself watch him as if she stood in the distance and could observe the scene play out before her. She recognized the change that came over his face when he realized she wasn't going to speak. She yearned to run into his arms, to sob and explain exactly who was behind the gunshot that had frightened her horse. She pleaded with herself to open her mouth and speak, but nothing would come.

Nick shook his head and turned to go. She reached a hand out to his retreating back but said nothing, and he did not turn around to see her gesture. She felt so small, so defeated, and dropped her hand. Nick lifted the tapestry that hid the doorway into the secret passageway and paused. He turned his head slightly and spoke. "If you decide to trust me, you know where to find me."

And then he was gone.

CHAPTER 22

*S*leep was nothing but a concept for Giulia that night. She made her nightly voyage to the kitchen for lemon tarts and hoped she would run into Nick, but he did not appear. She went to the locked tower on her way back from the kitchens and tried her hand at picking the lock, but to no avail. And then, when she could procrastinate no further, she sat before the dwindling fire in her room and opened her father's journal.

She knew what to expect, for she had seen her father's writing many times. She even anticipated the wave of grief and longing that washed over her as she began to read his words. What she did not expect, however, was that the more she read, the more she could hear her father's voice, and could nearly feel two warm arms wrap around her as if he was actually beside her.

Giulia read accounts of their journeys together, she read about the way he had loved and depended on Ames, and she even read the snippets here and there about his pride and joy, his Jules. Tears streamed down her face as she saw in her father's own words how much she had meant to him. A piece of her heart that had always felt less than adequate now brimmed over with love.

How had she ever thought that he had blamed her for her mother leaving? How had she convinced herself that he would have preferred to have Lily Cattaneo in his life over Giulia? Reading about his love and affection put to rest the years of doubts she had shouldered and the inadequacies she had felt.

She flipped the journal over to keep its place and retrieved a handkerchief to wipe the tears from her face. She was nearly finished, but the crying was making it difficult to read. Glancing at the window, she found that she had stayed awake all night as the swallows that nested above her window started to sing to the first rays of sunlight pouring over the edge of the earth. Giulia picked up the journal and moved to her bed before settling in and resuming her reading.

Jules made me proud today. We were visiting the village where most of the laborers for the Sutter's plantation come from, and a group of children began to follow us as we toured their village. Jules was making silly faces at the children, and the next thing I knew she had left my side and was teaching the little brats how to sing 'Baa, Baa Black Sheep.' Before I knew it, she had all of the children running around like sheep and she was chasing them as if she needed their wool. They do not share a language so I cannot fathom how she was able to convey the rhyme to them, but she has a gift with people, my Jules does. I do not know what my life would be without her.

Giulia chuckled as she recalled that day. She pulled her jeweled elephant from her bodice and kissed it before continuing to read. There were less stories as she neared the end of the journal and the entries became reminiscences of earlier times. She stopped dead as soon as she reached an entry dated one week before her father's death, with the first line beginning, *Lily would have been proud of my Jules.*

Giulia sucked in a breath and slammed the book closed. The culmination of her father's journal and the memories it evoked, Ames's stark absence, and her mother's recent reappearance were enough to make her nauseated. She sat up and held her stomach, closing her eyes and willing the nausea to go away.

When she opened her eyes again it was with resolve. Her fingers flipped through the pages until she nearly reached the end and found the place where she had left off.

Lily would have been proud of my Jules. It amazes me how the girl can look so much like her mother yet be nothing like her in any other way. She is brave and strong like me, but soft and kind and compassionate. I see so much of her grandmother in her fearlessness, but also in her acceptance and empathy. It saddens my heart to think those two had never met, and even more so that I am the reason they were kept apart. There were no two kindred spirits truer than my Jules and my mother.

I am grateful Lily left when she did. I did not see it at the time, but she paved the way for Jules to grow into the amazing woman she is today. Lily had no compassion, no heart. She had a craving for the treasure but never for the hunting, and if I had not cried broke when I did, she would have held on for all of Halstead, I am sure. Gresham was welcome to her.

I managed to convince her that Robert needed an heiress to save the estate, and I am certain it saved his life. She never seemed to care that I was the second son, and for that I feared for my brother. The woman was a mastermind of manipulation, and we were better off without her. I only wish I had not burnt every bridge when I chose to marry the love of Robert's life. Perhaps then I could have taken Jules home.

Giulia reread the last paragraph before closing the book and locating her slippers. She slid her feet into her shoes and ran her hand under the tapestry before thinking better of it. Pausing, she dropped the tapestry against the wall. She knew how to access Nick's room from the secret passageway through the next room over, but she would most likely become utterly lost if she tried to find it from her own.

She sped down the corridor and through the staircases as quickly and quietly as her feet would take her.

Knocking softly, she only had to wait a minute before the knob turned and the door opened, a groggy Nick standing in the open space with tired eyes and his dressing gown tied haphazardly in his haste. His eyes widened in surprise when he took Giulia in, and he glanced over his shoulder, where she was assuming he was reading the clock.

"Yes, I know it is early," she said quietly. "But you said when I needed you, then I knew where to find you. Or something along those lines."

He looked skeptical and she lifted the journal. "I have made a discovery, though I would prefer to discuss it when you are fully clothed. Should I wait, or...?"

He cleared his throat, pink tinging his cheeks. "Meet me in the breakfast room."

"That may be too public."

He raised an eyebrow. "Then perhaps you better come in."

"No." Giulia shook her head. "I am no longer your nurse, so that would not be proper."

He looked at her for a long moment and then smiled. "Go back to your room. I will come for you in a quarter of an hour." He shut the door and she stepped back, dazed from the sudden oak barrier in her face.

Nick lit the candle on his mantle before entering the secret passageway that linked his room to the west wing. He closed the bookcase most of the way, leaving a small gap to get back into his room, and turned to walk down the dark corridor.

A small smile tilted his lips as he made his way down the dirty passageway. Giulia was rattled by something, and she had chosen to come to him. He let the satisfaction sit momentarily before remembering her face the night before, and worry took precedence. That she was keeping something from him was unquestionable. Why she felt like she couldn't trust him was a mystery, and not the kind he enjoyed solving.

He had been hurt when she had asked for the journal back. The feeling mounted when she had refused to confide in him. He had stormed back to his room in a rage and slammed the bookcase door shut, throwing books from the shelves in his anger and creating havoc. Cleaning up the mess had sobered his vexation, but the hurt still simmered.

He cared for Giulia, and the idea of her not trusting him when he trusted her so greatly made him rethink how much he cared for her. Careful consideration did nothing to change his mind. He was thoroughly besotted with her. Giulia's charm and compassion were a small part of what made her so uniquely wonderful. And reading Patrick Pepper's journal had only reiterated what Nick already felt. Reading the journal had given Nick a window into the mind of Giulia's father. Patrick Pepper had had a gift with words, and particularly with storytelling. His journal was more of a compilation of stories than one man's rambling thoughts.

Nick had the impression that he'd gotten to read the *real* adventures of Patrick Pepper and his assistant, Jules, and the periodical that the man had produced was likely mere fluff. The thought gave him pride, and he was glad he had been honored with the opportunity.

If only he'd had the chance to finish reading it.

Perhaps Giulia had. She'd come to his room at such an early hour and in such disarray it was evident that she had not slept at all. Her braided crown was less braid and more frizz, her clothes were rumpled and the circles under her eyes had revealed her sleeplessness.

Nick avoided the turnoff that would lead to Giulia's room and continued straight. He planned to knock on her door like a gentleman. When he slid open the stone door that led into the room beside hers, however, he was surprised to find Giulia standing there waiting for him. She had smoothed her gown and fixed her hair, but she looked no more beautiful than she had before. He thought she looked brilliant either way.

"How did you know I would come this way?" he asked.

She lifted one delicate shoulder. "I just assumed."

"Follow me." He turned around and went back into the wall,

Giulia on his heels. He led her through the maze that made up the inner workings of the castle's secret passageways and up a set of rickety wooden stairs before coming to a short rounded hatch in the ceiling. He pushed it open and stepped aside to allow Giulia to pass through.

Cool air bit at his nose and he watched her face as she entered the top floor of the east tower. He was not disappointed by her reaction. She appeared to be awe struck. The floor they stood on was a perfect circle, with rivets that lined the top of the tower and an open expanse that showed the land for miles and miles. He picked up her hand and led her to the edge of the tower, reveling in the squeeze from her fingers as they neared the edge and looked out from the highest point on the castle.

"This is breathtaking."

"I quite agree." He smiled. "It has been a favorite place of mine since the dowager showed it to me."

"My grandmother?"

Nick was equal parts saddened and pleased by the hopeful expression in her eyes. "Yes, your grandmother. This was her favorite place in the castle, actually. She had an adventurous spirit."

"Is that why the doorway is hidden within the secret passageways?"

"No, that is because this tower is for the private use of the earl of the castle. We are not sure why they had it built that way, but the staircase leads directly into the doorway to the earl's bedchamber."

Giulia looked up to Nick nervously. "Will he be upset that we are up here?"

"No." Nick waved a hand dismissively. "He doesn't come up here."

"This is extraordinary." She chuckled, turning wind-chapped, pink cheeks on him. "Does every single bedroom have a secret entryway into the bowels of the castle?"

"No, actually. Most rooms do not." He smiled at her as she looked across the land. The sun was peeking over the edge of the earth, changing the light from pale to bright. Her face lit up and she grabbed his arm.

"Look!" she pointed over the top of a rivet. "That is Hattie's barn, is it not?"

"Yes, I believe it is. The Green's property begins there and stretches as far out as you can see. Next to Halstead, they are the largest landowners in the county. Now." He turned toward her and looked into her rich, sad eyes. "What is so urgent that you needed to speak to me before the servants themselves awoke?"

Giulia sobered quickly. He could see the light fade from her being as if whatever she was thinking about seeped energy from her. She let out a long, soft sigh and turned away from the view. Leaning against the wall, she lifted the journal and offered him a pitiful smile. "I have solved our mystery."

He raised his eyebrows. Had it really been that easy? Perhaps he should have just muscled through the whole journal in one shot. But that would have been *a lot* of reading.

Giulia opened the leather-bound journal and flipped it open near the end. She turned pages until she found what she was searching for and handed him the book, pointing to the middle of the left page. Nick read the passage, then read it again, at a loss for words; at least if he continued to read he would not have to say anything to her just yet.

Nick turned to the next page and asked, "Is there anything else?"

She looked away. "No. I skimmed the last few entries, but this is the only place he mentions my mother."

Nick nodded. "This explains a lot. Do you know what he means when he says that 'she would have held on for all of Halstead'?"

"No." Giulia shook her head. "I assume he is referring to his inheriting it in some way. He alludes to that enough. But I do not understand the context. My uncle would have had to die without heirs for that to happen."

Exactly. The woman sounded—in Patrick's viewpoint—as though money mattered to her above all else. "It is irrelevant anyway, I suppose."

"Perhaps not as irrelevant as you might think," Giulia whispered.

Worry lines formed on her forehead as she thought, and he wanted to take a finger and smooth away the wrinkles.

"At least we understand why he was banished from Halstead." Nick let out a low whistle. Stealing his brother's sweetheart? That was cold.

"Perhaps." Giulia shook her head, training her gaze on Nick with firm resolution. He could see in the way she set in her shoulders and straightened her spine that she was preparing for something. A little feeling within his gut told him to prepare himself as well, for he had the odd inclination that she was about to deliver a blow. He moved to reach for her fingers, to squeeze them in an offer of encouragement. But he dropped his hand, realizing that she didn't need it. She was courageous, brave, and strong, just like her father had described in his journal.

"Nick," she said, drawing out his name, "I do not want you to overreact, so you must promise me you will hear me out fully."

He nodded slowly, but it was an impossible promise to make. Why did people always insist that one should commit to a reaction before actually hearing what they were supposed to monitor their reaction to? Is not a reaction just that? Unpredictable?

Giulia pulled his hand into her own and looked him firmly in the eyes. "I saw my mother yesterday. She is here somewhere, and it was right after seeing her that I heard the shot that frightened my horse."

Nick felt ice travel down his spine and distribute throughout his body. He felt the paralyzing fear that had only taken hold of his body one time before, when he had thought that Giulia had been hurt. "Where was the gun pointed?" He heard himself ask the question, and the cold fear was replaced with hot anger.

"It was at you, wasn't it?" he yelled, stepping away and running a hand over his face. The sudden jerk sent a wave of pain through his shoulder. He ignored it, levelling Giulia with a fierce look. "That woman tried to shoot you?"

"She was hidden behind foliage, so I am unsure where she aimed the gun. She could have been hunting, for all we know. What would it gain for her to shoot *me*?"

He started pacing the length of the tower as he considered the new development. Giulia's mother, and Robert's old flame, was here. The woman had traveled clear from Italy, if her postmarks could be relied on.

The letters! He spun back to Giulia, who was watching him with alarm on her face.

"You've analyzed the letters?" he asked.

"Yes." She shook her head. "And I found nothing. Nothing beyond the jeweled key that she is seeking, whatever that means. I truly have no earthly idea what she is talking about." She threw up her arms in frustration and aimed her face at the sky. "Why must you have left, Father, right before the biggest adventure even began?"

Nick chuckled at the ridiculousness before him, despite his unease. Even in the face of such trials, she found a way to brighten his life. She was addressing the sky. Such an odd girl.

Giulia dropped her arms, facing him. "Should we inform the earl?"

"I'm not sure." Nick resumed his pacing. "I should think it would be prudent to warn him, but I cannot predict how he will take the news. He nearly kicked you out simply because you resemble the woman. Perhaps he still loves her."

"Then we must resume life as usual until we can discover more. Why she has come, specifically. I can only think that if we can discover what key she is asking for then everything else will fall into place."

"Yes." Nick nodded. "But how?"

"I do not know. I had hoped it would be revealed in the journal."

The way she spoke ripped at his heart. Nick stopped and looked at the small warrior who stood tall before him. Well, tall was relative, but her strong soul was apparent. He wanted to cross to her, to pull her into his arms and comfort away the fear she struggled to hide from him.

She looked weary, and he could not help but feel anger and envy toward the man who had his claim on her. *Ames.* Anger that the man had abandoned her, for all intents and purposes, and envy over the man's claim on her heart. He approached her cautiously and she remained still, watching him ease forward with a slight crease between her brows.

"Giulia," he said softly, "I will be by your side through all of this. Until your mother is gone, and you feel safe again, you need not fear." He laughed a little as he traced her strong jaw with his knuckles. "I would say that I will protect you, but I know you can take care of yourself. You must know, though, that you will not be alone. I will not leave you alone."

She crumpled forward and it took a moment for Nick to register that she was leaning into him, her small hands clutching the front of his shirt and her head tucked into his chest. He moved his arms around her and soaked in the feel of Giulia against him. His stomach tightened when he felt her shoulders heave in a sob and he pulled her in closer, holding her tight and stroking the back of her head. Nick could not recall feeling so equally content and disheartened before, and he memorized the feeling, storing it away for a time when Giulia would no longer be in his life. With another man in the picture, that was the inevitable future that he could neither ignore nor dispute.

She let out a long sigh and relaxed into him further before raising her hands and wiping her eyes. She lifted her face and gave him a soft smile. Her perfect lips were so close to his he could close the gap with nothing but a slight tilt of his face, but he did not. He respected her too much to cause her to be untrue to another. He used every ounce of self-control he had to look down and smile at her, to reassure her that he would be there for her.

When Giulia pushed away, he let her go with reluctance and offered her a bright smile to belie the malaise that had settled over him as soon as she moved away. They stood on the tower and looked at one another with an odd discomfort between them. She could see through his grin, he was sure, and he needed to remove himself from her presence. The air was too thick with unresolved feelings and there was too much on the line to play the heartbroken lover.

She lowered her eyes and smiled. "Forgive me for ruining your shirt."

"It is nothing." His smile widened and he moved toward the hatch in the floor. "I will go and change my shirt and then meet you for breakfast."

She followed him through the hatch and back downstairs. He felt her presence as strongly as he felt her emotional distance, and a renewed determination came over him. He needed to figure out what this jeweled key was about, but first, he would need to have a talk with Robert. Halstead needed to resort to its prior form—a fortified castle ready to protect and defend.

CHAPTER 23

*B*reakfast had never been so satisfying. Giulia filled her plate, emptied it, and then filled it again. Unloading her fears onto Nick's shoulders had released a weight within her she had not realized she was carrying. Her shoulders felt lighter, her mind less burdened. That, however, did not change the very distinct feeling that she needed to remain on her guard. There was now an urgency to discovering the source of the elusive jeweled key—what it could possibly be and, perhaps more importantly, where it was.

She sipped her tea as she pondered the facts. Her mother was searching for a key that she described as jeweled that had apparently been left with Giulia's father sixteen years ago. Father, now deceased, had never mentioned any key, let alone a key that was covered in jewels. *Was* it covered in jewels, or simply had a jewel somewhere on the device? Most likely not covered, perhaps, for that would be quite impractical.

The next question, and possibly the most important one, was what the key opened. Was it a door? Or could it be a chest? What did the key permit access to that was so valuable?

Heavy footsteps outside of the door betrayed the earl's approach and gave Giulia enough time to straighten up and throw a welcoming smile toward the doorway.

"Good morning, my lord," she said.

Lord Hart seemed taken aback by her pleasant disposition but recovered quickly. "You are up mighty early."

"Yes, it is quite early for me, that is true. I did wonder"—she turned in her chair to follow the earl as he crossed the room to the sideboard and began loading a plate with food—"if you would like to meet this morning to begin planning the ball? I should really begin writing the invitations right away."

He cleared his throat. "Yes, yes, right away."

An awkward silence overtook the room. The clank of serving spoons hitting dishes and the light thrumming of Giulia's fingers on her leg were particularly loud. There was really no sense in holding a meeting after breakfast if they were going to be seated together now, particularly when the planning of the ball could fill the very uncomfortable void. She cleared her throat, deciding to dive in. "And did you want to theme your ball, sir?"

He stopped piling bacon onto his plate and turned toward Giulia. "Theme?"

"Like a masquerade, perhaps. Or a black and white ball? I did attend one function in India where the hostess requested everyone to wear a shade of gold or red and it was absolutely breathtaking. That, however, would not necessarily be considered acceptable here in England, perhaps."

"I don't know about acceptability, but the folks of Graton would find it odd."

Giulia chuckled. "Indeed."

"Ah, Robert." Nick strode into the room. "Good morning, my lord."

Lord Hart grunted in return and took his seat at the head of the table.

She released a breath of relief at her buffer's entrance. "Perhaps no theme, then?" Giulia continued.

"Oh, right." The earl nodded as he finished chewing his eggs. "No theme."

"Am I to put any particular reason for the ball on the invitation? Will people not find it odd if we do not state why the castle is being opened again for festivities?"

"No," Nick called from the sideboard. "No reason necessary." He stopped and poked a fork in Giulia's direction. "Unless you would like to say that the ball is in your honor?"

"But it is not," she reminded the men. "It is in yours, Nick. We are going to find you a wife." She smiled facetiously at Nick's strangled expression and successfully covered the swirling in her own stomach.

"She's right, you know." The earl spoke into his plate, and Giulia and Nick shot each other a glance over his head. "We never threw you any sort of celebration to present you to the people as the next earl. It is reason enough."

Nick's eyebrows rose. "But I have lived here these last three years, and I believe I know nearly everyone there is to know. That is enough of a presentation for me."

"That is not how things are done. You will be the next earl and given our strange circumstances, we really ought to present you to the people. We Peppers do not shirk our duties."

"Very well, Robert. You may present me." Nick delivered a lavish bow before he moved to the table and gave Giulia a look of surrender, to which she responded with a slight raise of her shoulders and a terribly masked grin.

***

The rest of the party decor, guest list, and menu were discussed at length, each member of the conversation rising at least once to refill their plates, and twice, in the earl's case. Giulia had a decent idea of what the earl would like the ball to look like, and even more how Nick would like it presented, and found a decent middle ground in her mind that would certainly do well for the Pepper name. Which, fortunately, both Nick and Lord Hart cared about deeply.

If they were going to reopen the castle socially, then they must do it right.

The thought sent a shiver up Giulia's spine, and she shook her shoulders to release it. A warm hand closed over her arm and she turned toward Nick's concerned eyes.

"Are you cold?" he asked with a slight furrow between his pale brows.

She could not think to answer the man for a moment and stared instead at the soft curve of his mouth. She was seated in front of the fire of the parlor with a stack of cards before her on a writing desk. Nick had pulled his own chair beside her to watch her pen the invitations, but she did not realize before how close he had pulled his chair to hers. She didn't know what was keeping her from explaining what had caused her chill, for to say she was cold would be dishonest. The fire and the man beside her were sharing equal responsibility in keeping her warm and cozy, but to tell him that she was afraid seemed somehow wrong. Of course he was fully aware of the situation, and naturally he would not fault her fear, but something inside her gut was telling her not to make herself too vulnerable to him.

"I wonder if we should send an invitation to your family?" Giulia artfully redirected the conversation. "Lord Hart did not mention them, but I recall you telling me at one point that you have a sister?"

Nick reared back slightly and then a smile crept over his lips. Had she ever before noticed just how wide and perfect they were? Of course she had. He was very handsome.

"My sister would not appreciate an invitation. But thank you for thinking of her."

"What is so funny?"

"Perhaps one day you will meet her, and then you will understand."

Giulia eyed him a moment longer, the mirth dancing in his eyes betrayed a story somewhere in there, but she assumed he would share it if he wished. She turned her attention back to the tower of cards that had yet to be written on and resumed her duties.

"I would offer to help," Nick said lazily as he leaned back in his chair, linking his fingers over his stomach, "but my handwriting is atrocious. I would only create more work for you in fixing or rewriting the ones I touch."

Giulia shook her head, a small smile turning the corners of her mouth as she dipped her pen and started a new card. "Typical man."

He shot up straight, giving her a wary look that she caught from the corner of her eye. "I beg your pardon?" he asked haughtily, his tone jesting. "I have been an invalid. Sick. Bedridden, for heaven's sake! Now you claim I am lazy?" His mock anger would have been more humorous if there was not a load of truth to what he'd said.

"No, I'm merely noticing how very *male* you are being."

He was quiet long enough that she shot a look in his direction followed quickly by a laugh at his very offended face. Giulia placed a hand on Nick's arm and spoke calmly. "Do not be so offended; I only inferred that a man will not put forth more effort than he must." She then gestured to Nick and the cards, holding her quill over the ink pot and smiling. She had spent her life in the company of Ames and her father, and neither of them would have lifted a finger to help her pen the invitations if they could help it.

"And a woman would?" he countered.

"Naturally."

"So you are saying that men are lazy?"

"No, not lazy. Perhaps narrowminded is more accurate." She smiled, and a moment passed before Nick scoffed.

"That is not true."

Giulia's raised eyebrow was enough of a challenge. Nick sat up straighter. "It is not true," he repeated, this time with gusto.

"Very well, it is not true." Giulia turned back toward the desk.

"It isn't."

"So you said."

A frustrated grumble came from Nick, causing Giulia's smile to widen. He put his hand over hers and stopped her in the middle of writing 'in honor of' causing a nice long line to streak the page and rendering that particular card useless. She turned toward Nick with infinite patience etched in her raised eyebrows and the tilt of her head.

What was one more card when she had another forty to address, anyway?

Nick looked at her and squinted slightly, slowly tilting his head to match her own. "Perhaps you need a break."

The suggestion was surprising. "I have only written out seven cards. I could not possibly stop now. They are last minute enough as it is."

"Yes, but are there no other, more important things we should be doing?"

"More important than preparing for the ball at which we will find your wife?"

Nick's face did not change, but the tick in his jaw betrayed a clenched muscle. "What do you say to taking a picnic? It is nearly time to eat, and we can soak in the beautiful sun."

She froze. Any other day that suggestion would have filled her with excitement, but now she felt less than enthusiastic to be lounging out of doors. In clear view. After the earl had announced that everyone ought to remain indoors until Nick's attacker had been caught.

"Oh forgive me, I did not consider…" Nick's voice trailed off as his eyebrows pulled together. "On second thought, perhaps we ought to eat inside." His eyes lit up instantly and he shot to his feet. "You continue here," he said with a wave toward her writing desk, "and I will return for you shortly." He was gone from the room at once and Giulia watched him leave, fixing her gaze on the empty doorway he exited.

The empty place within her heart where Ames's desertion had left a gap was slowly being filled by the caring and attentive man who had just walked out that door. To say that she was falling in love with him would be just as true as it was terrifying. To explain why she felt the need to keep him distanced from her would be fruitless, for though she had come to the understanding that perhaps Ames did not intend to send for her after all—for how else could she explain his utter silence?—she could not release herself from her attachment to him until he'd written her back.

Regardless, she was wise to keep Halstead's heir at bay. The man was Devon's biggest flirt, according to the Swans, and Giulia was merely passing through anyway. That was how Giulia lived, always only passing through. She had only meant to stay at Halstead while she figured out her next step, her next phase in life—a life she expected to spend with Ames. Part of her felt like an imposter, staying in the castle, forming friendships and relationships with the people who lived in and around it, picturing a life there. Reality was always quick to smack her in the nose, reminding her that *permanent* was a foreign and unrealistic concept for her.

But aside from all of that, she had grown fond of her distant cousin. The man might not have any matrimonial designs on her, but his friendship was genuine.

Her reflections left her with two goals: first, to solve the mystery of her mother once and for all. Second, to enjoy every last moment with Nick before she would leave for good.

CHAPTER 24

*N*ick would be satisfied to remain in Giulia's company forever. He had half a mind to travel to London and call out this Ames fellow. But since he had no real reason for requesting a duel at dawn, that idea seemed a tad ridiculous. He could exercise his well-practiced skill of flirtation and convince Giulia to break off her relationship with Ames, but that, too, did not sound like a very wise course of action. He was loath to be the reason she was unfaithful to another or cause her to feel guilt for jilting the man she'd pledged herself to. He felt as though he was pushed into a corner with no clear route available to him.

He could always be her friend. Hard as that may be, he *wanted* to be her friend. It was better than nothing at all.

He made his way back to the parlor, picnic basket prepared, and a grin of anticipation graced his lips. He inched the door open and peeked inside, catching a glimpse of the wild-haired angel that had stolen his heart weeks ago. She was concentrating heavily on her task, pausing every few moments to stretch her fingers or roll her wrist. Yes, he had been right; it was most certainly time for a break.

Nick pushed the door open and hid the basket behind his back. "Come, my lady. Your meal awaits."

She turned toward him, and his breath caught at the direct gaze from her beautiful brown eyes. He hoped he hid it well, but he could not cease to feel awed by her or the magnetic force which seemed to link them together. A small part of him yearned to know if she felt it too.

Nick watched her rise and stretch her arms before strolling toward him. "And what have you planned?" she asked hesitantly.

"You will see." He held out a hand and was pleased when she took it, following him out the door and toward the grand staircase. He surprised her at the last moment by turning and walking under the stairs, moving aside a wooden panel and leading her into the belly of the castle.

A tingle of pride lit his chest as he guided Giulia through the intricate tunnels and once again up the rickety staircase to the solitary tower. Small shafts of light spilled between cracks in the hidden doorways or from the artfully hidden peepholes, lighting their way and allowing him to catch a few glimpses of interest from Giulia as they turned here or ducked there. He had come to know these halls as his own. And they *were* his, in truth. Or, one day they would be, no matter how hard that was for him to still believe.

Once they were both on the roof of the tower, Nick watched Giulia slowly pace the perimeter as he laid out the blanket he'd brought along and unpacked the food from the basket. He sat back, leaning on his hands with his head bent toward his shoulder and could not help the smile that crept across his lips as he watched Giulia fight her hair in the wind. Strands sprung free of the crown braid she religiously wore; for every bit she managed to tuck back in, three more would escape. A frustrated sigh traveled on the wind and he stifled a laugh when she stomped toward the blanket and plopped down.

"This wind is horrendous," she moaned.

His grin widened. "I rather like it."

She shot him a sardonic smile and then moved her attention to the low wall that shielded them from view. "This place is amazing. Do you think...?"

He waited a moment before assuming that she had become lost in thought. "Do I think?" he prompted.

"Oh, sorry." Her cheeks were mottled pink, but he knew it was not from a blush, but due to the wind. The woman just did not blush. "Do you think that the locked tower leads to the same thing? Simply a viewing point?"

"At one point it was probably a lookout. Though I could not say for certain. It is impossible to see from here what may be on the other side of the locked door."

She nodded slowly and he could see the wheels turning in her beautiful mind. He began plating the food that Cook had prepared for them. Sliced, cold ham, apples, cheese and a hunk of bread which he tore in half. A bowl of steamed peas was nestled into the corner of the basket and he spooned a fair amount onto the plate before handing it to Giulia, watching her eat absentmindedly and wishing all the while that he could hear her thoughts.

"I had a thought." She turned to him. He had not realized how close he had moved toward her when he passed her a plate and her nearness forced his breath to still. She had a similar reaction, for she had sucked in a breath and her eyes widened. He felt the invisible pull which linked their lips; the energy that ran between them was nearly palpable. He stared into Giulia's deep chocolate eyes and asked her a question with his own, a question he knew she could not answer.

He needed to stop.

He sat back on his hands and tossed back the rest of his lemonade before giving her his full attention. She seemed to collect herself, but her heightened color and rapidly rising chest betrayed that she was just as affected as he was. The revelation was as gratifying as it was disheartening. They cared for one another—they *had* to. If he could dream, then he would believe that she was on her way to caring for him on as deep a level as he was for her. Drat this Ames fellow.

"You had a thought?" Nick prompted.

"Oftentimes the treasure is given a name or even hidden within something obvious. In folklore, at least. Perhaps this key is in my father's things, and we have been overlooking it because we are thinking too literally."

"Your father taught you well."

She laughed lightly. "Well, it is a thought, but a fruitless one at present. I let Ames keep Father's box of treasure, so we do not have it here to analyze."

"He had a box of treasure? You did not think that a valid point to mention before?"

"I did not consider it before. He called it his treasure chest, but it was merely a box with remnants from our adventures. Scraps of paper with contacts he'd made or random drawings of things he'd experienced. The box aided his writing, but his real heart was in his journal. Ames had more of a connection with the box, so I did not feel the need to take it from him."

"And one day you would share your possessions anyway," Nick finished for her.

Giulia looked away. "It will not help us now. I wondered if maybe one of his scraps of paper had a hint for us, but it is far away in London."

She wanted to tell Nick that she had written to Ames. The letter was necessary to warn him, but she also hoped he would search her father's things for clues. She could not bring herself to tell Nick, however. What if Ames continued to ignore her? What if he received her letter, but never wrote her back?

They continued to talk as they finished their meal, but the conversation moved away from the dilemma and the key and more toward their differences in childhoods. She revealed more about her London home and Mama Jo, the woman who would make sure Giulia, and sometimes Ames, were fed while her father became mentally absent with his writing.

Nick described the farm he was raised on and the games he would play with his sister, Lettie, but stopped when he found Giulia fishing for more information about her. The woman was sly.

"Oh, come!" Giulia said as she realized he had caught her intent. "You cannot speak of your sister in such a way and then not tell me *why* she would hate to be invited to a ball at a castle! Particularly when you know my curiosity and need for solving riddles." She pouted, and a genuine grin spread over his mouth.

"I can, and I did."

Giulia scoffed. "And here I thought you were a gentleman." She raised her nose into the air and looked away.

"I am a gentleman of the highest order."

She peeked at him and he did not see it coming when she fisted her untouched peas and launched them at his face. He was stunned momentarily, before fisting his own uneaten vegetables and launching them right back.

"Not a fan of peas?" She laughed as she dodged the attack. He eyed the bowl of remaining mushy peas at the same time as Giulia, and they lunged forward in sync.

Nick managed to get to the bowl first and raised it high above his head. Giulia leapt for the peas but came crashing on him instead, forcing him to drop the bowl and roll with the impact. He shot an arm around her waist to protect her from hitting the stone ground with too much force and then found himself over her, his hand securely holding her close to him. Their chests rose and fell in rhythm and their eyes locked. Gravity aided the magnetic pull that brought him down and before he realized what he was doing his lips connected with hers.

Nick had only ever heard talk of fireworks before, but never had he been witness to them until this moment. He rather expected that this is what they were talking about when the papers described explosions of lights and beauty, one right after the other. The warmth that spread from his lips to the rest of his body was nothing to the heat that clouded his vision when Giulia began to kiss him back. He tilted his head and leaned in further, soaking in the feel of her mouth on his and her hand on his neck, her fingers working through the back of his hair. He rolled onto his back, bringing her with him, and felt immediate regret when she went as still as a board.

They held the position for another five glorious seconds before Nick felt her fingers leave the back of his head and her arms push away from him. The pang in his chest betrayed him when he told himself he did not mind the separation.

He froze when a thought came to him and guilt suddenly washed through him. *Ames*, blast the man! How was Giulia going to react to his blatant breach in propriety? How should *Nick* react? He had been so diligent about respecting her space and the unknown man who had a claim on her. How had he slipped so easily?

Giulia pulled herself up and crossed to the wall as Nick began to gather the plates and place everything back into the basket. He could not help the smile that curved his lips when he leaned over to reach the bowl that previously held the peas and packed it away. He had thought it bizarre when Cook added that to their basket. It was a strange addition to a cold luncheon. But now he could not be more grateful.

He hazarded a glance in Giulia's direction, but she had not moved from her perch at the tower's edge. Once the remnants from their meal were packed away and the blanket folded and set on top of the basket, Nick stood and crossed to Giulia. He had been fighting within himself to figure out what best to say but came up empty.

"Listen, Jules," he started. "I think—"

He was stopped by her stifled scream and her hand, which gripped his forearm so tightly he jerked back. He came forward and put his free hand on her arm. "What is it?"

Giulia felt the blood drain from her face. Cold swept over her body in much the same manner that warmth had filled it just minutes before. A hand came over her shoulder and she released Nick's arm when she realized the intensity of her grip.

"You are frightening me." Nick stepped closer, his eyes darting about rapidly as they swept her face. She tried not to notice the rise in her heart rate at his proximity, but that was near pointless after the moment they had just shared. She mentally shook it off. This was much more urgent.

"Behind those trees," she whispered, pointing in the direction that she had seen the woman. "Do you see the brown coat?"

Nick turned toward the trees and she watched him squint until recognition dawned. "I see the woman."

"That's not just a woman." She spoke so quietly, she wondered if Nick even heard her. "That must be my mother."

Nick nodded. He looked determined. When he turned to go she stopped him with a grip on his sleeve and he flinched. Had she pulled on his injured arm? "Do not go after her," she begged. "It is not wise. We do not know what she is capable of."

She watched the muscle jump in his clenched jaw. "Nick, I mean it," she pressed. "We must be smart about this. Besides," she turned back to the woman hiding in the trees, "she is alone."

"Then what do you propose we do about it?"

"We tell the earl," she said. "We cannot keep this from him. Especially when his safety could be in jeopardy."

She was right. And she could see that Nick agreed, whether he wanted to or not.

"Very well," he said with an exasperated sigh. He leaned over the turrets and gazed at the trees and she followed suit. What was the woman doing? She was weaving in and out of visibility, watching the castle and then moving away before coming back. Giulia had the odd sensation her mother was scoping out Halstead, but why? Was she intending to come search for the key herself? Could she not simply knock on the door?

Nick broke the silence. "Listen, Jules."

She brought up a hand to stop him without turning his way. Her voice soft, she felt the strain in her words as she spoke. "Let us not speak of it."

He turned and looked at her, but she did not face him, instead keeping her gaze locked on the woman who had once been her mother. If only she could see her face...

"Very well."

They watched the woman turn back into the woods and disappear. They stood there for a long while, hoping that the woman would come out of the trees again. From their vantage point, they would be able to see which direction she left.

Another few minutes passed in heavy silence before Nick let out a long, slow breath. "Perhaps we should go find Robert. I think the stable needs to be apprised of the situation as well."

Giulia nodded but did not remove her gaze. She was rewarded moments later when the woman left the woods on horseback. "Nick! There!" she called.

He dropped the basket and hurried back to her side. "Where is she going?"

"You would know better than I, but is that the direction of the Green's barn?"

Nick nodded. "And beyond that is the Green's property. There is no inn or pub in that direction."

They watched the woman ride off until she disappeared once again in a copse of trees on the property line beside the Green's barn and did not resurface.

"The mystery continues to build, I suppose. Shall we go find Robert?"

"I will leave that to you," she replied. "I really must return to my duties for your ball. The invitations will not write themselves."

"No, I suppose they will not." Nick locked gazes with her, and she felt the heat return to her chest. She could admit to herself that she felt for Nick in a way she had never felt for another man before. She should tell him about Ames's slight—that the man who had promised to build a life for her was instead failing to even write her a single letter. But...what if that broke the spell? What if telling Nick that she was less certain of Ames cut off the spark between them, making the situation too real? Too...possible? She had heard of Nick's reputation as a cad and still she broke her own rule to keep her heart guarded from his flirtations and charm. She had let herself enjoy it, naturally, but she could not place more worth there than there actually was.

And now he had stolen his kiss. The one he had tried for with each of the Swans when he had first moved to Halstead but had failed to achieve. He hadn't failed with Giulia. No, with her, he had conquered.

Casting him a lighthearted smile that was far from how Giulia actually felt, she turned toward the exit and lowered herself from the tower's roof. Swallowing hurt and her injured pride, she renewed her focus on the task the earl had given her. Perhaps throwing herself into the planning of the ball would benefit her in more than one way. She needed to keep her mind as occupied and controlled as her heart.

CHAPTER 25

*G*iulia had thought that once Nick apprised Lord Hart of the full situation, she would reap the consequences. Having been the obvious reason Lily Cattaneo was now stalking Halstead and its occupants, Giulia assumed the earl would become furious with her and demand her departure. Or, which could be worse, revert back to his solemn and ignoring ways. She was pleasantly surprised when the opposite, in fact, occurred.

Whether they were bonded by now sharing a mutual enemy, or Lord Hart truly felt a measure of protection was due to his niece— something she had a harder time believing—his demeanor toward her took a complete turn over the next week. He was warmer, more vocal. He did not run from her but, instead, pulled her into conversations. He invited her into his study on multiple occasions to discuss the ball, which felt more like an excuse to have her company, since their discussions often veered *away* from the ball. No topic seemed restricted, except her father, of course.

Patrick Pepper was the theoretical elephant that constantly joined Giulia and Lord Hart whenever they were together. Neither of them mentioned him, but he was always on her mind and, she assumed on occasion at least, on the earl's as well.

Giulia and the earl sat in front of the fire in his study and she shared with him the details of her stay in India when she was younger. Lord Hart compared them to his own experiences. He clearly had a fascination with other cultures that reminded her greatly of her father, and she filled him in on everything she could remember, including the story of her dreaded scorpion sting and how terribly ill she had become.

Her uncle nodded in understanding and shared how when he had taken a similar trip to India when he was younger, a man in his group had gotten stung as well. Lord Hart went on to reference the familiar phrase *look for the rainbow at the end of the rain* and explained how the man's illness eventually called for a nurse that had cared for him, fallen in love with him, and then married him. That particular friend remained in India to this day.

Giulia stilled at the phrase, having heard it so many times before. She had believed it to be a Patrick Pepper original and hearing it from Lord Hart's lips did nothing but pull at her curiosity until she considered asking of its origin. Breaking over that barrier and into the realm of Patrick Pepper was a risk she was not quite ready to make, though. She was building a relationship with an uncle who had wanted nothing to do with her just a few months prior. He was the only member of her family left on the earth that did not want her dead, and to jeopardize that now seemed unwise.

Her hand went to the chain on her neck and she toyed with it, pulling at it subconsciously while she thought of her father's unceasing optimism.

A knock sounded at the door and Wells poked his head inside.

"Visitors for Miss Pepper, my lord. I have placed them in the parlor."

Lord Hart nodded. "Thank you, Wells."

Giulia rose and curtseyed to her uncle. She reached out and took his hand before thinking better of it and gave it a squeeze. "I enjoyed our conversation today."

Before he could answer, she spun away and fled the room. Fear of rejection pushed her away quickly, but joy at their budding relationship kept a smile on her face. She followed the corridor to the front foyer and toward the parlor. The giggles that snuck from the room and into the foyer brought a larger smile to her face as she recognized who was waiting for her. She stepped inside and grinned at the bevy of swans perched on her sofa.

"But is today not the meeting for the Literary Society?" Giulia asked as she crossed toward the ladies. She stopped suddenly, "Oh no, Amelia, did you not receive my note?"

"I did." Amelia smiled back. "And today *is* the meeting. Since you could not come to us, we simply chose to come to you."

Tears welled up in Giulia's eyes and she blinked rapidly to push them away. The compassion and kindness of these ladies to someone they hardly knew was inspiring. She felt liked. And coming from other women, that was new to her.

Hattie rose and pulled Giulia to the settee across from where Amelia and Mabel sat. "Come, sit and tell us of this closed castle business." A stricken look took over her face. "Do not tell me the ball has been cancelled."

"No, the ball has not been cancelled," Giulia confirmed. "It is nothing, really, just..." She had been prepared to tell the women that the preparations were too great for the ball and kept her too busy to attend today's Literary Society, but she knew she should not lie to them. She also knew with a clarifying surety that she could trust them. "We have a threat. It is not serious, or...well, maybe it is. But until we can find out more it is just a better idea to remain safely within the castle walls."

Three sets of eyes widened in unison. "Safer for whom?" Mabel asked reverently.

"Currently Nick, myself, and potentially the earl. But please," she pleaded, "this information must not leave this room."

The three heads nodded in sync.

"What can we do to help?" Amelia asked.

"Nothing, really. The earl is aware of the situation and working with a man in Graton to get to the bottom of it."

Hattie gasped. "Mr. Pepper's attack! Is that what this is all about?"

"In part." Giulia nodded. "When I fell from my horse after our Literary Meeting last week, it was due to a gunshot scaring my steed."

Amelia's face blanched and Mabel and Hattie's jaws dropped.

"I am fine," Giulia said with a wave of her hand. "There is no evidence that the shot was intended for me."

"But still, how dreadful!" Hattie pulled Giulia into an embrace.

"Really, it is not so bad. I am safe here." She gestured to the castle at large. Lily could watch Halstead from the tree line all she wanted, but the castle was impenetrable. "We all are. And we have a bit of an idea of what they are after so now it is only a matter of time before we end this."

"Hattie," Mabel interjected, turning toward the freckled woman, "your father's intruder."

"Oh!" Hattie gasped and turned back to Giulia before addressing her in a low and serious voice. "One of our footmen found an intruder trying to break into our cellar just yesterday! The person got away before they could be detained. But the odd thing was…"

"Yes?" Giulia asked, resisting the urge to shake Hattie into spilling the details with better haste.

Her small, upturned nose wrinkled. "It was a woman. Surely a woman wouldn't have shot at Mr. Pepper. Or at you."

The room was quiet as each lady considered the implications.

Giulia rose. It could not be a coincidence. "I must tell my uncle at once."

"Absolutely," Mabel agreed. "Shall we leave you?"

Giulia halted. She was sorry to see them go, but this was a matter that needed tending to. Time was quite literally of the essence. "I hate to say goodbye so soon, particularly after you went out of your way to come visit me."

"We will see you again soon," Amelia promised.

Giulia hugged each of her friends and bid them farewell, leading them to the front entryway.

"We shall see you at the ball," Hattie exclaimed as she walked through the door. They left Giulia grinning, but the expression was quickly replaced with determination.

Now, to locate the earl.

She sped back to his study and rapped her knuckles on the door, opening it when she was bid.

"Oh good, you are both here," she said as she crossed to where Lord Hart and Nick sat on either side of the large desk. Their faces were turned toward her with mirrored images of surprise and she paused alongside Nick, clasping her hands before her. "There has been a development," she began. Lord Hart nodded at her to continue. "I have been visiting with Hattie Green, and she informed me that her father has recently found an intruder on his land. They could not catch her, but—"

"Her?" Nick asked, jumping up from his seat. "It must be your mother."

"My thoughts, also," Giulia agreed.

Nick circled the chair. "I must go out at once. Surely if I search the property between here and the Greens'—"

Lord Hart sputtered, his face mottled red. "But surely if Jolly—"

"Jolly has no scruples!" Nick yelled. "If the woman offered him more money than we did he would not hesitate to heed or assist her, regardless of his promises."

The men stared at one another and Giulia bit her tongue. Though she really would like to know who this Jolly character was.

"You must be right," the earl muttered. "If a person was found hiding on the Greens' property, then Jolly should have come to inform me. He would have heard news of it by now."

"We must devise a new plan. He cannot be trusted."

"Who? The man who shot you or this Jolly fellow?" Giulia asked. Both men turned to her as if only now remembering that she was in the room. "Well, which one isn't to be trusted?"

"Both, apparently," Nick responded. "We still do not know who shot me. But we should assume for the present that your mother did not come to England alone. She could not have done all of this without help *and* remained undetected. I shall go."

"No," Lord Hart said. "It should be me. I have other loyal informants if Jolly refuses to talk."

Nick lowered his voice. "I thought we decided that you would not leave the castle until this threat has been neutralized."

"Ha!" The earl laughed, causing Giulia to flinch. "*You* decided that, my boy. I hide from no one." He beat a hand to his chest. "I am a Pepper man."

"Then we shall go together. And do not bother arguing"—Nick raised a hand—"I am coming either way."

"Then I shall remain here and wait?" Giulia asked, irritation coloring her voice. Her hands found their way to her hips. "And if you discover my mother, will that threat be neutralized as well?"

"Never," Lord Hart said quietly.

CHAPTER 26

"What are you expecting to find?" Nick asked once they left the Pepper land and moved onto the main road toward Graton.

"Hopefully a dead man holding a gun," Robert replied in a low, threatening tone.

Nick lifted his eyebrows.

"Well, it would solve our problems."

"One of them, perhaps." Nick chuckled. He scanned the rolling green hills as they rode, watching for anything that seemed out of place. "Care to tell me about Giulia's mother now?"

Robert stared straight ahead. "There is nothing to tell."

The afternoon sky dimmed when clouds moved over the sun, casting a dull light over the earth and eerily coating the ground with orange and pink hues.

"I'm not buying it."

Robert grunted, his long, untamed hair moving in the wind. "Suit yourself."

They moved along in silence for a few more minutes before Nick broke it. "I see you have taken a liking to Giulia."

"Ha!" Robert chuckled. "You sure are fishing for information, aren't you, boy?"

Nick grinned.

Shaking his head, the earl let out a long breath. "I like her. She is nothing like her mother. She is like *my* mother, if you want the truth."

"That's what your brother said." Nick cringed after the words unwittingly left his mouth. He could feel the shift in the atmosphere and wished for a moment he could retract his statement.

"Is that so?" Robert asked through his teeth. He did not sound angry, exactly, but there was a significant taint of forced exertion in his words.

"Jules let me read his journal, actually. You know of the letters she received from her mother asking for the key?"

"Yes," Robert said.

"Well, I hoped to find some clue of the key in Patrick's journal."

"Any luck?"

"None. But I did get a good idea of the childhood that Giulia led, as well as Patrick's regret that she never could know her kindred spirit, your mother. Also," Nick forged ahead, figuring that it was all or nothing at this point. Besides, they were nearing the town so he would have to stop soon anyway. "Patrick regretted the choices he made that estranged him from his family."

They rode in silence the remainder of the road into town and then stopped off near the inn. A young boy came out and took their horses and Robert led the way inside, straight to the bar. A large man with a wide mustache and a round belly stepped forward, his face betraying the typical smile that dubbed his nickname.

"Jolly, can I have a word?"

"Always, my lord."

Jolly kinked his neck, indicating the gentlemen follow him into his private quarters behind the bar. They trailed behind him down a few shallow steps and into the cellar where Jolly's rooms were located and sat at the table he indicated.

"I think you know why we've come," Robert said. "There was a woman found on the Greens' property."

Jolly nodded, his smile never wavering. It made Nick wonder if he was in on a joke or the victim of one.

"She came and left, my lord. Stopped in for a bite and was gone in a snap." Jolly snapped his fingers to reiterate his point.

"Where to?"

Jolly lifted his shoulders and stuck out his bottom lip in an exaggerated shrug. "Beats me. I told my man, Digger, to keep his ear to the ground, but he ain't heard nothin' yet."

"Good. Keep him at it. And remember, there will be *sufficient* compensation for information."

Jolly's eyes gleamed at the mention of payment. There was enough of a thirst there to confirm to Nick that at this point Jolly was on their side. Whether or not he had been the evening prior.

Robert stood and Nick followed suit.

"Actually, gents," Jolly said, fingering his mustache, "I may have remembered a little something." He stopped, his mouth clenching shut, and Robert stared at him, waiting.

"You'll get paid when I get my information, Jolly. You know how I work." Robert's voice was calm, but Nick could hear the desperation behind the words.

Jolly seemed to consider this a moment and nodded. "Heard tell the woman was here a few months ago. Poked around and then left for a while. Foreign, they say."

The silence was pregnant with various feelings. Jolly holding out, Robert trying not to seem too eager. Nick nudged the earl and he pulled a pouch from his pocket. Jolly's eyes lit up as Robert slowly untied the twine, cinching the bag open and dumping half of the contents onto the table. He looked back at the innkeeper expectantly.

"She's staying in a cottage near Hampton Park. Abandoned or some such thing."

"If she is hiding in a cottage near Hampton then why was she found on the Green's property?" Nick asked.

Jolly shrugged. "Begs the question; what's her *target*?"

Nick got a sick feeling in his gut. He knew the target. Jules. *His* Jules.

Robert's fist came down on the table in a quick thud, causing both Nick and Jolly to jump and the coins to scatter. "What do you know?" he said, the words coming out between his teeth in a slow, deep rhythm.

Jolly swallowed, the lump moving down his neck as his eyes twitched nervously. "It's the girl. She wants the girl. The woman thinks Miss Pepper's got something of hers and is holding out on her. It ain't you they want, my lord." He glanced between Robert and Nick. "Neither of you."

"Then why shoot at her?" It was Nick's turn to be angry.

Jolly's hands came up in surrender. "I don't know nothing about anyone shooting anyone. Alls I know is that if it was *me* and I was wanting something from this young girl, I'd maybe try to scare her into handing it over."

"But she doesn't have it!" Nick yelled.

Robert's hand came to Nick's shoulder, squeezing it firmly. He took a deep breath and watched as Robert threw the pouch at Jolly. "There's more where that came from. You give me information, and you are compensated."

"Yes, my lord." Jolly greedily picked up the fallen coins and refilled his pouch as Nick followed Robert back up the stairs. They mounted their horses as the first raindrops began to fall.

"Where to, Robert? Hampton?"

"Not tonight." Robert shook his head. "We know where she is. That is enough for now."

Not enough for me, Nick thought.

CHAPTER 27

Giulia paced in front of the parlor fire. She stopped occasionally and watched out the window at the growing darkness for a pair of men on horseback, but to no avail. The dinner hour had come and left, and she wrung her hands in anticipation. She had nearly jumped on a horse of her own and followed the men but quickly realized the flaw in that plan. She did not know the area and was surely destined to get lost.

Picking up the poker from the side of the hearth, she stoked the fire, pausing to watch the flames lick the sharp tip of the instrument, the vision beautiful and mesmerizing.

The hair on the back of her neck stood up in unison, and she knew at once that she was not alone.

Someone was watching her.

The prickling on her skin was the same feeling she had received moments before the shot had fired and she'd seen her mother; it left her feeling altogether nauseated and frightened. She straightened, closing her hand tightly on the poker's handle, and pivoted to the window.

Right in the center of the window was the face she expected to see. Lily Cattaneo.

Somehow, Giulia took in the figure without flinching. She watched her mother for a moment, curious how she was remaining dry when it was clearly raining. The woman must be standing under the roofline, protected from the rain. In fact, she must have been standing beneath it for quite some time, since it had been raining for at least a quarter of an hour, and the woman was completely dry.

Giulia shivered. Her gaze unflinching, she studied the woman's same dark hair and brown eyes as her own. The wrinkled face belied the woman's years, yet she was still beautiful, far more beautiful than Giulia. Still, the resemblance between this older woman and what Giulia looked at in the mirror each day was uncanny. It felt very much like she was looking at her future self.

Except, she would never make a *game* of terrorizing her daughter.

Had Lily Cattaneo known the men were gone? A slice of fear ran through Giulia before she held the woman's gaze and nodded. Perhaps her uncle's absence was a blessing. If she could talk to Lily, perhaps they could sort through this mess.

Surprise reflected back at her on the other side of the window. Lily's gaze followed her as Giulia moved to set down the poker and then leave the parlor. When she opened the front door of the castle and slipped outside, she was not startled to find her mother waiting for her, bathed in light from the nearby windows and slightly damp from crossing the distance to the door. They stood apart as the rain fell around them and looked at one another in a quiet, observational manner. Giulia was not going to break the silence; that was not her job. She simply stood there and waited until Lily was ready to speak.

"My darling girl," Lily whispered in a thick Italian accent as she stepped forward, her hand rising up as if she meant to cup Giulia's cheek.

Giulia stepped back and lifted both of her hands. She couldn't trust the woman. Not yet. "Please say what you have come here to say. I know you cannot still be asking for the key, for you must know by now that I do not have it."

Lily's eyes flashed, her jaw tightening. "Is it so wrong for me to want to see my little girl? To assure myself that you are well?"

Giulia could see how the woman had stolen both of the Pepper men's hearts. She was beautiful, her voice seductive. She was reeling Giulia in with the desire to know her. "I have not been your little girl for quite some time. And you can plainly see that I am doing well."

"I do," Lily agreed, nodding. "I can see you have grown to be a *bellissima* young woman in spite of me."

Giulia shivered at the words. That was exactly what her father had written in his journal. "Then you must also know that my father raised me to be kind, honest, and good. I am not lying to you when I say I know not what you are asking me for. I do not have a key."

Lily seemed to consider this for a moment. She clicked her tongue, shaking her head. "Patrick would not have let it go."

Giulia had the impression that Lily was speaking to herself instead of her daughter, but she responded anyway. "Perhaps he did not have a choice."

Lily's eyebrows rose at this. "My Patrick was no fool."

They stood in silence a moment longer and Giulia realized that the romanticized image she had connected to her mother all of these years was as false as it was absent. No longer did she see the woman who left her to be glorious and romantic. Instead she now saw Lily for what she was—a pathetic fortune hunter who would never be satisfied. The sound of hoofbeats brought them out of their collective trance and before Giulia could register what was happening, Lily had vanished without a word.

She stood in front of the door for a moment longer before it opened, and a panicked Jack pulled her inside.

"What were you doing out there?" he asked, his frantic gaze searching the dark before he closed the door. "Tilly could not find you anywhere."

She could not find the words to explain the distinct loss of simultaneously confirming her fear that she had not been missed these last sixteen years and letting go of her small hope that her mother had not, in fact, chosen to walk out on her and never look back. Her face crumpled with a sob and Jack reached forward, his arm rubbing her back in a show of comfort.

Since his death, she had not yearned for her father as keenly as she did in that moment. She needed his strong, caring arms to come around her and comfort her, to remind her that she was loved and needed and cared for. She found her thoughts drifting to Ames and was only slightly surprised to realize that she was not wishing for his capable arms to be holding her in that moment, but for Nick's arms instead.

As if she had summoned him forward, the door swung open and Nick raced through, his clothes dripping, and his face panicked. "Are you well? Is she well?" His face went from Giulia's to Jack's and back before deeming her well, apparently, and relaxing.

Robert stormed in behind him, however, not as relaxed. "Was it her?" His voice was near thundering. "The woman on the porch! Was it *her?*"

Giulia straightened and wiped her eyes on Jack's offered handkerchief before nodding.

Robert froze. He turned and looked back through the empty doorway and the wet darkness beyond. The room was silent, waiting to see what its master would do.

Robert moved to the door and hesitated before closing it. He walked past the group in silence.

Nick speared his valet with a glare, boring his eyes at Jack's arm still around Giulia's shoulders. "I ought to change. Why are you not preparing my evening rig?"

Jack dropped his arm from Giulia's back, clasping his hands together behind himself. Offering a tight smile, he said, "I was helping Tilly search for Miss Pepper."

"I have returned now. You are no longer necessary." He held Jack's gaze, waiting for the man to leave.

Giulia glanced between the men. If Nick's possessive behavior was odd, Jack's defiant stare was simply shocking.

She broke the thick silence. "I will see you again shortly." She stepped away from the men, remaining composed as she moved into the parlor and closed the door behind herself. When they were gone from sight, she expelled a shaky breath and crumpled into a chair.

Giulia did not have heaps of time to compose herself. The men returned dressed for dinner within minutes. Each of them was solemn and pouty, but for different reasons—or, so she imagined. They moved into the dining room and continued to eat in silence, the air thick from all that had occurred. Nick's outburst toward Jack was as irritating as it was strange. By the time he had returned, Giulia had built the moment up in her mind until she was near fuming. She refused his arm for dinner and continued to ignore him at the table.

There were obviously more important things to worry about than whether or not it was acceptable for her to accept a servant's comfort. Her own uncle had not cared, so why should Nick? Besides, she had not even noticed the man's arm about her when Lord Hart and Nick returned. To be singled out was embarrassing enough as it was. To bring such pointed attention to it was outside of enough.

"Did you have a successful outing?" Giulia asked the earl, careful to keep her eyes from flitting in Nick's direction. She didn't care if she was being childish. He deserved to be ignored.

"You could say that," Lord Hart answered with his mouth full. He finished chewing and she waited for more. "Found out where she is staying. Now we need to determine our plan of action."

Silence permeated the room once again, and Giulia startled when her uncle spoke. "What did she want?"

Giulia lifted her gaze. "Nothing."

"We have to be honest with each other if we are going to handle this efficiently."

"I speak the truth." Giulia looked at her uncle. "She did not ask for anything. She still wants the key, and that is all. I told her I did not know anything about this key. The strangest thing..." Giulia trailed off as her brow furrowed and she considered the interaction. She could feel both sets of men's eyes boring into her, but she turned to the earl only. "I think she believed me, that I do not know anything about the key. But I feel as if she still thinks I have it. Whether or not I know." She shook her head and went back to eating.

"That sounds like Patrick," the earl muttered.

Giulia glanced up at Nick without thinking, the surprise in his face no doubt mirroring her own. She glanced away quickly, but not before seeing the small smile of victory on Nick's perfect lips.

"He would have hidden it somehow," Lord Hart continued. "Patrick cared for the hunt. He was clever about it, too."

"Do you think it could be in my things?" Giulia asked. She had not considered this before.

"Yes, or in his. What have you done with my brother's possessions?"

"He didn't have many. I kept what was important to me, and Ames kept the rest."

Lord Hart sat back in his chair and linked his fingers over his belly. "Then it could either be hidden in your things or somewhere in London." He sat up suddenly. "Have you warned your friend? Lily is clever, too. I am sure she knows of him."

"I have," Giulia nodded. "I wrote to him as soon as I could after I saw her the first time." She continued to ignore Nick, but she could feel his stare with gusto at this point.

"Perhaps we should write again, request that he bring us anything that may have belonged to Patrick," the earl suggested.

"Oh, I do not see how that—"

"That is not necessary," a familiar voice cut in.

Giulia's head whipped around to find the very man they were discussing standing beside Wells in the doorway, a boyish grin spread across his face. Ames's coat dripped and his hair was plastered to his forehead, his hat hanging limp in his hand.

She pushed away from the table and stood, drinking in the sight of the only person left on earth who afforded her a distinct connection to her father. She hesitated slightly, her hand gripping the back of her chair. This man had not written to her in months. He was a link to something familiar, but he also felt a stranger. It was disconcerting, to say the least.

But his eyes told a different story. They danced with pleasure, seeming to appreciate the sight of her every bit as much as she cherished the sight of him. Before she could convince herself otherwise, she allowed a grin to spread over her lips, released the chair, and all but jumped into Ames's arms.

———

Nick felt his jaw hanging open. Intellectually, he knew that closing it would be the right move. Yet somehow he could not get it to obey. All he could do was stare at the tall, wet man hugging his darling.

As quickly as the shock overcame his body, it was replaced with gut wrenching nausea. Oh, no. He was going to be sick.

Well, at least that got his mouth to close.

"Giulia, introductions are in order," Robert said authoritatively.

Good, Robert. Gain control over the situation.

"Yes, right..." Giulia stammered. She turned back toward their table, her hand clutching Ames's arm. Her eyes shot right to Nick's before looking away again. Was that...yes. It *was*. Giulia had the decency to blush. The first time Nick finally got to see her perfect cheeks tinge the most beautiful shade of pink and it was because of *Ames*. Brilliant.

"Ames, I'd like you to meet my uncle, Lord Hart, the Earl of Hart. And his heir, Mr. Nicholas Pepper." She took his hand and pulled him closer to the table. "And Lord Hart, Mr. Pepper, I would like you to meet my dear friend, Mr. Ames."

"Just Ames, please," the man said.

Well, there went my jaw again, Nick thought. At least the action of dipping his head in a semblance of a bow was enough to cause him to close his mouth this time. She had done it. After all of that, she had actually called him *Mr. Pepper*, and she hadn't even flinched. Giulia had blushed, and she called him Mr. Pepper. Could this evening get any worse?

"You have come to help, then?" Robert asked, gesturing to the seat beside Giulia's usual place at the table. Wonderful, so now it was time to get down to business. Let the poor man change into dry clothes first, at least.

"In a sense, I suppose." Ames glanced at Giulia with another grin before following her to the table and sitting beside her. She could not stop staring at him. Why on earth could she not stop staring at him? His dark hair was unfashionably long and fell over his forehead, and his smile did not even reach his entire mouth, it was an abominable sort of half-smile. There was no way she found that attractive.

Except, she must.

"I came as soon as I got Jules's letter." His expression transformed into one of concern as he narrowed it at her. "Have you seen your mother again?"

"Yes, actually."

Ames's face hardened, his voice matching his expression. "Did you speak to her? Did she wield a gun this time?"

"I did speak to her. But I believe her to be harmless. I'm not even certain she meant to shoot at me that day."

"Shooting a gun is not harmless, Jules," Ames said. "Regardless of the intent."

"On that we can agree," Nick said with a raise of his glass. Ames glanced at him and then back to Giulia. The disregard he showed Nick made him bristle. He was the next earl, for pity's sake! And besides that, *he* had been there for Giulia for the last few months while Ames had been absent.

"What is your plan, my lord?" Ames addressed Robert.

"We know where she is staying. You brought Patrick's things, I assume? We need to search everything for a potential hiding place. Patrick was smart. He would have hidden it somewhere indispensable to assure that it never got thrown out, yet obvious enough that he knew it would be found by the right person."

"Which begs the question," Nick intercepted. He was going to have a say in this whether Ames or Giulia wanted him to or not. "Who would he have wanted to find the key?"

"Jules," Ames said at once.

"I am not so sure about that." She shook her head, gazing into Ames's eyes. "I would not be surprised if he left it for you to find. He trusted you so much."

He appeared to think over that, his dark brows coming together as his eyes shot skyward. "Perhaps. We would do well to search everything."

"Then it is settled. We find the key, and then we deal with the woman." Robert stood. "We will adjourn until tomorrow. I assume you would like to rest from your journey, and I can speak for this household in saying that we have had quite an adventurous afternoon."

Everyone stood, bidding the earl good evening as he walked away. Ames made no move to leave. Which, in truth, made sense. He probably did not know where he was meant to go.

"Shall I fetch Wells to show our guest to his room?" Nick directed his question to Giulia.

"I believe we shall sit in the parlor for a spell," Giulia replied before turning her attention back to Ames. There was a sudden fierce glint in her eye and Nick was grateful he was not at the other end of her ire.

"I will leave you to it, then. Goodnight." He received a halfhearted reply from each person and then spun toward the door. Ames better not have planned on a long stay, for this was essentially Nick's castle. And if it was Nick's decision, Ames was not a welcome guest at all.

CHAPTER 28

*J*t was refreshing how one could be reunited with an old friend and fall back into the same comfortable ease in manner and conversation as they were wont to have. It was almost as if Giulia had been given a gift to travel back to a time when her evenings were filled with her father and Ames. Only presently, the conversation was strained with unspoken feelings.

She was glad to see Ames. But despite her delight at his appearance, they had more important things to discuss than how she went on in the lush, Devon countryside.

Giulia leaned back against the settee beside her friend, spearing him with a look so full of promise, she heard an audible swallow. "It might interest you to learn that I discovered, upon arriving at Halstead, that the letter I received from my uncle had been forged."

Ames held her gaze, his firm jaw unmoving. She refused to speak until the man beside her did, and she watched him with no uncertain consideration until he finally opened his mouth.

A guilty look passed over his face. "I had no other choice, Jules. Your father asked me to write it."

She drew in a quick breath. "But when? Why?"

"You were in the room, though you were asleep." Ames smiled at the memory, his head tilting in compassion. "You were so exhausted sitting beside your father day and night. No one dared wake you whenever you managed to fall asleep."

She had felt guilty, regardless. It had been clear that her father was not going to live long, and she had been determined to spend every single moment with him that she could. "Please, Ames," she said softly. "Just tell me."

"He was not afraid for your wellbeing, of course. He spoke to me briefly about his plans. His will was unalterable at that point and he knew everything was coming to me. I told him I would see to it that you were cared for."

Cared for? Ames had not promised her father that he would marry Giulia? She had little time to absorb this information before he continued.

"He believed that if you arrived at Halstead alone, the earl would take you in. He told me a little of their history with your mother and asked that I not repeat it. But suffice it to say that Lord Hart's qualms were with Patrick, and not you." Ames reached across the sofa, picking up Giulia's hand and lightly squeezing her fingers. "Your father wanted you to have a chance to know his family. This was the only way he could conceive to make it happen."

"You must have known that I would realize when I arrived that the letter was forged."

"Not precisely," he said, shrugging. "I had hoped the earl would try and save an embarrassing situation by claiming the letter as his own."

"*This* earl?" She cocked an eyebrow. "He would have sent me away instantly if I had not struck a bargain to nurse Nick in exchange for room and board. I was never a guest in the beginning. I was little more than a servant."

"That cannot be." Ames sat up, irritation dancing in his eyes. They'd pulled the settee beside the fire so Ames would dry quickly. He had shed his wet coat but remained damp, still. They would need to retire upstairs soon, or he could catch a chill.

219

"The earl had a valid reason to hate my father and wish me gone." Giulia nearly burst with frustration. Things may have worked out for her benefit, but some small part of her needed Ames to know she had struggled. The very human part of her wanted at least a little sorrow from the man who had sent her on an adventure alone. Especially when he had been her partner for the last fifteen years. "And you, who promised to write to me, did not do so once. Not even after I wrote to warn you of this dratted jeweled key business."

Ames dipped his head. "I planned to write," he said, casting her a guilty smile. "I waited to hear that you'd arrived safely, and that the earl had welcomed you. When I did not hear from you, and you did not return to London, I figured that you were well off here."

"But you were wrong."

"You've not been well?" he asked.

Had she? In truth, the struggle to gain the earl's favor had been unceasingly tiresome. But now...now she almost felt as though Lord Hart did not wish her gone whenever she stepped into a room. She had slowly, painstakingly built a bridge between them and felt it strengthening with each passing day.

To say nothing of Nick.

"I am sorry, Jules. I thought your father's plan was good. We only meant it for the best." The sorrow in Ames's eyes touched her.

"It is all well now," she said. She felt a strange barrier between them, and his shifting gaze was telling. "What is it you are not telling me?"

He glanced up. "I am doing rather well in London," he said. "I've not had much time to do more than chairs, so far, but they are selling rather well. In fact, I've taken on a little help with the store front. Little things, you know. Cleaning and whatnot."

"Oh?" she asked. Why did Ames seem so shifty?

"You know her, actually. The woman I hired." His sheepish look gave him away. Had he fallen in love with this woman?

Giulia tried to search her heart for any feelings of jealousy or hurt, but instead she felt a small bud of joy on his behalf. Relief rushed through her, though she failed to credit why.

"Who is she?"

"Josephine," he said.

"Little Jo? As in Mama Jo's little girl?"

"Yes." He laughed, nodding. His grin grew wide and unrepentant. "Although, she is not such a little girl any longer."

"I would hope not," Giulia said, laughing. "Oh, Ames." She took his hand in her own. "I own that this is quite odd, but I am so very happy for you."

He looked at her intently for a moment before saying, "You mean that." It was not a question, but a statement, rather. He could tell she was pleased for him. Perhaps, all this time, they truly had the sibling relationship Giulia used to imagine. She certainly loved him as though he was her brother.

"What will you do?" Ames asked. "Shall you remain here?"

"Lord Hart has asked for my help regarding a ball he is putting on in Nick's honor. After that"—she lifted one shoulder in a shrug—"I suppose I ought to find a position as a companion or governess."

Ames dropped his chin, not unlike Nick's odd display at dinner earlier. Whatever had that been about? The man seemed to have lost some of his marbles.

"You cannot work in service, Jules. You are the granddaughter of an earl! You deserve to marry and raise children and live a life of peace. I promised your father…"

She did her best to give Ames a look of reassurance. "Father's wishes were well-intentioned, but you and I both can accept that it is better for you to marry for love than to marry me for obligation."

"But it is not an obligation, Jules. I do care for you. I promised your father I would see you taken care of."

"I believe when you made that promise you meant as a sister," she added. "It was always that way for you, wasn't it?" She expected to fear his answer but found that she wasn't frightened at all.

Ames looked at his hands. "I know your expectations were somewhat different. But I loved you for so long as a child, Jules, as I would a little sister. I didn't want to hurt you."

Giulia nodded. "I know, Ames."

"And I will care for you, Jules."

She smiled warmly. "I can promise you now that if I find myself with nowhere to go, you will find me on your doorstep." She could not help but grin. "I am sure your new wife will appreciate that very well."

"If she agrees to become my wife," Ames said. "I have not so much as breached the subject, for I needed to speak to you first."

"And when had you planned on doing so?" Giulia asked, before she could think better of it.

Ames shook his head. "You have never been one to shy away from difficult conversations, have you? To be perfectly honest, I have written you a half-dozen times, at least."

Giulia lifted her eyebrows. She had not received a single letter from him.

"I did not send them," he said, his mouth tilting into a half-smile. "I could not find the right way to explain the situation to you. None of them seemed to feel quite right."

She nodded. He'd caused her undue pain over the last few months, but the end result had been good. She had been forced to examine her own feelings and came about right in the end. Ames would always be her brother. Her youthful fancies were just that—a desire for love, perhaps. But it was not the real thing.

"We better locate Wells," Giulia said as she rose. "I am sure you are exhausted from your trip."

He nodded and joined her, stretching his arms high above his head before following her out the door. She turned before they made it to the hall and embraced him once more. "I am so glad that you have come."

"So am I, little Jules. So am I."

Giulia could not sleep. She tossed and turned on the feather mattress long enough to claim that she had given it a valid try before pulling her trunk out from under her bed and dragging it toward the fireplace.

Stoking the embers, she revived the fire, warming herself and warding off the chill emanating from the cold, stone floor.

Facing the fire, Giulia opened the trunk and emptied the contents onto the floor. The stack of periodicals featuring her father's stories beckoned her, but she pushed them to the side. She would have time to enjoy them later.

Surveying the interior of the trunk, Giulia felt along every nook and cranny for a bump or latch out of place. Anything to indicate a hidden compartment or sewed-in key. Nothing felt out of the ordinary, so she took a deep breath and began tenderly ripping the seam out of the lining until she had thoroughly investigated the trunk and determined that it was, in fact, void of any key. She tamped down her disappointment and frustration at the work ahead of her when she realized she would have to resew the lining back into the trunk and moved on to her valise.

After checking her two pieces of luggage, her small sewing box and slightly larger letter box, the seams of her few books and even the lining of her beautiful fur-lined pelisse, she determined that her father had not hidden the key within her things. The setback was discouraging, but there were always the things Ames had brought from London. They would be able to sort through them tomorrow and she was certain they would discover it then.

A small piece of her wished she had discovered the key within her things. To prove to herself that her father had trusted her as much as he had trusted Ames. That given the choice, he was sure his darling Jules could be counted on.

Shaking off her disappointment, Giulia placed everything back where it belonged and climbed back into bed. It only took a few minutes for her to get back out, throw on her dressing gown and sneak downstairs for a lemon tart. If ever there was a time that she needed a sweet and tangy treat to wash away her woes, it was now.

When she opened the kitchen door to find Nick sitting at the work table in the center of the room, licking his fingers, she felt her blood rise in temperature a degree or two. Now that she was free from obligation to Ames, would things shift between her and Nick? The possibility was frightening.

He glanced up and halted when their eyes made contact, his thumb halfway in his mouth and his eyes round with surprise. She watched as his expression turned sheepish and she knew from that and the empty plate beside him that Nick had eaten every last tart. Spinning on her heel, she turned to go right back upstairs.

"No, wait!" Nick called, his voice sounding garbled. Oh, yes, he must still be chewing on her tart. "Jules, come back!"

She halted halfway up the stairs and he collided into her, sending her down hard onto a step. He immediately reached for her arm to pull her back up and she yanked it from his grip, smoothing down her dressing gown as she stood. "Do not call me that, only my *friends* may call me that."

She knew she was being childish, but she did not care.

"Of course," he said, irritation coloring his own tone. His eyes flashed. "Now that Ames is here you have no further use for me, is that correct?"

She glared down at him from where she stood a few steps higher. Her own chest heaving, she studied Nick's guarded expression. He was irritated, clearly, and trying to hide the depth of his feelings. But she did not have the strength for an argument. "Ugh!" Throwing her hands up in the air she spun around again and began making her way up the stairs. She had no time for games.

"Jul—Giulia, wait!"

"What?" she all but yelled, spinning around and glaring at him. Anger and sorrow and frustration warred within her, and she vented them all on Nick with a single word.

"Forgive me for finishing the lemon tarts," he said. "It is so late, I assumed you'd already eaten what you wanted for tonight. If I'd had any idea you were coming down, I would not have touched your tarts."

She glared at him. She was being irrational, and she knew it, but she did not care. They were her tarts! Hers! He could have eaten something else. There was probably something more manly some-where in that kitchen for him. A leg of ham, or a chunk of cheese. But the tarts? Those were hers.

"I see that you are still upset," he began, cautiously.

"Of course I'm upset," she said through gritted teeth. "I travel all the way down to the kitchen in search of the one thing, the *one thing* that I want to soothe my aching heart, which Cook makes and sets aside especially for me, and come to find them gone." She tried to ignore the way Nick was appraising her. No, she had not gone mad, thank you kindly.

He spoke softly, his words slow. "I have a feeling this may be about something more than the tarts, do you perhaps—"

"What else could it possibly be about, Nick?" she snapped. "Have you eaten something else of mine as well?"

Amusement danced in his eyes, and the smile that spread across his lips was contagious. She had to fight hard not to mirror it.

"Why don't you come back down to the kitchen and let me make you some tea?"

"I don't want tea. I want tarts," she said.

"Well, I cannot provide those for you at present."

"Then I am going to bed." Giulia turned away again but stopped when his hand pulled her back.

"You would not go to bed angry, I hope."

Giulia slowly turned to face him, aware of the warmth spreading from his hand to her own. She tried to fight the smile he ignited within her and cast her gaze to the stairs, shaking her head.

Nick tugged softly, guiding her down a step as he closed the distance a little, leaning forward. From her vantage point, they were nearly eye level and she found the novelty enjoyable. "Is there any particular reason you cannot sleep?" he asked.

"Many reasons," she said, a wry smile twisting her lips. She sighed. "I checked everything. There is no key hidden among my possessions."

Nick's eyebrows pulled together in compassion. "That does not mean your father did not intend for you to find it. He could not control everything after his passing."

How did Nick know what she was thinking? How did he know so well what she needed to hear? She was startled by his intuition and gratified by his support. She lowered her voice to nearly a whisper. "Ames asked to be released from his obligation to me. He has fallen in love with someone else."

Nick stilled. His face took on a foreign expression and she wished she could hear exactly what he was thinking in that moment. She had taken a big risk in telling him of her freedom from Ames, and yet, a large part of her regretted the admission. How would this change things between them?

His face was serious, his voice low and firm. "Shall I call him out? I am an excellent shot, you know."

"No, you shall not call him out." She chuckled. "I am not all that surprised, to be honest. And I am truly very happy for him."

Nick searched her face once more and then he nodded, accepting this information. His hand came up and cupped the side of her face, his fingers wrapping over her hair and tangling themselves in her disheveled coronet braid. "You aren't spoken for then," Nick whispered.

"I'm not spoken for then," she whispered back.

Giulia did not know who closed the gap, only that she was kissing Nick, and she was being thoroughly kissed in return. He tasted sweet and tangy, and her lips curved up in a smile when she realized she was tasting her lemon tarts. A small laugh escaped her throat and his answering smile told her that he was thinking the exact same thing. His arm came around her waist and pulled her closer to him, his fingers splaying across her back, before he broke the kiss and held her against him.

"Can I walk you to your room?" he asked.

"No, but you can walk me to the top of the stairs," she replied.

Nick took her hand and led her to the top of the servants' stairs and into the foyer. He guided her to the grand staircase and stopped on the landing that separated her wing from his. He pulled her in for another sweet, small kiss, his lips resting on hers long enough to force her heart into an erratic rhythm.

He held her gaze. "Goodnight."

Giulia turned to walk away and felt her body take flight. It did not matter what happened now. Lily could have the key for all Giulia cared. She had something more valuable. She had Nick's heart.

CHAPTER 29

*L*emon was not an easy taste to rid oneself of. But in this case, Nick wasn't bothered by that at all. A smile grew on his lips as he stretched in bed, recalling the moment in the stairwell the night before and the way Giulia had fit ever so perfectly in his arms.

She had been a willing participant. Nay, she had been an *instigating* participant, in his view of things. She had ignited his soul and settled his nerves and he knew, from the moment she kissed him, that he would never want anyone but her for the rest of his life. He was sunk.

He was in love.

"What is that foolish grin for?" Jack asked, stoking the fire.

"You'd like to know." Nick pulled himself up, stretching his arm and rotating his shoulder against the soreness. The morning light streamed through the windows as Jack threw the drapes back and Nick sat on the edge of his bed, leaning his hands on the edge of the mattress and grinning.

Jack crossed the floor and threw open the clothes press before selecting a shirt and trousers for Nick. He paused, his eyebrows drawing together, and stared at Nick, who couldn't wipe the smile from his face. "Have you gone mad?" Jack asked.

"No. Maybe foolish, perhaps. But not mad."

Jack straightened. "What happened?"

"Nothing."

"That is clearly not true." He laid a cravat over the back of the chair and faced Nick, disappointment on his brow. "You've not compromised her, have you?"

Fire shot through Nick's veins and he swallowed his affront. Jack might have become something of a friend when Nick brought him to Halstead, but even in that capacity he had no right to tell Nick how to live his life. "Mind your place," Nick said. "I brought you here to be my valet, Jack, not to run my life. You have no business approving or disapproving any of my choices." He swallowed, holding Jack's gaze.

"Mind my place?" Jack sputtered, his face mottling with rage. A lock of hair flipped over on his brow as he shook his head. "Your head's grown bigger than your station, if you ask me."

"No one did ask you," Nick said. Regret clutched his heart from the words spoken in anger and he shook his head. This wasn't right. This was not how one spoke to a friend.

Jack stood by his clothes press, chest heaving and eyes wild. He was spitting mad and Nick didn't blame him. He'd be just as angry were the roles reversed. This was a man he'd fished with as a boy and though they did not remain close as they'd aged, he owed Jack the decency of respect.

"Forgive me, Jack," he said, dropping his head into his hands. "I just cannot handle the pressure sometimes. And now the earl wants me to marry—it is all just too much."

Jack's expression was tight. He did not appear eager to brush the argument under the carpet. Instead, he nodded once and went about dressing Nick for the day. There was discord between them and evidently one simple apology was not going to fix it.

Nick swallowed his irritation at his valet. It was not worth his energy at present. He would fix things eventually.

Giulia stepped quietly from her room, meandering down the hall while her mind floated somewhere far above the castle. Kissing Nick had felt like coming home. He was just the sort of man to inspire fanciful, affectionate poetry. If Giulia was the sort of woman who wrote fanciful, affectionate poetry, that is.

Her mind was constantly wandering back to Nick, the dim staircase, and the lemon-infused kiss, but she was aware enough to recall the important matter at hand. Ames was here, and he'd brought her father's things. He sent a note to her earlier that morning asking for help going through the trunks and papers, and she was prepared to search meticulously for any clue. The mystery was beginning to wear. She was ready to quit feeling the constant need to look over her shoulder.

She reached the landing connecting her to the east staircase and nearly ran into Jack, he had been racing down the steps so quickly.

"Good heavens," she said, resting her hand on her heart. "You are in quite a rush."

Jack bowed, irritation clear on his brow. Was he bothered by her? She hadn't *tried* to step in his path. What was he doing on the main steps, anyway? She was certain he used the servants' stairs most of the time.

"Forgive me, Miss Pepper," he said stiffly.

"What is it, Jack?" she asked, her mind drifting back to the moment when he'd stepped forward and comforted her despite the impropriety. He had not bothered to hold back when she was in despair. Surely she could return the favor.

She had not grown up gallivanting about the oceans without gaining an appreciation for human beings of all social classes.

Jack paused, gazing at her with such focus, she was nearly positive the man had begun wool-gathering.

"You are being careful, are you not?" he asked, startling her. His deep voice permeated her cheerful, dreamlike state.

A cool chill ran up her arms. "I have only left the castle one time since seeing my mother, if that is what you—"

"I am referring to Nick," he said, a hint of derision shining in his eyes. "I do not scruple to tell you that I have known the man since our infancy, and his behavior has cycled much the same since our youth. He attaches himself to a woman until he gains their affection, and then he grows bored. And when Nick finds himself bored, he moves on to the next conquest without delay."

A cool wave washed over her heart, and Giulia reminded herself to breathe normally. "What do you mean, Jack? Are you trying to tell me that Nick is not *sincere* in his attention?" She would have blushed, had apprehension not taken root in her chest.

"I do not presume to tell you what is in anyone else's mind," Jack said, softening. "But I will have you know the truth of Nick's history and you may do with that information what you will. I cannot sit idly by and watch the same thing happen to you that has happened time and again to other, unwitting females."

He held her gaze so firmly, Giulia would have shrunk away were she made of lesser stock. But she was a Pepper. She did not shrink from the truth any more than she hid away and allowed the Pepper men to solve this key riddle for her.

Jack had nothing to gain from sharing this bit of information with her, and everything to lose. Had Nick overheard their conversation, he could have turned his valet away without a reference. What man would abide their servant speaking ill of them in such a way? Giulia certainly would not.

She could not help but feel that Jack was only trying to help. Furthermore, she could not fight the overwhelming feeling that his warnings were not unfounded.

"Thank you," she said. "I realize that this could not have been easy for you to say."

A small smile graced his lips. "It is no large sacrifice, I assure you."

She watched him bow before he turned and continued walking down the stairs. She could not recall the embrace she'd shared with Nick without her heart warming and a youthful giddiness overtaking her chest. But Jack's warning called to mind the stories Amelia, Mabel, and Hattie had shared with her at the tea so many weeks ago. Nick had made each of them a target directly after arriving at

Halstead—much as he'd made Giulia a target soon after her own arrival.

As loath as she was to admit it, the cycle of behavior, as Jack had aptly called it, spoke for itself.

Giulia leaned back against the bannister, her eyes drifting closed. She had been so naive to imagine that Nick's flirtations were genuine with her when he had made a game of her friends.

She was such a fool.

CHAPTER 30

"*I*t just does not make any sense." Ames dropped the last of the notes into the rectangular wooden box and leaned back against the wall. The bedchamber Wells had designated to him in the east wing was near Nick's room. Tilly sat in the corner with a basket of mending—bless her soul, the maid had been willing to sew the lining back into Giulia's pelisse—and the door was propped open.

Giulia and Ames sat on the floor, defeated. They had checked every last thing that had once belonged to Patrick, Giulia, and even some of Ames's own belongings. They searched linings and potential hiding places, they checked the more obvious places like pockets or boxes, they even went through every last note or drawing in the box where Patrick Pepper compiled the documents he'd used in research for writing his periodical, but nothing pointed them in even remotely the right direction.

"Perhaps we are missing something," Giulia said as she stood, wiping her hands along her skirt and moving to sit in the chair beside the fire.

"Your father was not a materialistic man, despite his adoration for treasure hunts. There was not much left by way of possessions when he died."

233

"I know," she said in agreement. "That is partially why I am sure he would have left this key for us. He would have delighted in the mystery he left behind."

"Unless," Ames said, "it was too dangerous. Perhaps he rid himself of it to protect you."

Giulia shook her head. "Not Father." She lowered her voice. "The danger is simply—"

"Part of the fun," they finished in unison. They shared a smile at the memory of a constant phrase uttered by her father. A deep voice cleared in the doorway and Giulia snapped her head up to find a scowling Nick perched against the door frame, his arms crossed against his chest.

"Am I interrupting?" Nick asked dryly, his mouth lifting in a sardonic smile.

"No." Giulia sighed, doing her best to appear unaffected. The man was too handsome for his own good. And she had foolishly fallen for his charms. "We have found nothing."

"But it still doesn't make any sense," Ames said. "Patrick would have hidden it, if it was as valuable and important to him as your mother is leading us to believe. Why else would she come back for it *after* his death? She must believe that he would have held onto it."

"She does not merely 'believe' anything. She is utterly convinced," Giulia said with conviction of her own. She had seen it in Lily's eyes on the porch the evening before. Lily knew the key was hidden somewhere. Giulia was worried about what her mother would do if it was not found soon.

"I have come to see if you would like to eat," Nick asked, regarding her closely.

"I, for one, am starving," Ames offered.

Nick's smile was forced. He indicated the corridor with a sweep of his arm. "There is a luncheon served in the breakfast room." He shot Giulia a questioning glance, but she turned away, watching the floor until Nick's footsteps could be heard retreating down the hall. He muttered something incoherent as he walked away. Was he bothered she hadn't jumped up to greet him? That she hadn't thrown her arms around him and expounded on her gratitude that he had deemed her worthy of a late-night dalliance? Her skin prickled with shame. She'd been warned of his reputation. If only she had listened.

Ames threw Giulia a questioning glance. "That was odd. Did he not seem a bit agitated to you?"

She lifted her shoulders in a shrug, reminding herself that it was better this way. She could not forever fall at Nick's feet. It was time she started guarding her heart better.

Ames moved to clean up the rest of his things. "Well, whether you're willing or not, I won't say no to a nice meal." He reached for her hand and helped Giulia to her feet before guiding her from the room. She chuckled, noting his lost expression as he glanced down the corridor in both directions.

"The castle takes a while to learn," she said, patting his arm.

"So I see." Ames laughed and followed Giulia to the dining room where a nice spread was set up on the sideboard much like breakfast had been. The earl was already seated and his plate half empty, but Nick was nowhere to be seen.

"Ah, Giulia," Lord Hart started when she entered the room. Food clung to his beard and jiggled as he finished chewing his mouthful. "Tell me you've had some luck?"

She waved off Ames's offer of a plate and moved to sit beside the earl, her stomach not quite in the mood for sustenance at the moment. She could not get Nick's irritated face from her mind. Where was he, anyway?

"Giulia?" the earl prompted.

"Luck? I am afraid not," she reported sadly.

"Do not give up yet," the earl said with a serious eye and a fork poised midair. Where had this man come from? He was a far cry from the grumpy ogre who had nearly booted her out on her first night at Halstead. He was beginning to remind her more and more of...of her father.

"Perhaps you have some insight, my lord?" she asked hopefully. When he did not immediately grunt his disapproval, she took it as a sign to proceed. "It had to be in my father's possession nearly twenty years ago, at least, if Lily knows of it." Lord Hart's shoulders tensed at the mention of Patrick, and Giulia waited for his anger to lash out. She had broken their unofficial agreement and broached the subject of the metaphorical elephant that stood between them. Nothing happened, however. She could feel the unease slip from her spine as smooth as a rejuvenating breath.

"I have no insight," Lord Hart said. "No keys. We only had the trip to India alone before we met your mother, and after that...we did everything together, the three of us." The earl's voice dipped quieter and Giulia found herself straining to hear. She faintly noticed Nick hovering in the doorway again as Ames sat beside her, his plate over-flowing. "There were no secrets between us until then. Until Lily, I mean." Lord Hart's gaze took on a glassy quality. "I wouldn't know about the key if he picked it up after he and Lily..." He shook his head. "That was when he stopped telling me things."

The earl stood quickly, surprising everyone in the room. He glanced around but his gaze didn't settle on anything in particular. Instead, he nodded distractedly before fleeing the room, swiping past Nick so quickly the younger man had to jump out of the way to avoid being pummeled. Everyone seemed frozen in place, the earl's vulnerability so bizarre it left a trail of unease in his wake.

Or was the unease caused by Nick and his perpetual hovering in the doorway?

Giulia stood to cross to the sideboard and fill a plate of her own. The strawberries on Ames's plate looked juicy and tantalizing and made her stomach growl. No sooner had she scooped a pile of the vivid fruit onto her plate than a tall form sidled beside her and began loading up a plate of his own. Her pulse quickened with the memory of the previous night in the dim stairwell and confusion clouded her mind as her heart was telling her one thing and her brain another.

She could not dispel the fact that she had enjoyed kissing this man immensely. Regardless of Nick's lack of good intentions, the feelings he invoked within Giulia had been real. For *her*. Suddenly heat infused her cheeks in a very uncharacteristic manner that made her want to run from the room and hide until her face returned to its natural pale color. Twice in two days? What was happening that she would actually blush *twice* in two days?

"What is it, Jules?"

Nick's kind whisper only added to her embarrassment as chills started behind her ear and traveled down her arm. Frustrated, she shoved her plate into his hands and turned away, running from the room and toward the staircase.

She groaned with claustrophobia at the thought of being confined in the castle for another moment and changed direction, sprinting for the front door. She blew through the doorway and across the bridge that covered the moat, before turning again and racing toward the stables. Halfway there she recalled the ban and knew that the earl's loyal men would never let her take a horse out for a ride. She was aching for a bruising ride, or run, or anything really that could burn off the pent-up feelings inside her and let her feel free again.

Giulia reached the stables but didn't stop. She circled back to the castle and began running along the moat, lifting the hem of her gown and following the perimeter of the large, ancient structure. She relished the stretching of her lungs and the thoroughly purifying feeling of utilizing her muscles. She gazed up the wall of the castle when something caught her eye. Halting mid-stride, Giulia nearly stumbled, but she righted herself quickly and stopped to catch her breath.

Screwing her eyes, she strained to see what it was at the top of the tower that was glinting, for something was definitely shining up there. She craned her head back until she was nearly off balance again and caught herself before she fell. Checking to make sure there were no witnesses to her fumbling, she took one more glance upward in vain, for it was much too high and she could not quite see what was causing the sun to glint off of the top of the tower.

She froze as recognition dawned; this was the west tower—the one which led to the locked door. A renewed sense of adventure flowed through her veins as one more piece of the seemingly unsolvable puzzle presented itself and she found herself wondering what Nick would think of this development.

Well, that did the trick. Giulia sobered and turned back to walk along the moat. Sneaking inside through the front door, she trod quietly up the stairs and down the hall in the west wing, away from her room. She rounded the alcove that led into the west tower and ran straight into something solid.

Two hands came under her elbows to steady her, and she commanded the butterflies in her stomach to calm when she recognized Nick's blond hair and deep green eyes.

"I thought I would find you here," Nick said with a devastatingly handsome smile.

"I was just out for a walk. I saw…" She swallowed. She could not trust this man with her heart, evidently. But the mystery was different.

"Yes?" he prodded, leaning closer.

Giulia let out a breath and stepped out of his reach. The flirt was going to have to realize that she was through with his games. She could be his friend, but nothing more. Which would be significantly easier if the man would simply step back a bit.

"When I was outside I saw a light shimmer off of the locked tower, at its very highest point."

His eyebrows drew together. "You should not be outside alone."

"I am safe. But the light—"

He shrugged. "It is not so bizarre. It was probably a window that you saw."

"That is what I thought," she agreed. "Except that it was the strangest thing, but the window appeared to be colored."

Nick pursed his lips together in thought and swung around to face the door. "Has Ames tried his hand at the lock yet?" he asked while he faced away. His voice was low and controlled.

"No, I have not asked him."

"But he is willing?"

"No. Or, well, I am sure he would if I asked, but I thought…"

Nick turned around to face her. His expression was shuttered, and it caused her to step back a fraction. "You thought?"

Giulia swallowed the lump in her throat. She had no idea why she was fighting tears, but they were there just the same. "I was hesitant to admit another person into our mystery."

"And why is that?" He stepped forward.

She inched backward again. "I did not want to ruin..." She could not find the words to explain her feelings. The mystery felt like theirs, Nick and Giulia's, and bringing Ames in would have felt like a betrayal of sorts. Though why she felt the need to protect it now was puzzling.

A smile tilted Nick's perfect lips and his gaze strayed to hers. That was enough to pull her from her daze and she straightened her spine. She stepped back again and spoke in clipping tones. "Of course, the fact remains that he is rather skilled and could gain us entrance should we wish it. But I will leave that up to you. Let me know if you would like me to ask him to help us. Now, if you do not mind." Giulia stepped back again. Good. More space was better. More space made it easier to breathe. "I am going to take care of a few things for your ball. Good day, Nick."

Giulia nodded curtly as she spun and walked away. She was in her room with her door locked within moments and slunk back against the wall until her breathing slowed. At this point there was only one thing she could do. She needed to fully immerse herself in the planning of the ball.

CHAPTER 31

$\mathcal{R}$obert cleared his throat, his gaze sticking to the pile of books on the edge of his desk. His large, thick fingers tapped the desktop before he strung them together over his belly.

"Did you wish to go over the details for the ball?" Giulia asked. Wells had fetched her from the parlor, explaining that the earl needed to speak to her. But thus far, the man had not said anything beyond an initial greeting.

"The ball..." he said, drawing out the word. "Yes. In a sense."

Giulia waited for him to continue. His thick, white eyebrows danced a rhythm on his forehead, drawing together before rising. He was clearly contemplating something. His gaze flicked to the doorway and he muttered something incoherent under his breath.

"Would you like me to inventory my expenses?" Giulia asked. "I have managed to keep the decor at a reasonable—"

"No," he said, shaking his head. "I have asked you here to introduce you to someone, but she is late." Lord Hart glanced to the door again.

Giulia peeked over her shoulder, but the solid wood door remained closed. The silence in the room was reminiscent of their earlier dinners at Halstead and she graciously thanked the heavens that they had managed to move past those quiet, awkward moments—her gaze flicked to the uncomfortable earl—at least, for the most part.

A knock at the door preceded Wells and he stepped aside to allow a short, gray-haired woman in a plain, violet gown to bustle inside. She carried a work basket on her arm and wore a look of determination, mixed with a dose of apprehension, if Giulia was correct in her assumption.

"Madame Chastain, please come in," Lord Hart said.

The woman dipped in a curtsy before setting her work basket down and crossing the floor, narrowing her gaze as if to inspect Giulia.

"Beautiful," Madame Chastain said. "Emerald green, perhaps? Or a deep violet would do nicely."

Lord Hart rose, his hands coming up in the air. "I will leave the details to you." He made to leave, but Giulia was no more enlightened now than she was before the woman had entered the earl's study.

"My lord, wait," she said, gathering his attention.

He paused, turning back. His face displayed his desire to be anywhere but his own study at the moment.

"Forgive me," she said, "but I still do not know what is going on."

Lord Hart's cheeks grew rosy. "I have ordered you a gown."

A scoff escaped Giulia's throat and she clamped her mouth closed.

"Well," amended the earl, "I have sent for Madame Chastain so *you* might order a gown of your own choosing."

"And I will have my hands full completing the order in time for your ball," Madame Chastain said, her French accent so thick it caused Giulia to wonder at its authenticity. "Come," she said, motioning for Giulia to stand, "we have no time to waste."

Giulia stood, stepping around the older woman and gazing at the earl with such gratitude in her heart. "You've done this for *me?*" Never before had someone taken measures to gift Giulia such an extravagance. Never before had Giulia owned a formal ball gown. It simply was not practical.

Lord Hart grunted, but he sounded more uncomfortable than bothered. A smile erupted on Giulia's face, matching the burst of joy in her heart.

"I cannot thank you sufficiently," she said.

Lord Hart paused, his body growing still. Something of a smile flickered across his time-beaten face and he dipped his head. "You needn't thank me. I believe it is I who has some making up to do."

"Nonsense," Giulia said. "But I will take the gift, regardless."

"How polite of you," Lord Hart returned, amusement dancing in his eyes. "I am certain Madame will not forget the entire order, but I will have you know that I directed her to fulfill whatever it is you are in need of."

Giulia's heart stopped. All jesting left her tone as she said, "That *is* too much, my lord."

"No," he argued. For once, his gaze remained firmly fixed on hers as he spoke with authority. "And I won't hear another word about it. You are my niece—my family."

He turned, fleeing the room before Giulia could wrap her head around the situation. He had accepted her role in his life. He had called her family. Could this mean the man had softened his opinion of her? Of course, she had imagined in recent weeks, and more certainly in recent days, that the man was beginning to grow fond of her. He had done his best to cover his amusement, but she could see that he claimed much of the same sense of humor that his brother had.

Madame Chastain bustled to the desk, laying fashion plates atop it and pulling a measuring ribbon, pencil, and sheet of paper from her basket.

Giulia tamped down her mounting elation and nodded to the modiste that she was ready to begin, but all of her best efforts were unable to dampen her smile. The kind gesture from her uncle stuck with her and she felt buoyed up by his generosity. If nothing else, Giulia felt, with very little doubt, that her uncle cared for her. And that brought her a level of contentment she had not felt in quite some time.

Robert appeared to be happy with the preparations for the ball thus far and Nick assumed he would be too, if Giulia deigned him worthy of previewing any of her ideas. The woman was blasted mad. She was running around the castle and even the town with the trusty bodyguard, Ames, by her side nonstop. Nick had never actually been involved in the planning of a ball before, but he knew that Giulia had not either, and it seemed to him she was now creating jobs for herself, simply to keep busy.

Truly, there were only so many times she could go into Graton to check on the gown she had ordered or the cakes she had commissioned or the draperies she had arranged with the dressmaker's sister to design and create.

Crossing a foot over the other ankle, Nick leaned back in his chair and fixed his gaze on the door to the ballroom. There had most definitely been a shift between Giulia and himself since the morning after the lemon tart kiss, and he could not figure out what caused her to be so distant.

Now with the ball two days away she was completely ensconced in the ballroom where Nick, conveniently enough, was not allowed to enter under her guise of keeping the decor a surprise.

Nick let out a frustrated breath and stared at the door to the ballroom as if his gaze could penetrate it. From where he sat in the library he had a clear view of the oversized oak double doors and found himself watching them open and close repeatedly as people came and went. The dressmaker's husband had arrived not a quarter-hour ago with the draperies Giulia had ordered; that must have been a load off of Giulia's mind.

And then there were Jolly's nephews, who had appeared a solid hour before and had not yet left. Jolly's nephews—as untrustworthy as their uncle—were the reason Nick was so absorbed with watching the door to the ballroom, or so he told himself. What on this green earth would Giulia need Jolly's nephews for? Halstead boasted plenty of men. Denny the footman, Jack, Nick *himself*, Ames...just to name a few. It was absurd. Nick was stronger than both of Jolly's nephews combined. He and Ames could easily accomplish whatever Giulia was delegating to those unruly brats.

Footsteps sounded in the hall and two maids approached the door, each laden with trays of food. Not a simple tea service, no. They were armed with ham and chicken, cheese and bread and all manner of fruit. Good heavens, was Giulia feeding an army in there? Nick's stomach rumbled on cue and his scowl deepened. Like he had thought earlier, Giulia was blasted mad.

But she was incredible, too. He sighed out his frustration, rubbing the sockets of his eyes. His mind wandered to the way she had made him chuckle when he was mostly unconscious from the gunshot, to the adorable way her dark eyebrows pulled together when she was concentrating, even to the confidence and tenacity she exhibited in her determination to keep her distance from him now.

He chuckled as he shook his head back and forth. He had been so jealous when he went to Ames's room that day and saw their easy banter and close proximity. And his envy had only grown the longer Giulia insisted on keeping Nick at bay.

But now she refused to give him her full attention. She'd kissed him, thoroughly, and then...grown bored of him. Or so it seemed. Had his touch been so repulsive?

He dropped his chin onto a fisted hand, narrowing his eyes as the maids slipped through the doors and closed them securely. Nearing the end of his patience, he was quite ready to storm the ballroom. Perhaps that was exactly what he should do. He chuckled as he pictured himself, donned with the armor displayed in Robert's study and beating down the door, demanding entrance.

"Mr. Pepper, sir?" Wells said from the doorway, cutting him from his musings. How long had the butler been standing there?

Nick straightened in his chair. "Yes?"

"Tea is served in the breakfast room."

"Very good. Thank you, Wells."

The butler nodded and turned away.

"Wait, Wells?"

"Yes?" He turned back, his older face etched in stone.

Nick gestured toward the ballroom. "What precisely is going on in there?"

Wells glanced toward the ballroom doors. When he returned his gaze to Nick, it looked as if the older man was fighting a smile. But that would be uncharacteristic of the old retainer.

"Preparations for the ball, sir," he said.

"Yes," Nick said patiently, "but *what* preparations, exactly?"

"I am afraid you will have to question Miss Pepper, sir."

"She's got you under her spell too, then? Very well, off with you," Nick growled, doing his best to tamp down his annoyance. Evidently, even Wells had switched allegiance. Not that it surprised Nick at all. He would pledge himself to Giulia as well if he was given the option. If she would acknowledge him or even look in his direction once in a while.

He resumed his brooding, putting his afternoon tea and growling stomach on hold while he continued to watch the ballroom doors open and close, admitting every other person in the entire castle.

As the door opened once more, Nick shot to his feet. "Ames!"

The dark-haired man had a few years on Nick, but their height was equally matched, and Nick felt that he would easily win in a battle of fisticuffs. Sizing up Ames, he no longer felt inferior to the man. Jealous on occasion, maybe—no matter how unfounded. But no longer inferior.

Ames waited for Nick's approach, impatience in his eyes.

"I have a favor I'd like to ask of you."

"Oh?" Ames's eyebrows shot up as he cocked a hip and leaned against the wall. It was no wonder Patrick Pepper adopted this man into his family—Ames had the curiosity to fit in well.

"My sources inform me that you are skilled at lockpicking," Nick said, doing his best to affect nonchalance.

"I may be," Ames answered skeptically.

"Splendid. I have need of your services if you would be willing to help me. It is time sensitive, you'll understand. I have a surprise for Giulia."

Ames watched him a moment before delivering one concise nod. "I am free right now."

Perfect. The man followed Nick as he turned toward the stairs and the west wing.

Ames shot him a guarded look as they mounted the stairs. "So she told you, then?"

A prickle of dread gathered in Nick's stomach and he banished it with a clearing of his throat. "I am not sure. What should she have told me?"

Ames halted in the corridor. "That she is leaving with me after the ball."

"Oh." Nick felt the air rush out of his lungs in one fell swoop. "No, she did not tell me."

Ames glanced sheepishly away. "Sorry, mate. I thought you knew when you said that it was time sensitive."

"Right."

Panic rose with each step they took closer to the tower. Was that why she'd grown so distant? It did not make sense. What had gone wrong during their lemon tart kiss to incite a desire in the woman to *leave*?

They arrived at the alcove, the urgency to see Giulia—to talk to her —clawing at Nick's chest. He felt all the more eager to do this for her. He gestured toward the thick, ironclad door. "This leads to a staircase and another door with an ancient lock. I am not sure what is up there. It might be nothing but an empty room. But Giulia has been trying to solve this mystery since she arrived here, and I want her to be the first one to open it."

"I understand." Ames shot an arm out and stopped Nick before he ascended the stairs. "Listen, for what it is worth, she is not leaving to be with me. I am only taking her home, to care for her as I promised her father I would do. But I am still marrying Jo."

That was a funny name for a woman. "Of course." Nick brushed off the man's hand and tried to appear as though he did not care that his heart was being ripped from his chest and torn to shreds. Why should he, anyway? She was leaving him.

No wonder she had been avoiding him so thoroughly.

When they reached the locked door at the top of the stairs, Ames crouched down, lifting the lock and letting it drop with a heavy thud against the door. He let out a low whistle, shooting Nick an unsure glance before pulling a knife from his boot and getting to work.

"It's a shame, really," Ames said as he jimmied the knife back and forth, methodically moving it in a way that appeared random but was most likely a very practiced art. "She is really flourishing here." He paused for a moment and glanced at Nick. "That was always her gift, you know."

Nick had not known that, but it did not surprise him at all.

Ames returned his attention to the lock. "No matter where we landed, Jules would acclimate right away and make it a home. She would put forth an effort to get to know the people and everyone loved her. It is probably why Patrick had always been comfortable leaving her behind on all of those excursions. He knew she would always be fine."

"Fine, maybe. But that does not lessen her need for consolation or reassurance."

"Reassurance? Little Jules? No." Ames shook his head decisively. "If there is one thing about Jules I know to be indisputable, it is her ability to thrive. She is very comfortable in her own skin."

Nick grunted, focusing through the arrow slit in the stone wall at the expanse of land that would one day become his. How could a man that claimed to know Giulia her whole life, know her so little? Of course she needed reassurance; everyone did. The woman's own mother had abandoned her at the tender age of four. She had not needed to be left alone on various continents with strangers while her father and friend left for the real adventures. She had needed extra love, extra support, and extra reassurance that she was cared for, that she was needed.

A click reverberated off the walls in the narrow, curved stairwell and Ames looked up, triumphant. The padlock hung on the door open, and Nick felt a surge of excitement flow through his veins.

They were likely to find a storage room full of covered furniture and old, tattered portraits of ancestors long forgotten, but that was irrelevant. He was finally going to watch Giulia open the door. Her eternal optimism made even the mundane activities exciting.

They turned in unison and descended the stairs, parting ways as they reached the foyer once again.

"Shall I fetch her for you?" Ames asked.

"No, she is busy. It can wait another hour or so," Nick said, thanking the man again before heading off to drink his tea. The last thing he wanted was for Ames to be around when he took Giulia to the tower. This was their mystery, and they were going to open the door alone.

CHAPTER 32

*G*iulia released a sigh of contentment as she stood in the center of the ballroom and spun slowly, taking in her masterpiece. This place had begun to feel like a home and working with the people to prepare for the ball had given her such a glorious feeling of fulfillment and companionship. She swallowed the bitter taste in her mouth, reminding herself that she had never been welcome to remain at Halstead forever. Ames's offer to return her to London and give her a place to stay at Mama Jo's while she figured out what she was going to do with her life was timely. While it was a generous offer, she knew it would be best to refuse.

Little Jo would not appreciate another woman encroaching on her home, particularly at this crucial time of the engagement and start of her marriage to Ames. Giulia and Ames might be well aware of their lack of romantic feelings for one another, but that did not mean that Jo would welcome her around. Perhaps after they had been married for some time, or Giulia had someone of her own…

But what choice did she have? She couldn't imagine staying on at Halstead Manor with Nick, not with the way things stood between them. Where would she go when he tired of her? Or when he moved on to the next woman, or the woman who would eventually become his wife? Maybe she wouldn't go with Ames, but she had to go *somewhere,* that much was certain.

She shook her head and looked back to the beautiful shimmering drapes Mrs. Tubbs had designed for her. The woman should be applauded. The bunched fabric fell from the ceiling in swoops, artfully avoiding the three massive chandeliers and running down the length of the walls. It gave the illusion of the room being turned into an enormous, fantastic tent. When the chandeliers were lit and the room aglow, it would shine off of the glimmering fabric and look even more magical. It was such a simple design, so masterfully assembled by those Tucker boys. It gave Giulia a heavy feeling of contentment.

The door swung open and Nick stood tall and determined, framed by the light behind him in the foyer. He looked almost dangerous, his eyes fastened on her, and Giulia's breath caught. She'd done her best to avoid him since that wretched morning after their lemon tart kiss. Or ensure that Ames would be nearby to act as a barrier between them.

And now they stood alone in the ballroom. Dinner was over, the earl and Ames both had gone off to bed, and not a servant stood in sight.

"Good evening, Nick. I suppose I must bid you goodnight?" She moved toward the exit, roundly avoiding him as he stepped into the room.

"Jules, this is..." He spun slowly, soaking in every detail that she had designed and orchestrated over the previous week and a half until his gaze landed on her. "This is breathtaking."

Literally, she thought. "I am glad you approve. Though I believe I requested that you stay away so you might be surprised."

He dipped his head. "I am awfully surprised. I have never seen anything like this."

"Lord Hart seemed pleased as well."

"I cannot imagine a more perfect setting for reopening the castle for social events."

She nodded her acknowledgement and moved through the door, hoping to silently make her escape. She made it to the base of the stairs before Nick caught up to her, his hand coming to rest lightly on her arm. "Giulia, wait. I have a surprise for you."

"Can it not wait until tomorrow?" she asked, manufacturing a yawn. "I am dreadfully tired, you see, and I really do not think I can stay awake another moment."

"It can wait, but I would much rather show you now."

She couldn't ignore the warmth of his hand on her arm, the pleading in his eyes. Her resolve slipped away. "Very well."

Nick's face lit up and his hand slid down her arm, grasping her hand and pulling her up the stairs, toward the west wing. The moment they turned away from the corridor that led to her room, she knew where they were headed.

"Is it unlocked?" she asked as they made their way toward the tower.

"It is." Nick grinned down at her. "But no one has opened the door yet." He answered the question she was thinking.

Excitement pulsed through her veins as they rounded the alcove and slipped through the door, running up the stairs of the west tower hand-in-hand, her free hand holding up her skirts. They paused at the door, their breath coming in equally rapid beats.

"Ames?" she asked.

"Yes," Nick answered.

She nodded and gripped the padlock, slipping it from the ancient handle and hanging it on a nail beside the door. Nick took another candle from his pocket and lit it with his before handing it to Giulia. She took it and inhaled a deep breath before pulling the door open and stepping inside the dust-covered room.

Silence muffled the tears that gently slid down her cheeks as Giulia walked to the center of the room and spun in a slow circle, taking in each tiny detail of the room as the candle lit it section by section.

"So this is where it all began," she whispered. And it had to be true. A tattered sofa sat against the wall, covered by an abundance of pillows and a quilt thrown over one side in a way that reminded her of the Swans' Literary Society and their makeshift meetinghouse. An elaborate painting of a tree covered one portion of the wall, its branches stretching high onto the ceiling. A small ladder came away from the tree at an angle and ended at a hatch, no doubt leading to the roof of the tower.

Every bit of wall that was not claimed by the painted tree was covered in shelves and shelves of books. It was an oasis. A grand and beautiful playroom that undoubtedly fed Patrick and Robert Peppers' love of adventure and danger and intrigue.

"This is amazing," Nick said in awe, filling Giulia with pride. She had known this room was somehow related to her father—she had been able to sense it deep within her. "I can see why Robert has ignored it, though."

She nodded. "He must have locked it up when their relationship ended."

"How do you feel?" Nick asked as he crossed toward her.

She took stock of her emotions and a smile spread across her lips. "I am well. I truly am." She spun again in a slow circle, pausing when she reached the window above a low-sitting bookcase. "Nick, this must be what caused that odd shimmer I saw outside. It is stained glass."

They both raised their candles to reveal a beautiful stained-glass window depicting a sun shining over hills and valleys of green earth. The window boasted every color of the rainbow and would undoubtedly shine beautifully in the daylight.

"Come." Nick pulled her arm away from the window. "Let us return tomorrow when it is easier to see."

Giulia allowed Nick to lead her from the tower. She breathed contentment. The ballroom preparations were finished, the tower mystery was solved, and she was well on her way to healing Lord Hart's scars.

Now, if only she could figure out what to do about her mother and the wretched, nonexistent key, she would not have a care in the world. Well, none that didn't involve the future earl of Hart, at least.

Nick was overjoyed. Not for the ball that was going to take place that evening, of course, but for the tower. The tower was better than he could have hoped. There was about as much dust as he expected to find, that was for certain, but the contents of the room were far more valuable than he could have guessed. Not in monetary terms, of course, but to Giulia they were even more precious. She got to glimpse her father's childhood.

It was no wonder the earl had locked away that particular room. For a moment, Nick had worried they were crossing an invisible barrier that would evoke the anger of the earl, but then he decided it did not matter—this was just as much Giulia's history. Particularly when her time at Halstead was quickly drawing to a close.

The morning after they had finally unveiled what was hiding behind the padlocked door, Nick had returned to the tower early to find Giulia reverently scanning the books that lined the walls. He'd watched her for some time before slipping away quietly, leaving her to grieve her father and remember him in peace.

He intercepted Ames later in the morning and explained what they'd found in the tower room. He was grateful when the man agreed that Giulia should be left alone. The only problem he came up against was directly before dinner when Robert had asked where Giulia had gone off to, for she had skipped their afternoon tea. Nick explained that she was doing her best to research more on her father's past belongings.

No doubt Robert interpreted this as research about the key, but Nick did not elaborate. They went through the evening in companionable silence, but Giulia's lack was felt acutely by both of the Pepper men.

He'd almost convinced himself to beg Giulia to stay at Halstead, but better sense prevailed. If she chose to remain at Halstead, Nick wanted it to be her choice and not the result of guilt. She knew how he felt. She must, if their chemistry had anything to say for him.

The local dressmaker, Madame Chastain, spent the morning with Giulia in the parlor delivering the ballgown the earl had commissioned for Giulia and slinging requests for more clothing orders—if Nick had to guess. That woman could be ruthless. But, when Nick had first arrived in town, Madam Chastain and her horde of little ones had made him feel at home and welcomed. She was a gossip, but he didn't mind. The woman was as warm and nurturing as she was ruthless in her sales.

Nick made his way downstairs for luncheon and wondered if he would find Giulia there today. According to Jack, who'd heard from Tilly, Giulia had only eaten the day before when the maid brought a tray to the tower. It was the only break she had taken from the tower the day before and he had been glad, for he had feared she would forgo food for the entire day in favor of her father's old playroom.

He arrived at the luncheon room to find Robert and Ames eating from their overfilled plates. He turned around directly and made his way toward the tower. If she was not going to come down to eat, then perhaps he needed to remind her to take a break.

Giulia was overwhelmed as she flitted back and forth between joy and grief. Going through her father's old books and journals was equally rewarding and painful. Mostly rewarding. She found stories he had written dating back to when her father was only twelve, many themes within them ones he had later repeated in his periodical. She was not surprised to find that the only women featured in his youthful stories were the maternal figures.

As she scanned the book titles lining the wall, she noted a distinct range in themes and levels of reading. What likely began as a child's playroom had grown with the boys as Robert and Patrick added to their collection. An entire section on one shelf was dedicated to India; Giulia assumed it was their research done in preparation for the trip they took as young men prior to meeting Lily. She found many books about countries on the Continent, but only one Italian language sampler. Frowning, she returned it to the shelf and continued to browse.

"Ahem."

Giulia spun around to find Nick leaning in the doorway, his arms casually folded over his chest.

"Good day," she greeted him before turning back to the books.

"I have come to escort you downstairs. You must eat, Jules."

"I am not hungry," she said over her shoulder, promptly returning her attention to the spine of the Italian language sampler.

"Be that as it may" —Nick's voice grew softer as he drew closer— "you must eat, Giulia. You cannot hide here all day."

"I can," she argued, "and I will. Besides, I have spent the morning with Madame Chastain and have only just recently come up."

"Are you pleased with your gown?"

"I am." She was surprised by his change in tactics. "And I am quite grateful to the earl for supplying it. To be honest," she confided, pivoting to face him and plucking at the skirt of her dress, "I am quite thrilled to be rid of this dratted gray."

Nick chuckled beside her, leaning against the bookcase. "Is this room everything you hoped it would be?"

"That, and more." She smiled back. This was it; her opportunity to explain. Leaning her shoulder against the bookcase, she crossed her arms over her chest in a mirror of Nick. She lowered her gaze, licking her lips. "Listen, I must tell you something."

She searched for the words to tell him she was leaving Halstead but did not know how to explain. She was equally frightened to tell the earl, particularly after their recently budding relationship and the man's admittance that he considered her family, but she knew she must. When the swans had come by the day before to visit and Mabel had offered Giulia a place to stay, she had instantly accepted. She needed to get away from Nick but knew that returning to London with Ames was not the answer.

Hattie had offered Giulia a home as well, but Mabel lived the farthest away, and that was appealing to Giulia. It had been a buoying revelation when Giulia had explained that she wanted to set off on her own, and they'd immediately come up with ways to keep her around. Giulia cried tears of gratitude and joy and was hugged in three directions by her new friends.

She was creating her own life, her own adventure, and the control she had over her direction was exciting and thrilling. But would Nick understand?

Oh, what did that matter? The man had just been trifling with her, anyway.

Nick held up a hand, pulling her from her thoughts. "No need to explain. I know you are leaving." He swallowed, glancing around the room. "When do you go?"

"I planned to stay a day or two after the ball to help return the castle to its natural state. Perhaps Monday, I suppose."

Nick nodded curtly, his gaze flicking about the room.

"Listen, Nick—"

His eyes narrowed. "What is that?"

The most glorious light streamed through the stained-glass window, landing upon the sofa in a colorful reflection. "It looks like a rainbow," Giulia answered quietly.

"Yes, a perfect rainbow," Nick agreed in awe.

They moved to the center of the room in unison, drawing their hands through the flawless arc and marveling at the simple beauty.

"My father had a fondness for rainbows," Giulia said softly.

"Perhaps this was why."

She nodded as her hand followed the rainbow to where it ended on the sofa, sitting softly and playing with the light on her fingers. Nick followed her over and she glanced up when he grew still.

"What is it?" she asked.

"A crack in the wall," he answered quietly. Giulia leaned over the sofa and saw what he was referring to. The walls of the room were the same gray stone as the rest of the castle, but there appeared to be a crack along the bricks behind the sofa. "I am going to move the couch," Nick explained as he crossed to the end of the furniture. Giulia moved to the other side and helped him push it away from the wall. She gasped. The crack moved down and formed a perfect rectangle about as long as her forearm.

"Could it be?" she asked.

256

"Perhaps," Nick responded, kneeling on the floor. "This whole place is littered with trapdoors and hidden cabinets."

Giulia knelt beside him and watched as his fingers dug into the cracks of the rectangle, perfectly illuminated by the beam of rainbow light from the stained glass. The stone gave way, scraping as Nick slid it from the wall, revealing a small, dark space.

He gestured to the space. "Would you care to do the honors?"

Giulia swallowed before reaching into the dark compartment in the wall. She quickly pulled her hand back and shivered. "You may. I don't fancy pulling out a dead rodent."

Nick laughed. "Or a live one? It is too bad we don't have a candle."

Giulia shuddered again but the humor only partially covered the anxiety building in her gut. She watched as Nick's large and capable hand moved into the dark space in anticipation.

"There is something here," he said, his voice full of excitement as he slid something from the dark recess in the wall.

Giulia gasped. Then she felt herself grow cold, her gaze seeking Nick's. If this is what she thought it was, Lily had been right all along.

CHAPTER 33

"It's locked," Nick said, pulling at the lid of the beautiful, ornate box. It was not large, by any means, but it was absolutely breathtaking. The box was gold—or perhaps brass—the lid covered in precisely cut, clean jewels of every shade that came together to form the image of an elephant.

A beautiful, ornate, jeweled elephant.

Nick glanced up to find Giulia staring at the box, her eyes wide with fear and hesitation, her hand resting over her chest. "Giulia, what is it?"

She glanced up to him and then back at the box as if a magnetic pull kept her vision from moving elsewhere. Her hand went to her throat and hovered there before Nick reached forward, grabbing her hand and squeezing her fingers with his own.

She seemed to swallow with effort. "We've found it, Nick. We've found the key."

"Key? But Jules, this is locked." Nick dropped her hand and pulled at the lid, demonstrating for her once again. The poor woman had probably spent too much time in this tower, for she was acting strange.

She gave him a look as if to say that *he* was the one acting strange, and he set down the box, lifting his hands in surrender.

Nick watched as Giulia lifted the box, examining it thoroughly. Then he was wholly surprised to see her lift the chain she always wore around her neck and pull a pendant out of her bodice. The pendant was an elephant, identical to the one on the top of the box. His jaw went slack, but he did his best to close it quickly. "You think..." he started, quieting as she nodded.

Giulia placed the box on the floor before her, kneeling directly in front of it. She unclasped the chain around her neck, holding the elephant by its tail. Bringing it to the front of the jeweled box, she inserted the pendant into the slit on the front, trunk first, before wiggling it for a moment and then turning it to the right in a quarter turn. A satisfying click bounced off of the stone walls and Nick found himself holding his breath as he watched Giulia slowly lift the lid.

Giulia and Nick sat in silence as they looked at the contents of the box. He could not be certain, but it appeared to be filled with folded missives. He watched as Giulia sifted through the paper and confirmed that it was, indeed, full of letters.

"Most of these appear to be from my father," Giulia said in confusion, lifting some from the box and combing through them. "They are rather old. Oh, they are letters to his mother." She quietly gasped. "Here are a few she had written to him."

Nick watched as Giulia continued to sift through the letters that filled the box.

She glanced up with a puzzled expression. "But why would they be in this box in this tower if she wrote them to him?"

"Did she post them?"

Giulia turned one of the folded letters over. "No, it appears that she never even addressed them, she simply wrote them. And it looks like she stopped eighteen years ago." She lifted her gaze. "Or maybe she stopped putting them in this box."

Nick noted the sorrow in Giulia's expression as she tried to make sense of the treasure. He yearned to pull her in and comfort her. But he couldn't. This was her story and her trial, and she needed to process it on her own. Didn't she?

"Oh, Nick!" Giulia surprised him with the force of her words. "You see what this means?" Suddenly her tone became more solemn, more calm, as her watery, brown eyes sought his. "Father *did* trust me with the key."

Nick smiled encouragingly as Giulia grinned at him and then went back to sifting through the letters. Her face displayed a wealth of various emotions with each passing missive. She laughed, she smiled, she frowned. He could have sat there all day and watched her. Then, when she froze, he followed suit.

Giulia sat too still and too quiet for far too long. Nick placed a hand on her shoulder, and she startled. Had she forgotten he was there?

"I am sorry," she said quietly. "This was the last letter."

He glanced over, noting that it was from Giulia's grandmother. "To your father?" he asked.

She nodded. "She wrote this to him but never sent it, same as the others. She must have locked the box at that point, too." Giulia raised the letter in indication, then explained as she skimmed the words again. "She wrote that she thought he had made a mistake in marrying Lily. He was disgracing his family by stealing his brother's betrothed and would no longer be welcome at Halstead. She also told him how much she loved him and wished things had gone differently." Giulia sought Nick's gaze. "Of course, she describes in this letter how she could not possibly say such a thing, for it would be terribly un-Pepper-like of her to admit vulnerability." Giulia laughed. "I have to assume she left that part out of the actual note that she sent."

"How do you know that she sent anything at all?"

"Because she sent him this," Giulia said, lifting the elephant pendant. "And then he must have waited until he was in India to give it to me so I would not question its origin. Apparently..." She stopped, clearing her throat. "Apparently my grandfather gave this box to my grandmother when they were newly married. It was a gift given to him by a Raja when he visited India with his own father and was said to bring good luck. That is what my father told me as well. It has been my good luck charm ever since."

She brought the elephant to her lips and kissed it once before securing the chain around her neck and hiding it in her bodice. "It is funny," Giulia said, her unfocused eyes in a slight daze, "my father told me not to flash it about because of thieves and robbers. He wanted to protect the necklace and, in turn, protect me. I kept it hidden away until the point that it became habitual. But that must have been his intention all along."

"Most likely," Nick agreed.

Giulia piled the letters back into the box and closed the lid with a click. "Shall we take this to the earl?" she asked as she rose.

Nick stopped her with a hand on her arm before rising as well. "It can wait. We have the ball this evening and the last thing Robert needs is to dig up all of this old history again before facing Graton's genteel set."

"True." She nodded in agreement before crouching down and looking at the hiding place. "There were no vermin?"

"None." Nick chuckled. He took the box from her and placed it back in the dark space before picking up the stone covering and fitting it back into the wall. Together they slid the sofa back into place.

Nick sat on the sofa, pulling Giulia's hand until she sat beside him. She pulled the elephant from her bodice, fingering the jewels.

"I assume I must hand this over to my mother." She held his gaze. "She was right all along, I did have it."

"You will do no such thing," Nick said with force. "We will do what we must to have her removed from English soil. I will convince the woman that Patrick Pepper died with the necklace around his own neck if I must."

Giulia laughed. "She just might believe that. But I am afraid it would only drive her to search out his resting place. This necklace must be awfully valuable."

They sat in silence for another moment as the heaviness from the previous hour weighed on their minds. "Shall we go eat?" Nick asked, rising and offering his hand.

"Yes, lets."

CHAPTER 34

The ball was off to a fabulous beginning. Giulia stood beside Nick and the earl in the receiving line and met each and every person as they came into the room, listening humbly as they marveled at the decor and praised her ingenuity. Giulia played the perfect hostess. She was gracious and kind, laughed when it was necessary and deflected rude or snide remarks as if she had not even heard them. Above all, she was wearing her favorite color.

Madame Chastain had used a beautiful blue silk for Giulia's gown that was a deep enough blue to make her pale skin look creamy, her brown eyes rich, and her horrid hair shiny and lustrous —though her coiffure might be better credited to Tilly's skill than to the gown.

The gown was magical. And in it, she felt like a princess.

Nick and Ames had both looked upon her in awe as she had descended the stairs to check on the last-minute preparations, and Lord Hart had averted his gaze, his eyes suspiciously shiny.

She stepped away from the men as the receiving line grew, unable to watch Lord Hart introduce beautiful, eligible women to Nick.

"I think every unwed woman in the county has come," she said, sidling up beside the bevy of swans on the far side of the room.

Hattie wrinkled her nose in apology. "Word has spread that the future earl is in want of a wife."

"I'm sure every household claiming an eligible daughter accepted their invitation," Mabel added.

And Giulia knew how many invitations went out in the post, for she had penned each of them. There were doubtless going to be plenty of women this evening for Nick to sort through. She was glad she was about to leave Halstead so she would not be forced to watch him court those women as well.

Amelia strung her arm through Giulia's. "Is it true, though? He is trying to find a wife?"

Giulia nodded. "The earl has requested it."

"How will he manage that when he's put off every woman in Graton?" Amelia asked ruefully.

Hattie scoffed. "Those little dalliances are easily forgiven when a title hangs in the balance."

Music filtered through the grand hall as the musicians tuned their instruments. Ames caught her eye from across the room and raised his eyebrows. She nodded softly and watched as he picked his way through the ever-growing crowd.

Nick had lent Ames a set of evening clothes and he was dashing. Giulia wished she had the ability to draw his likeness so he could take it home and show his sweetheart. Little Jo surely would have appreciated the vision Ames made.

A man approached, requesting Hattie for a dance, and then Dr. Mason followed shortly after, asking Mabel.

When Ames approached, she was gratified by his chivalrous bow and introduced him to Amelia.

"I have heard about you," Amelia said, curtseying with poise, a secret smile upon her lips.

"I hope it was all good things," Ames said, his eyebrow lifted.

Giulia and Amelia exchanged a look.

Ames cleared his throat. "You know I cannot ask you to dance, but I wondered if you would like to borrow my name for an excuse this evening?"

"That would be quite helpful, thank you."

Amelia's brow clouded.

Giulia leaned closer to her friend, lowering her voice. "I cannot dance."

"In truth?"

"Yes," Giulia said. "I never learned English dances."

The mourning swan's face broke into a laugh. "You did not think to tell your uncle when he requested your help planning the ball?"

"Of course not," Giulia said. "Then I would have had to learn."

They watched Mabel and Hattie dance with different men as Ames led Giulia and Amelia to two available tufted chairs along the wall by a window.

"Will you forgive me if I leave early?" Ames asked, his face screwed up. This was not a scene in which he felt comfortable, regardless of how well he appeared to fit in.

Amelia leaned over, snaking an arm around Giulia's shoulder. "She has friends."

The statement was meant to encourage Ames, but it also did its part to comfort Giulia. He bowed to them both before snaking through the crowds and leaving the ballroom.

"You were correct in your assumptions, I assume," Amelia said, arranging the skirts of her black gown around her knees. The stark contrast of black against her milky skin and copper hair was sharp and elegant.

"Indeed." Giulia craned her neck, attempting to find the men in the receiving line and failing. She turned her attention to watching the dancers, instead. "Ames is to marry another woman."

"Does it pain you?"

"No. My father would have liked for us to marry, and neither of us had any objections to the scheme. But while we cared for one another, we were never *in love*. Ames has found that now, and I do not fault him for it."

Amelia nodded, understanding.

Giulia smiled wryly. "Though, perhaps he could have directed me to Halstead differently—no, I do not mean that. I am not sure I would have forged a relationship with my uncle had I simply arrived with a desire to know him better. My survival instincts kept me at Halstead, and I am glad the situation forced us together."

Amelia shook her head, a smile playing on her lips. "I suppose I ought to be glad too, for it brought you to us."

A tall, handsome man with chestnut-brown hair and a Grecian nose stepped before them, causing both women to startle.

"Good evening, Charles," Amelia said smoothly. "Allow me to introduce my friend, Miss Giulia Pepper."

The man bowed over her hand. "How do you do, Miss Pepper?"

"Giulia, this is Mr. Charles Fremont. He is good friends with my brother and a cousin to our dear Mabel."

"Good evening, Mr. Fremont," Giulia said, dipping her head in response. "Welcome to Halstead."

"Thank you. I am much obliged." He turned, gesturing to the decor with a swiveling wrist. "It is a magnificent design, Miss Pepper. Simply stunning."

"Thank you, sir."

"Amelia," Mr. Fremont said with caution as he turned toward the beauty in black, "I was hoping you would partner me in the quadrille. I believe it is coming up shortly."

"Oh, that I could," Amelia said with false melancholy, "but I am in mourning, as you see, and I think it very improper to dance while one is in mourning."

Giulia shot Amelia a sideways glance.

"Perhaps next time?" Mr. Fremont asked, undeterred.

"Perhaps," Amelia replied, noncommittally.

Mr. Fremont nodded and walked away, and Amelia gave way to slight laughter.

"Whatever was *that* about?" Giulia asked when the man was out of earshot.

"He is horrid. He has been after me since we were children. I think it irks him that I've married three men in my young life and none of them were him. He'd like to make himself the fourth Mr. Amelia Fawn."

"I see," Giulia said, feeling sorry for the man. "And does he stand a chance?"

"Not on this green earth," Amelia said before hiding her chuckle behind a fan.

Amelia quickly recovered and went on to educate Giulia on the local gentry, pointing out who they were and then expounding on the gossip each person had connected with their name.

When she arrived at the fair-haired beauty who was being led about the dance floor fluidly by Nick, Giulia felt her spine stiffen.

"That is Fleur Lamont."

"French?" Giulia said with surprise.

"Yes, but she's lived in England longer than she ever lived in France. She keeps her accent thick, however. Very proud of her heritage, that one."

Giulia's eyebrows rose. "Even with the war?"

"Even with the war." Amelia nodded. "In London she's an Incomparable, too. She graces us with her presence as her uncle is a local peer, but she will not settle for any of our lame country folk."

"Unless they are a future earl?" Giulia asked as she gestured to Nick. The couple was absolutely stunning and watching them move gracefully in sync gave Giulia the strong desire to throw a fork at something.

"Perhaps," Amelia replied with a delicate shrug. "Though I will be surprised if she settles for anything less than a current duke."

"Are there any unmarried dukes in England currently?" Giulia was quickly realizing that her knowledge of the peers was sorely lacking.

"Only two, I believe. One is rather old, however, and the other is quite difficult to catch."

"Oh."

"He is our neighbor, actually. Though he's hardly seen away from his estate."

"Except for at Lords, I would assume. He does partake in Parliament, does he not?"

"Not even then," Amelia confided. "I have heard that his seat has been empty these last five years."

"That is interesting," Giulia said. "Do you know why?"

"There are plenty of rumors," Amelia said with a flick of her fan. "But who really knows the truth?"

Giulia nodded, not fully satisfied with the lack of information following that revelation. How had nobody mentioned that they were neighbors with a duke? Perhaps it was not very exciting news to the Halstead household since a duke would outrank Lord Hart.

"Good evening, Dr. Mason," Giulia said as Amelia's brother approached.

"I see you have been accosted by Charles already," Dr. Mason said after bowing to the women, a smile in his eyes.

Amelia shot her brother an annoyed look and went back to surveying the dancers. Dr. Mason began a joke about men not knowing when to walk away but Giulia was only half-listening. Her gaze was fixed on the open door to the ballroom that led out into the hallway and the figure she saw perched at the foot of the stairs.

She held the woman's eye for a brief moment and then Lily was gone.

Giulia rose so quickly that Dr. Mason had to take a step back to avoid being hit. She placed a hand on his arm and said, "I apologize, Dr. Mason, I must beg your forgiveness. I only just remembered something, and I must attend to it immediately."

She curtseyed to the pair and set her path straight for the foyer, weaving through strangers and acquaintances alike as she made her way toward the exit. She faintly noticed Nick dancing with a raven-haired beauty, his confused gaze following her as she passed. She shot him a smile to let him know everything was fine before she slipped from the ballroom and into the empty hall. She glanced either direction and was stunned to see not a footman in sight. Denny had been perched beside the door all evening, so his absence was surely odd.

Giulia raced up the stairs, pausing to listen for sounds indicating which way Lily may have gone. She turned down the east wing first, checking the men's chambers before running back toward the west wing. She glanced in her own room before running down the next hall, and then the next, treading lightly and listening for any noise to indicate where her mother was. It was not until Giulia reached the alcove that she heard steps above her.

Lily was in the west tower.

CHAPTER 35

*G*iulia climbed the spiral staircase swiftly and paused in the doorway, pushing herself flush against the wall. She watched her mother move along the wall, pulling out books and feeling the shelves in a hectic, thorough manner. Giulia considered her options before stepping into the room.

"It is not there," she said.

Lily stopped cold. She turned to face Giulia with a crazed smile painted on her face. "How do I know you are not lying to me?"

"Because I was raised to be honest. You would know if I was lying, actually. I'm rather horrid at it."

Lily stood against the far bookcase, sizing up her daughter before turning back to the last shelf left intact and dismantling it book by book.

A frustrated cry rang out as Lily flung the final book on the floor, pushing and prodding the bookcase to no avail. She spun, shooting Giulia a maniacal look that shook her. "You have it," Lily snarled, pointing at her daughter. "You *must.*"

Giulia jumped back as her mother started toward her, but she fell as her foot slipped on a book and she hit the floor hard. Pain shot up

Giulia's back, knocking the breath from her lungs as Lily crouched over her, her face distorted with greed and passion.

Had Giulia actually thought her mother beautiful before? Lily looked absolutely dreadful now.

Lily searched her face. "Patrick would have put it here. This was his favorite place in the world," Lily said, her accent growing thicker as her mania deepened. "He was forever going on about this wretched room and how positively *magical* it was. His mother created it for them, you know. It was all her idea. She shared that adventurous gene with her sons."

"You knew my grandmother?" Giulia could not help but ask.

"Knew her?" Lily sat back on her heels, her face screwing up in derision. "Of course I knew her. I lived here for nearly a year before Patrick and I eloped."

Giulia's jaw dropped. She had been told her parents met in Italy and married there.

"But you lived in Italy."

"Yes, after we married. The earl forced us out and we went to live with my *famiglia*. He did not like scandal, the earl, so he made us go. Patrick hated Italy, though, so we came back. But we were forced to stay in London."

"And then you left."

"Of course I left!" Lily said with feeling, rising and stepping back. She was restless. Obsessed. It was frightening. "Patrick was forever jumping from one adventure to the next, spending all his money and forcing me to wear rags, to cook and to clean! I am not a woman made to cook. Or to *clean*."

Giulia refrained from mentioning that Lily was a woman who'd had a child but felt that an unnecessary point in that particular moment.

"And when that old woman sent Patrick the key, well, then I knew that we would be rich again. But the idiot refused to sell it." Anger flared in Lily's eyes. "I did not have to remain poor when a wealthy viscount hung on my every word. So I made Patrick choose. He could sell the key and keep me, or he could keep the key and lose me to Lord

Gresham—who was both wealthy *and* willing to leave his wife and return to the continent with me. Patrick chose the jeweled key. So I left."

Giulia was shocked. Never before had she thought to comprehend that her good luck charm held so much power. She wanted to stroke the chain out of habit but kept her hands by her sides with simple force of will.

"How very impractical," Giulia said instead.

"*Scusami?*"

"A key which is covered in jewels does not sound very practical. That is what you are looking for, is it not? A key that is covered in jewels?"

"*Si*. But it does not open anything, it is merely decoration."

"Oh, I see." Giulia nodded slowly. Lily was unaware of the box hiding in the wall directly behind her—a box that was worth ten times its key, most likely.

"But you waited all this time to retrieve it. How do you know it is still here?"

"Gresham died last year and left everything to his wretched wife. When I heard that Patrick died, too—" Lily stopped, turning her gaze on Giulia. She narrowed her eyes and said slowly, "How do I know you aren't trying to distract me now?"

"Because I don't have any keys covered in jewels," Giulia said, rising. She threw her arms out in her frustration, hoping the woman would see reason. "You must believe me. You can tear this castle apart stone by stone, but you will not find a decorative key covered in jewels."

The room itself seemed to hold its breath as Lily watched her daughter in wide-eyed panic. The woman was mad. Had she not realized after tearing the room apart one book at a time that it was nothing more than a playroom?

Lily deflated, her eyelids drooping as her shoulders slouched, and Giulia let out a slow, silent breath. She needed to figure out a way to get Lily out of the castle for good and sneak back into the ballroom before anyone noticed her absence.

"Lily?" A voice called from the stairwell. It was deep and masculine, causing shivers to trail down Giulia's spine. Lily shot her a look full of fear before glancing around the tower in haste.

"Quick!" Lily said in a rushed whisper, "to the roof! He must not find you alone."

"I thought you came alone," Giulia said as her mother grabbed her arm, pulling her toward the ladder.

Lily shook her head, and Giulia scrambled up the ladder as quickly as her feet would carry. But the wooden hatch was stiff from years of neglect and it took a couple of hard shoves with her shoulder before it gave way.

"Lily," the voice called again, sounding strange and yet familiar. "Have you found it?"

Giulia nearly made it out of sight before the man came into the tower, and she caught a head of dark brown hair before she quickly closed the latch. She backed slowly toward the edge of the tower wall and stopped, glancing down the sheer stone wall. Fear gripped her as she realized she had nowhere to run.

Light poured onto the earth below from the brightly lit ballroom and shadows jumped and swayed on the lawn as the dancers inside moved, blissfully unaware of the woman standing high above them and her deadly predicament. She pulled the elephant from her bodice and kissed it once for luck and then again—for an extra dose, of course—before shoving it back away from view.

The hatch slowly raised, sending prickles down her spine as light seeped from the opening and onto the stone floor of the tower roof. Fat, cold drops began to fall from the sky, landing on Giulia's bare arms and sliding down her neck.

A dark head rose from the floor, an eerily joyful smile crossing the face of the man who'd stood by her side for weeks while she had nursed his master back to health.

Jack.

Giulia straightened up, calling forth every ounce of courage and strength that she could either summon or feign.

"Well," Jack said, climbing onto the roof of the tower as rain began to fall harder. He looked taller, broader than before, and his eyes darker. "Lily tells me you don't have the key. But you know what I think?" He leaned down, pulling Lily by the hand and dragging her onto the roof. "I think that you *do* have it." Jack threw Lily to the floor and she slumped in a heap. Fear trickled down Giulia's spine as she swallowed, trying to hide her anxiety.

"You've heard us searching, Jack," she said, trying to sound reasonable. "We trusted you. Do you not think you would have known if we had it? Are we not friends?"

He came toward her, eyes narrowing, and she stepped back, bumping into the wall.

"I am not in your confidence," he argued. "And we are not *friends*. I was good enough to share your company while you nursed Nick, while the earl treated you as a servant. But the moment Nick healed, and Lord Hart accepted you, I became scum."

"You were never scum—"

"When did you spare me a glance, eh? When did you find a minute to converse with me? Am I not a man, too, worthy of consideration?"

Giulia gawked at him. She feared for her life, the way Jack was leaning toward her with a wild look in his dark eyes. She needed to tread lightly. "I believed myself *engaged* to a servant, Jack. I never thought myself above you."

He shook his head, sorrow reflecting in his eyes. "But you did. When the earl started paying you attention, and Nick decided to play with you—"

"Nick never—"

"I am speaking," Jack spat, his face coming within a hand's width of her own. "Nick never cared for you. He never cared for anyone. He just chases women for the fun of it and leaves me to tend the broken hearts. When we first came to Halstead, Nick dallied with a dozen women, all in the first year. His new position got to his head and he cared nothing for the lives he wrecked."

Jack's chest was heaving. "And then you arrived, and I figured you would be different. I thought you were a strong woman who could resist him, but you let me down. And still, when I tried to comfort you and Nick disrespected me, you *let him*."

It took a moment for Giulia to recall the situation Jack referred to. But when she did, shame fell over her. She hadn't corrected Nick in Jack's hearing, but she had been bothered by the way he'd spoken to his friend.

If she had spoken up, would all of this have been avoided?

Lily moaned from the floor a few paces away.

No. Giulia had to think that nothing would have been different, regardless of how she had acted. Jack knew her mother; he had said her name. Something was clearly afoot here, and she did not have all the information.

"Let me tend to my mother," she said, "and then I will do whatever you wish."

"It is too late for that," Jack said, stepping closer and running a finger along her jaw. "You will take me to the key, and you will hand it over, and then you will distract the household until I am safely away. Or, you can die up here on this tower and no one will know until morning. What sounds more appealing?"

Giulia swallowed. The rain began to fall harder, and she glanced to the hatch and then to Lily, lying in a lump on the floor. She wished she had not searched out Lily alone and wondered whether or not anyone had noticed that she had not returned to the ball yet. Surely someone would notice, wouldn't they? Perhaps if she simply stalled for a while, then…

Jack cut into her thoughts. "What is it going to be? I will not wait all night. I have been patient long enough, and it ends now."

She needed him to keep talking. A man who had kept silent for so long was likely bursting to speak his feelings. She held his gaze. "How long have you known my mother?"

"Mere months," he answered with disdain. "She sought me out after learning that I was Nick's valet. She knew she could never get the key alone. But together—"

"Are you the one who shot at Nick, as well?"

Jack's eyes grew darker and Giulia's stomach roiled. "Why?" she asked.

"I did not aim to kill. Just to create a diversion so Lily would have time to sneak inside and search Halstead—though, we had mixed up our meeting place and by the time I located her and returned to the house to send Robert out to search, you had arrived." Jack lowered his voice. "It didn't work, but I do not regret it. Nick has always gotten whatever he wished. He has always been lucky. If anyone deserved to be plucked from their dreary life and given a seat of luxury, it was not *him*."

Giulia stared at the man in astonishment. Had he not been plucked from his life as well and given a fine position with relaxed propriety? The longer she gazed into Jack's face, the further she saw the greed which consumed him.

"Why now? You have been his valet for three years, have you not?"

"I am not mad, Giulia," he said. "I would never risk my life merely to teach the imbecile a lesson. But Lily presented an opportunity to me that I could not resist."

He looked to be growing impatient, and Giulia was nearing the point where she would have to give up the necklace or her life. Or both, for once she gave him the key, her leverage was gone. Jack would have no reason not to shove her from the tower then and there.

She *must* find a way back inside the castle.

"I take it you shot at me, too?" she asked. "Two targets, and two misses. I suppose you are not a very good marksman."

"No one shot at you. Your mother was hungry. I could only sneak her food occasionally, so I gave her a gun in case she needed to obtain a pheasant."

Lily *had* been hunting.

"We are getting away from the point," Jack said through clenched teeth. "Make your choice, Giulia."

"No, there is no point!" Giulia shouted. "I do not have a key. You, who sat and listened to Nick and I try to *find* the wretched thing should know this best of all."

Another moan cut through the rain and Giulia looked to Lily's form curled on the stone floor behind Jack.

"What did you do to her?" Giulia asked.

A brief look of concern flashed in his eyes but was quickly replaced by a hard expression. "She was in my way," he growled.

Giulia ducked around Jack and crossed the open hatch, dropping on her knees beside her mother's still form. The light of the moon was enough to show her the large purple lump that had developed on Lily's right temple, and the trickle of blood oozing down the side of her face and over her ear, helped along by the rain.

Lily groaned again and shifted sideways as a large hand came down and knocked Giulia on the side of the face, stunning her.

"Where is it?" Jack roared.

Giulia staggered back on her heels as she recovered from the blow, but not before a hand grabbed at her hair and lifted her, her scream piercing the quiet as he yanked her to her feet. Hot breath tickled her neck as Jack came closer and asked through his teeth, "Where are the jewels?"

Giulia held her breath and clenched her teeth, the pain from being lifted by her hair was nearly blinding and she could not form a rational thought.

Fury shone in his eyes as he turned her to face him. "I suppose it is a tragic death on the tower that you choose, eh?"

Giulia tried to gain her bearings. If she could kick Jack hard enough, he might drop his hold long enough for her to get to the hatch. Rearing back, she kicked hard, and he released her, sliding his hand around her waist and holding her flush against him.

She opened her mouth to scream when a shaft of light poured through the floor, surprising them both. She was blinded momentarily but felt Jack's grip slacken. Sliding out of his arms, Giulia crawled across the floor until she bumped into the wall. Using it as a reference point, she followed it around the tower and put as much distance between herself and Jack as she could.

"Jules?" A voice pierced the dark and Giulia gulped in a breath of relief.

"Nick!" she yelled as a head appeared above the hatch, a lamp in hand. Her vision adjusted as he climbed onto the tower and she gasped, "He's behind you!"

Every muscle in Giulia's body tensed as she watched Nick spin around with catlike finesse and hit Jack across the side of the head with a heavy iron padlock.

Jack slumped to the ground in a heap and she felt equal parts relief and grief.

Within a moment Nick was beside her, his arms around her, pulling her against his chest. She felt dazed as his hands held her close, rubbing her back and stroking her head as rain pounded down on them.

"It was Jack," she said softly, then looked up. "It was all Jack."

"Shhh," Nick soothed, rubbing his hand along her back as his arm kept her close. "He cannot hurt you anymore."

"The threat is gone?" she asked timidly, almost afraid to hear the answer.

"Yes," he said, the warm sound vibrating against her head and combating with the sorrow she felt in her heart. "The threat is gone."

CHAPTER 36

*A*fter helping Lily onto the post coach with a bandage around her head and enough money to get her back to Italy—and a bodyguard in Ames who would assure Giulia through writing that her mother had made it on the boat and sailed away—Giulia returned to Halstead with the distinct feeling that she had aged about fourteen years.

Any future potential of a relationship with her mother was now at a complete end, and while there was a sense of catharsis to that farewell, it was bittersweet as well. It was only natural to mourn the loss of one's mother in one's life, even if she had never been present to begin with.

Giulia wished she had not ruined the ball for Nick, but he had been immensely supportive through the entire ordeal. Most of the guests hadn't realized he'd gone missing at all when he arrived back with Giulia on his arm—after Giulia's hair was braided again, of course, her silk gown changed into a plain green evening gown Madame Chastain had managed to deliver with the ball gown, and her mother safely deposited in one guarded room, and Jack in another.

Jack had been sent to the magistrate first thing the following

278

morning and taken into custody, unlikely to come away from the confines of prison again. His dark eyes haunted her, the jealousy and greed lurking within them forever searing her mind. She mourned the loss of Nick's friend but praised heaven he'd been apprehended before he could do any real harm. Aside from Nick's shoulder, of course, which had almost healed to perfection.

"All packed?" Giulia asked Tilly as she moved into her room, removing her bonnet and swinging it onto the bed.

"Yes," the maid answered. "Thank you again for taking me with you, Miss Pepper. I promise I won't let you down." Tilly gushed and Giulia could not help the smile that spread over her face.

"Lord Hart insisted, Tilly, and I am glad he did. I could not survive without you."

"You are too kind, miss."

Giulia reached forward and grasped Tilly's hand. "I am not being kind, Tilly. You earned the job as lady's maid when you helped me into that gown and fixed my hair for the ball. Madame Chastain will not make me gowns I can fasten myself. I need you, and I am thrilled you accepted the position."

Tilly beamed and Giulia pulled her in for a hug. The maid covered a suspicious sniffle and Giulia turned away to afford her privacy.

The earl had taken her departure with a blank face and tone of voice void of feeling. She'd felt hurt for a moment, but the man was covering his emotions as well as he hid his face with an overgrown beard and bushy eyebrows. The strides they'd made since her arrival were considerable progress, and she was only going to be a few miles away at Mabel's home. Their relationship did not have to be at an end yet.

Nick, on the other hand, was taking the transition far too well. She had the sense he knew why she was leaving, the independence she needed to exercise. She let out a breath. And regardless, the more formal of a relationship she had with Nick, the sooner she would be able to move on.

Wells appeared in the doorway. "Miss Sheffield to see you."

"Wonderful! Thank you, Wells," Giulia said as she followed him into the corridor and down to the parlor. Mabel sat in the chair near the window and stood upon Giulia's entrance.

"Are you ready?" Mabel asked.

"I am," Giulia said softly as she stepped toward her friend. "Are you certain this is not an inconvenience?"

A grin spread over Mabel's face as she looked down to Giulia, pure kindness written in her expression. "Do not back out on me now," Mabel said in mock seriousness. "I am looking forward to your company far too much. My grandmother is near deaf and my sister is a tiny rascal. I could use a force of reason to keep me sane."

Fully gratified, Giulia nodded. She watched the footmen carry her trunk and valise to the carriage outside, as well as the three additional boxes Madame Chastain had delivered the day before. The earl was anonymously adding more gowns to her after-mourning wardrobe— she was not supposed to know but Madame Chastain had told her— and she was delighted by the colors which had been added back into her daily wear. At the moment she donned a butter yellow walking dress and a matching— "Oh, Mabel, I left my bonnet upstairs. Would you mind waiting while I run up to retrieve it?"

"Not at all."

With quick feet Giulia rushed toward her room, considering the cold stone walls and massive tapestries that had somehow began to feel warm and comforting over the course of her time at Halstead. They had begun to feel like home. She passed the corridor that would lead her to her father's tower and turned away regrettably.

It was not her last time in the castle, she reminded herself. She would be back.

Giulia turned toward her bedchamber and came up short when she found Nick sitting on the edge of her bed, the yellow ribbon trimmed bonnet swinging from his fingers. He glanced up and gave her a half-hearted smile that hardly touched his lips at all.

"This is not goodbye, Nick," she said as she hovered in the doorway. She felt the unmistakable pull that linked them, and would always link them, or so she assumed. But stepping any closer was dangerous if she was to remember that they were to remain friends. She laughed lightly to dispel the heaviness in the air. "I am sure I will see you again soon."

He stood, walking toward her and pausing just out of reach. "Of course. Robert would not let you leave forever. Not now that he has his mother's spirit and spice back in his life."

"No," she agreed. "Nor would I choose to leave permanently. I look forward to regular visits." She gave him an amiable smile. "We shall remain friends."

"Regular visits," Nick repeated. "*Friends.*" He said the word as if he was trying it out on his tongue for the first time and wasn't certain he liked the way it tasted. His eyes were fastened on her firmly and she found she could hardly breathe under his direct gaze.

She reached a hand for her bonnet, but he put his own in it instead, squeezing her fingers. She caught sorrow in his eyes and wanted to laugh at the absurdity. He had been so understanding before. What had gotten into him? "*Really,* Nick, I am only going to be a few miles away."

"What do you mean?" he asked quietly, hope surging in his vivid eyes.

"You said you knew," she reminded him, confusion drawing her eyebrows together. "I am only going to live with Mabel."

"The Sheffields?"

"Yes, the Sheffields."

Nick's face brightened with urgency and magnitude. Before she knew it, he picked her up and swung her about the room, her skirt billowing as she flew in circles, Nick's masculine hands securely holding her waist.

He placed her feet on the floor, his chest rising and falling rapidly as his hands clutched her waist. "Ames said you were going to London."

"I was invited, yes, but I declined. Mabel could use some help with her elderly grandmother and her younger sister, so I offered my services." She raised a hand to halt the dispute on his lips. "I am going as a friend and companion, not a paid servant."

Contentment settled over his features. "You are not leaving Graton," he said quietly.

"I am not leaving Graton," she grinned back. Had he gone mad? He was acting so strange.

Before she knew it, Nick pulled her up onto the tips of her toes as he placed a sweet, gentle kiss on her lips. It was over before she realized it was happening, and she looked up, her face flushed and her pulse racing, to see the smile that he aimed down at her. "Perhaps I should address your uncle first, but I have it on good authority that you are the sort of young female who governs yourself. Jules, will you marry me?"

She stilled, a thousand thoughts moving through her brain and efficiently stunning her into silence. Her heart ached from hearing the very words she desired above all else, while knowing it was not meant to be. She cleared her throat and took a minuscule step back, pushing on his chest to force space between them. "I will not be toyed with."

"What do you mean by that?"

"I've heard of your exploits, Nick—"

"From Jack?"

Giulia held his gaze. "Yes, among others. I will not subject myself to a relationship with a man who dallies with women the moment he meets them."

"Dallies with—" Nick stepped back, shaking his head. "I am not a rake, Jules."

"But Amelia, Hattie, and Mabel all said—"

"Yes," he said, nodding. "I will admit to the folly of my youth, but that was three years ago. When I arrived at Halstead and the future title of earl got to my head I was too forward in my attention to the local women. I was not careful, and I flirted recklessly. But Robert quickly put an end to that."

"To flirting?" Giulia asked, raising her eyebrows.

Nick scrubbed a hand over his face. "One does not simply cease *flirting*, Giulia. One learns to become circumspect."

A moment of silence passed before Nick dropped his hand, piercing her with a look so deep his eyes turned the most vivid shade of green. "You imagine that I did to you what I did to your friends. That I flirted with you, stealing kisses with no intention beyond the fun of it."

She held his gaze, daring him to dispute it.

"I put aside youthful games the moment Robert caught wind of my despicable actions and forced me to see reason. And every word I said to you, every single moment I held you in my arms, all of that was real," he said earnestly, shaking his head. "I love you, Giulia. I thoroughly, completely love you."

Her heart flipped over in her chest, but she subdued the feeling. Aching, she smiled sadly at him and spoke quickly before he could argue further. "Even if I share the sentiment," she put a hand up to halt his advance, "I have promised myself to Mabel for the time being, and I intend to keep my word." Giulia noted the emotions warring in Nick's expression as he flitted between confusion and complacence. His tall, broad shoulders were those of a future earl. She could sense the truth in his words. Furthermore, she trusted him.

She should not have let Jack poison her mind against him. Nick held and directed himself with honor and care, and regardless of where he came from, he was primed and prepared to take on the role that awaited him. And he was going to be great.

"You are a Pepper man. When the time comes for you to step in Lord Hart's shoes, you will do a remarkable job."

"And so will you," he said, stepping closer. "I know what you were doing when you prepared for the ball. I know that you were using as many resources from Graton as you could, giving money to the community, hiring help from the people and then feeding them beyond your obligation. You were doing precisely what a good countess would do for her people; you were looking out for them."

Giulia cast her gaze to the floor. She did not know what to say. That had been her intention, of course, but she had not realized anyone had noticed.

"*Together* we could be great, Jules," Nick continued, gathering her hands in his own as he dipped his head to secure eye contact. "I know that to be true. You care for the people, you are smart and resourceful, and you have Pepper blood. You were made for this." His voice dropped to a heartfelt whisper. "Please do not refuse me, Jules."

"I cannot marry you right now. I have made a commitment to Mabel." She paused, her pulse thrumming, and said in a softer tone, "Though I would not refuse if you were to come calling, of course."

"You would like me to pay a call at Mabel's house?" he said in disbelief, dropping her hands and stepping back a fraction. He scoffed as he raked his hands through his hair, frustration evident on the planes of his face.

She would have to speak plainly if he was to understand her meaning, evidently. Could he not see that she was opening the door to the possibility of a relationship? She could not commit this very day—she needed more time than that. But time was something they had plenty of.

Reaching for Nick's hand, she held it in her own. "And maybe take me out riding. Or perhaps escort me to Graton's assemblies. They do hold balls in Graton, do they not? You would have to teach me English dances first, of course."

Recognition lit Nick's face and he turned back to her, a small smile widened his mouth, pushing the creases in his cheeks further back. "I see. So, Giulia Pepper, I suppose I must beg your permission to court you."

"Oh, Nick, what a splendid idea," Giulia said.

Nick chuckled as he took her hand and placed it on his arm to escort her outside to where the carriage, Mabel, and Lord Hart awaited.

"You know what this means, don't you?" he asked as he ushered her down the stairs and into the foyer.

"What is that?"

"That by this time next year," he whispered into her ear, "you will be Mrs. Giulia Pepper."

She turned to give him a look of confusion. "I already am Giulia Pepper."

"Well," he said with an air of annoyance, "you know what I mean."

"I think I do," Giulia replied facetiously. She knew precisely what he meant. For *Mrs.* Giulia Pepper did, indeed, sound absolutely marvelous to her.

EPILOGUE

*G*iulia glanced at Tilly over her shoulder in the mirror and grinned. "I never thought you'd be able to tame this rat's nest of hair I've been cursed with, but I truly think you've done it."

Tilly beamed. "Practice, miss. It's not so bad with the right number of pins."

Giulia waited for the final few pins to find their placement and then rose, stepping away from the dressing table. She shook out the soft green gown, smoothing the wrinkles and admiring the way the fabric fell.

"You look beautiful, miss, if you don't mind my saying so."

"Thank you, Tilly. That is very kind of you." She gave her maid a squeeze on the shoulder and drew in a fortifying breath before leaving her room and making her way downstairs to meet with Mabel and Mrs. Sheffield, Mabel's grandmother.

Mabel was elegant in a gown of deep mauve, her hair pulled back and styled low on her head with an ivory lace shawl draped over her arms. She tapped her fan against her hand. "Are you ready for your debut?"

"I am not coming out," Giulia said, mocking affront. "I am merely celebrating an engagement."

Mrs. Sheffield started for the door and Mabel linked her arm in Giulia's. "I meant your dancing, you ninny."

Apprehension pooled in her stomach. "I suppose so."

Giulia followed the Sheffield women to the waiting carriage, her nerves rising as they drew closer to Halstead Manor. She'd been working with a dancing master—with Nick's help—to fill in the gaps in her dancing education. She was prepared to accept dances this evening at her ball, but she was inordinately nervous to do so.

The castle's drive was lit with torches that reflected against Halstead's windows and caused the stone to glow. A steady stream of carriages extended before them and it was some time before the Sheffield women and Giulia were let out at the drawbridge.

Giulia's body shook with impatience as she walked across the ancient wooden bridge and up the steps. She'd been at the castle only the day before to go over last-minute preparations with Lord Hart's housekeeper, but now that the ball was in full swing, it felt transformed.

The stone entryway was not much warmer than outside, and Giulia handed her pelisse to Denny before moving to the side to wait for Mabel, who guided her grandmother up the steps.

"You go along," Mabel said, a knowing smile stretching her mouth. "We will be in shortly."

The ballroom doors sat closed before her—no doubt to contain the heat inside—and Wells bowed crisply before reaching for the door.

"Not yet, Wells," a voice called from behind them. A tremor ran down Giulia's spine and she glanced over her shoulder to find the door to the library open across the corridor, a man seated on a plush chair with his gaze directed at her.

Spinning to face him, Giulia clasped her hands before her and waited as Nick rose, pulling at his cuffs and running a hand down his jacket before approaching her.

"You look stunning," he said, his low voice washing over her like a low-burning fire.

She reached forward and allowed him to take her hand, causing a thrill to run up her arm. She'd yet to feel unaffected by his touch, his presence.

"Where is my uncle?" she asked.

He nodded toward the ballroom but tugged her in the opposite direction, a secret smile pulling at his mouth. She found she could not look away from his lips and followed as he led her into the library, away from Wells's watchful eye. The moment they rounded the corner, Nick released her hand, sliding his arms around her waist and backing her against a bookcase.

Her heart beat an erratic rhythm as his head bent slowly toward hers, his hands coming up to grip the bookcase on either side of her head. "I missed you," he said, his mouth hovering above hers.

"I saw you yesterday," she whispered back.

"And enduring your absence this entire day was torment."

Chuckling, Giulia ran her hands up his coat, gripping the lapels and tilting her head, resting it against a row of leather spines to better see his eyes. "You've only a fortnight left before the wedding, Nick, and then you won't be able to get rid of me."

"And I cannot wait."

He closed the distance, pressing his warm lips to hers. Releasing the bookcase, Nick slid a hand behind her neck, pulling her closer and deepening the kiss.

A throat cleared in the doorway and they both stilled. She felt Nick smile against her lips and lightly kissed him once more before pushing against his chest.

He obeyed, stepping away from her, his hand sliding down her arm until it grasped hers.

Lord Hart stood in the doorway, his unruly hair combed into a semblance of order and his black coat brushed to perfection.

Giulia's heart pounded hard, blood rushing past her ears from being caught in such a compromising position. Though given their recent months of courting, this was not the first time Lord Hart had come upon them in such a manner.

"'Tis a good thing you're marrying her in a fortnight, or I'd be forced to call you out," her uncle said, spearing Nick with a glare.

Nick smiled back with unabashed humor.

"Now," the earl said gruffly, his gaze darting between them, "this ball is halfway over and they've yet to see the people being honored. I should think you owe us an appearance, at least."

"Of course, Uncle," Giulia said, "we will come now." She pulled at Nick's hand and he followed her from the room, passing by Lord Hart as the man muttered something like, *it's bad enough now, how am I supposed to live with the two of you once you've wed?* and shaking his head.

Giulia's cheeks warmed and Nick squeezed her hand, pausing just before the ballroom doors. "Are you ready to become my wife?"

"I have been ready for ages."

He chuckled. "I know the feeling. Now, the question of the hour. Are you ready to dance?"

Trepidation skittered through her. "Much less so, that."

Nick took her fingers and placed them on his arm before nodding to Wells. The doors opened and they were announced, signaling attention from the room at large. Lord Hart followed close behind them but paused at the perimeter of the dance floor as Nick and Giulia made their way to line up for the quadrille.

"You'll be marvelous," Nick said into her ear before moving to take his place. Shivers crept over her shoulders and down her arms as she looked into his green eyes and relaxed. She could accomplish anything with Nick's love and support.

The music began and Giulia danced. Fear and unease slowly lifted from her as she moved through the familiar steps, growing more comfortable as the dance progressed. She found Hattie grinning at her further down the line and passed Mabel and Amelia on the edge of the ballroom. Bolstered by the support of her friends and the gentle love shining in Nick's eyes, Giulia's heart soared.

She was home.

ABOUT THE AUTHOR

Kasey Stockton is a staunch lover of all things romantic. She doesn't discriminate between genres and enjoys a wide variety of happily ever afters. Drawn to the Regency period at a young age when gifted a copy of *Sense and Sensibility* by her grandmother, Kasey initially began writing Regency romances. She has since written in a variety of genres, but all of her titles fall under sweet romance. A native of northern California, she now resides in Texas with her own prince charming and their three children. When not reading, writing, or binge-watching chick flicks, she enjoys running, cutting hair, and anything chocolate.